REVENGE IS NOT JUSTICE

ALSO BY TONY SPALLONE

Murder at Breeze Canyon

Murders in the High Desert

Murders on Pigeon Mountain

REVENGE IS NOT JUSTICE

By
Tony Spallone

REVENGE IS NOT JUSTICE

Published in the United States of America by Long Walk
Publishing.
www.TonySpallone.com / Tony@tonyspallone.com

ISBN-13: 978-0-9864271-5-2

Edited by Stephanie J. Beavers Communications
www.StephanieJBeavers.com / 610-247-9494

Cover design by @coverbookdesigns

To Lyn Kelly

ACKNOWLEDGEMENTS

Thank you, Patti, for your advice and positive reinforcement. You are my heart and soul.

To my editor, Stephanie Beavers, for her meticulous, cogent reviews and edits of my novels.

My sincerest thanks to Lynn Ingersoll for her incisive critiques and support.

Thanks also to Terry Work and Fran Bergstein.

PROLOGUE

Santa Fe police detective Clay Bryce woke at five o'clock, put on his running gear, then turned on the porch light on his way out the door for his predawn run.

He stood for a moment, hands on hips, on the front landing of his adobe-style house on Via Santa Clara and breathed in the juniper- and sage-scented air of New Mexico's high desert. It was his favorite time of day. He listened to the sounds of the early morning—coyotes yapping in the distance, mourning doves droning their laments, and crows cawing as they tormented their target, the great horned owl.

With the help of reflected light from Santa Fe, Clay's eyes quickly adjusted to the darkness. Clay walked down to the empty street and began with a slow jog before picking up his tempo and turning right onto San Gabriel. The forty-one-year-old was well over six feet tall and packed 240 pounds on a muscular frame. His effortless running stride belied such a large physique of solid muscle.

He weaved his way through empty neighborhood streets for another two miles and reached East Santa Fe High School where he ran four laps on the synthetic quarter-mile track behind the school.

Most mornings, he did not see any cars. Today, however, when he was on the track, he noticed that one had entered the school parking lot adjacent to the track. The driver stopped and turned off the headlights but kept the engine idling.

Probably the school janitor. When Clay left the track and began his run back home, he was unaware the car was following him, its headlights still off.

1

Clay was a few hundred yards from his home and starting his cool-down walk when the driver of the car flicked on the car's high beams. Clay moved to the far left side of the road, close to the curb. He waved to the car to indicate it was safe to pass, but the car continued to trail Clay at a speed that matched his walking pace.

Clay did not understand why the car did not pass. He stopped and turned to see if he recognized the driver, but the car pulled into a driveway and doused its headlights. *That explains it. He lives on Santa Clara.* Clay resumed his cool-down walk, now only two houses from his own home.

The trailing car backed out of the driveway, turned on its high beams, quickly caught up to Clay, and followed him again.

Clay heard the car suddenly accelerate, its tires burning rubber. He turned in time to see the car coming right at him. He took a step first one way, then the other, trying to avoid being hit, but the car fender struck his right thigh with a glancing blow that flung him five feet into the air. Clay landed hard on his left shoulder, then slid and tumbled another ten feet, ending up against the curb on the grate of a storm sewer. His knees and elbows were scraped raw and a deep cut bled from his temple.

The driver pulled up alongside Clay, hesitated, then sped down the street out of sight in seconds as Clay lay dazed and defenseless, unable to make sense of what had just happened to him. A few moments later, from the corner of his eye, Clay saw headlights turn onto Via Santa Clara from San Gabriel.

He's coming back to hit me again.

Clay tried to crawl over the curb into the adjacent yard, but electric shocks surged through his legs and he fell back onto the storm grate.

The headlights advanced slowly toward him, the driver of the vehicle searching for Clay, now only several yards away.

Clay's neighbor, Alan Strickland, was awakened by screeching tires in the street. He flicked on his front porch lights and stepped outside.

The driver of the hit-and-run car saw Strickland and quickly doused his headlights, then fish-tailed down Santa Clara out of sight again.

CHAPTER 1

Strickland saw a man lying at the front edge of his yard and shined the flashlight from his cell phone in the direction of the injured man. He hurried down to the street and immediately recognized the man as his neighbor Clay. "Oh, my God! What happened?"

Clay twisted his head in the direction of the elderly neighbor. "I got hit by a car, Alan. Help me up."

Strickland shined his flashlight on Clay and knelt beside him. "You're bleeding pretty bad. I'm calling 911."

"Just help me... get up," Clay repeated. "I'm... okay. I don't need an ambulance."

"Yes, you do." Strickland dialed 911 and gave the dispatcher his address."

"I told you I'm okay."

"No, you're not. You shouldn't move until the ambulance gets here.

Alan's wife appeared at the front door. "Alan, what happened?" she shouted.

Alan shouted back, "It's Clay Bryce. He got hit by a car."

"Oh, no," said the woman.

"I called 911. He's bleeding. Bring some towels. Hurry!"

A minute later, Harriet Strickland, dressed in bathrobe and slippers, carried a half-dozen towels down to the road as fast as her arthritic knees allowed. "Oh, you poor soul." She folded one towel in half and gingerly slid it under Clay's head, then used another to apply pressure to the cut on his temple.

Alan took two other towels and wrapped them around Clay's bloody knees.

"I'm okay... I can walk it off."

4

"No, you stay right here," Harriet said sternly and put a hand to Clay's broad chest to restrain him. "Alan called the ambulance. They should be here any second."

Two minutes later a cop car arrived at the scene with his flashers on. The cop exited his car and left his flashers on. He recognized Clay. "Detective Bryce, what happened?"

Strickland answered for him, "He said he was hit by a car."

The cop looked around but did not see a car. "Detective, can you describe it so I can radio it in?"

Clay shook his head. "It was dark. I never saw it. I think it was an SUV—white or silver—but I'm not sure."

The cop saw that Clay was dressed in running shorts. "Do you think maybe he didn't see you jogging in the dark?"

"No. The sonofabitch hit me on purpose." Clay turned to Harriet. "Excuse my French, Mrs. Strickland."

"You're excused," she said with an understanding smile.

The cop asked the Stricklands, "Are you the ones who called 911?"

"Yes. I'm Alan Strickland. This is my wife Harriet. We live here." Alan pointed to their house.

"Did either of you see what happened?"

Alan answered, "No, I was awakened by the sound of tires screeching, then I heard a thud. When I went outside to see what had happened, all I saw was the taillights of a car racing to the end of the street. A minute or so later, the same car drove by—at least I think it was the same car. The driver saw me, but he took off again down the street before I could get a good look. Everything happened so fast I can't tell you what kind of car it was."

Harriet, who continued to apply pressure to Clay's head wound, said "I didn't see anything, Officer."

Clay was becoming more alert. "He... got me pretty good, huh."

"You're going to be okay," Harriet reassured him.

The cop asked, "When you called 911, you asked for an ambulance, right?"

"Yes. Where the heck is it?" Alan muttered. "They should have been here by now."

Clay tried to sit up again but was still dazed. "Where's the car that hit...?"

The cop said, "The car that hit you left the scene. Looks like it was a hit-and-run."

More neighbors hurried out to see what had happened. The cop asked if anyone had seen the car that hit Clay. No one had.

A paramedic ambulance entered Santa Clara, its siren painfully shrill as it neared. The flashing lights of the ambulance along with the lights of the cop car created a shower of colored lights against the fronts of neighboring houses and lit up the accident scene.

A female paramedic and male EMT jumped out of the ambulance. The EMT opened the back door to pull out monitoring equipment while the paramedic knelt next to Clay to assess the extent of his injuries.

Alan exclaimed, "What took you so long?"

The paramedic answered, "We were at the opposite end of town. We got here as fast as we could."

"You shouldn't have been called. I'll be okay," Clay uttered. He again tried to sit up but fell back in pain.

The paramedic said, "Whoa, hold it, sir. Let's check you out first. My name is Allie and my partner is Evan." She removed the towel that Harriet had pressed against Clay's head wound. "We need to get that taken care of."

Alan said, "His knees and elbows are pretty beat up too."

The cop said to the Stricklands, "The EMTs will take care of him. Let's move out of their way."

Clay was angry. He insisted, "Just... help me up, I said. I'm all right."

"I'll be the judge of that," the paramedic said with a smile. "That's why they pay me the big bucks."

"Allie, you're pretty." Clay was half out of it.

"Well, so are you." The woman had a sense of humor.

"No, you really are." He managed a grin.

Her outfit was hardly one that elicited compliments. She was dressed in cargo pants and a jacket with the word PARAMEDIC printed in reflective material across the front and back. Her hair was tucked under a baseball cap. "Nice try, but flattery isn't going to change my mind. I need to stop your bleeding. And you have to tell me what else hurts."

"Nothing does. I'm okay."

"You're a tough guy, huh," she said. "That's adrenaline talking. We're going to take some vitals."

Clay's only thought was to find the car that hit him. "Lady, I need to get up to find that SOB who hit me."

The paramedic said, "Just give me another minute to finish my examination."

"I said I'm okay. My house is right there." He looked for his neighbor. "Tell her, Alan. Tell her it's the house with the flag in front." He pointed to his house without lifting his arm. "You can see it from here. It's only two houses away. I can walk to it. It's right there. Do you see it?"

Allie turned to look at Clay's house. With a nod she said, "I see it, but you're in no condition to walk to it. Now, I want you to behave yourself and let me do my job," she scolded.

"You are one mean lady."

"Yep. Now hush up for a minute so I can take your vitals."

Clay calmed down, took a deep breath, and said, "Okay, get it over with. You're lucky you're pretty. I wouldn't let just anyone do this to me."

"Behave yourself, sir." She took his blood pressure. "One ten over seventy. Pulse, fifty. You just got hit by a car and your vitals are excellent. What are you, the bionic man?"

"Yes. So let me go home," he snapped.

Allie ignored Clay's pleas and applied quick-clotting gauze bandages to his head, knees, and elbows. "You'll need stitches to the wound on your head and your knees and elbows need cleaning from your road rash. You've got gravel embedded under your skin. We're going to get you to St. Vincent's to have the ER doctors remove the gravel and stitch your head up. They'll also want to examine you for broken bones or internal injuries."

"You're kidding me. I keep telling you I'm okay."

She disregarded Clay's comment. "Sir, where did the car hit you?"

"The back of my leg."

She turned him enough to examine his thigh. "I'm surprised you think you can stand, much less walk."

Clay was more and more perturbed. "Come on, lady. I said I'm fine."

She examined his eyes for signs of shock. "Can you tell me exactly what happened?"

"Some jerk hit me when I was out for a run. His high beams were in my face so I couldn't see the driver. I think the car was an SUV. When I heard him coming at me, I tried to jump out of the way, but I zigged when I should have zagged."

The paramedic asked, "What's your name, sir?"

Clay did not answer.

"Sir, I need your name for our records. What—"

"His name is Clay Bryce. Detective Clay Bryce," said the cop on scene. He was standing alongside the paramedic, jotting down information about the accident.

"So, what's your last name, Allie? It's only fair you tell me yours since you know mine," Clay said. He was acting like a schoolboy.

"Marland. Allison Marland. Allie for short."

"Marland. Like Maryland, only without a *Y*?"

"That's it," she said. "My partner and I are going to take you to the ER now. Your road rash will get infected if it's not taken care of. You'll be out of there in no time at all."

"No way," Clay said. "I'll be there all day."

"No, you won't. I'll make sure they get you out of there in half an hour," she said, although she knew that would not be the case.

"No person on earth has *ever* been out of an emergency room in half an hour."

"Let's do it anyway, okay? Have faith in me."

Clay was mellowing, but he was not ready to accept the paramedic's suggestion. "I told you my house is right there. How about if you walk me there? You and your partner can have a cup of coffee with me and then I'll drive myself to the hospital. I'll sign a waiver if you want me to. Seriously."

"Seriously, I can't force you to go to the ER, but I strongly urge you to go." It was Allie Marland's turn to be riled. "Detective, c'mon. Let's do it, okay? It's been a long night. You can thank me later."

Clay finally relented. "Yeah, okay."

The EMT wheeled a gurney over to him. "I need you to get on the gurney. We have to strap you in before we can take you to the hospital."

"Oh, for Christ's sake."

The paramedic showed her pluck. "Listen, Detective. We've got to do this right. I'm not going to lose my license because you're being hard-headed. Understand?"

Clay sighed. "Okay, Maryland. No need to get bent out of shape."

"My name is *Marland*, not Maryland."

"Yeah, whatever." Clay thanked the Stricklands for their help. "I owe you some new towels," he said.

"No problem, Clay. Take care of yourself."

CHAPTER 2

Allie Marland and her EMT partner wheeled Clay into St. Vincent's emergency room and provided the ER medical staff with the monitoring data of Clay's injuries taken at the accident scene. They left the hospital with a "Good luck, Detective Bryce."

Clay gave them a half-hearted wave in return and a sarcastic, "Yeah, thanks a lot."

Two emergency room nurses flew into action. They took Clay's blood pressure, pulse rate, and oxygen level. The on-duty trauma doctor ordered a whole-body CT scan to rule out injury to Clay's lungs and other internal organs.

Two hours later, the tests showed there were no broken bones and no indication of internal injury, although Clay's right hamstring had a large, spreading hematoma at the point of impact. The wound on Clay's temple required a dozen stitches and he had suffered a slight concussion. The physician told him he would not have to be admitted—not that Clay would have stood for that edict anyway.

* * * * *

Allie Marland's shift ended at seven that morning. She did not normally inquire about the status of a patient she had treated at an accident site, but an hour later she called the hospital to find out how Detective Bryce was doing. She learned he was still in the ER and decided to pay him a visit. She had never before visited a patient she had taken to the ER and was not sure why she was going, except that Clay was a big, strong guy with an attitude to match—the kind of man she was attracted to.

11

"He's in exam room six," the ER admission clerk said.

"Buzz me in, please." The curtain was open in his room. "Knock, knock."

Clay was surprised to see Allie. "Hey, Maryland. Back again? What are you doing out of uniform?"

"It's Marland," she corrected—again. She was dressed in a simple white blouse and black skirt and explained, "I'm off shift. I came back to check on you to see if you were behaving yourself."

"I've been a good boy."

"Yeah, I bet you have."

"No, really, I have. Ask anyone."

"I'll take your word for it." She gave him a bright smile. "How do you feel?"

He was hurting but did not admit it. "I feel great. A little hit-and-run to kick off my day is all I usually need to get started in the morning—either that or a cup of coffee."

Allie laughed. "You know, you're incorrigible. What's the diagnosis? Anything broken?"

"No, I'm good. X-rays were negative. No internal bleeding. A couple of stitches to my head. You want to know why I have stitches?"

"To close up your wound, of course."

"No. That's not it. It's to close up the hole in my head for letting you bring me here. I've been waiting hours to get discharged."

"It's hardly been hours. What about the gravel you picked up on your knees and elbows—your road rash?"

"The wise-ass doctor said she pulled out enough stone to rebuild the Great Wall of China."

"She really said that?"

"Yeah, she did." Clay's pretend anger turned to a smile. "Okay, I hate to admit it, Maryland, but you might have been right to bring me in. I guess I should apologize for giving you such a hard time."

"That's nice to hear. I'm glad you're doing okay. Anything I can do for you?"

"No. Oh, wait a second. How about you pull your weight and get me out of here? I gotta get to work and I'm late already."

"You shouldn't be going to work today. I'll be happy to call your boss to tell him what happened and that you can't make it in."

"What? No. I don't want you to call him. Of course I'm going to work. I'll call him when I get home and explain why I'm late."

"I'll check to see if you can be discharged now." Allie left to search out the ER doctor. As she walked off, Clay stretched his neck to follow her walk. He liked what he saw. She was tall and slender, with a toned, athletic figure and wore her strawberry blonde hair in a bob cut. Clay was taken by her effervescent smile and girl-next-door look that featured a band of small freckles across the bridge of her nose. He guessed her to be in her early- to mid-thirties. *She's cute as hell.*

Allie returned a few minutes later. "The doctor's trying to expedite your discharge. That's the good news. The bad news is they told me you haven't been a very good patient."

"Really? They said that?" Clay paused. "Well, maybe not *very* good, but I was... All right, okay, I'll apologize when I leave."

"Not a bad idea. Oh, and I was also told you had a *slight* concussion. Apparently, you have what I suspected from the beginning—a hard head."

"Very funny."

"You also had a dozen stitches on your head wound."

"A dozen stitches? No kidding! I wondered why it took so long to sew me up. Those are bragging numbers," he said with a crooked grin.

Allie shook her head. "Bragging numbers? You are *some*thing. I am sorry it's taken so long to get you treated, but you were pretty beat up—and it takes time to make sure you don't have underlying injuries. Listen, excuse the pun, but I've got to run. Take care of yourself. I'll see you around."

"Not so fast Maryland. Since you drove me in here against my will, it's only right you drive me home."

She smiled her bright smile again. "You think, huh? Are you *asking* me if I *might* be able to drive you home?"

Clay smiled back when he realized he was still coming across as a pain in the ass. "Sorry. Yes, I am. I guess I should say 'please.' *Please* can you drive me home?"

Allie looked into Clay's eyes and believed he was being sincere. "Okay. Sure. I'm going in that general direction."

"I guess I'm still not making a very good impression on you, am I?"

"No, not the best. But you did say 'please' this time."

A nurse gave Clay prescriptions for antibiotic ointment and a painkiller and reviewed instructions for him to care for his wounds. She ended her discharge instructions by handing him crutches. "Use them. I've seen you in here before. It seems to me you needed crutches back then too."

Clay had been in the ER twice before. The first time was after a serious car crash while chasing a murder suspect and the second time was when he was shot in the leg during a hostage situation.

"Yeah, I remember you. I'm aiming for frequent flyer miles."

The nurse laughed, "Yeah, you're close to qualifying for a free visit."

"I don't really need the crutches. Save them for someone else."

"No, take them, and use them. You're a big boy. You need to keep pressure off your damaged knees."

"Yes, sir, Sergeant, sir."

The nurse smiled at Clay's attempt at humor and gave a secret wink to Allie which said, "He's hot, isn't he."

On the drive to Clay's house, Allie gave Clay more care advice. "Detective Bryce, you're going to be hurting. You should take those pain pills as you need them. Don't be a martyr. Do you want me to stop at the pharmacy to get your prescriptions filled?"

"No. I'll do it on the way to headquarters later on." He had no intention to fill the prescriptions.

"Something tells me you won't get them filled. You're going to play Mr. Tough Guy, aren't you? I think you should reconsider your decision about going to work. Tomorrow you'll be hurting worse than you are right now."

Clay grimaced as he turned toward Allie. "Nah, I'm going to be okay."

"Detective Bryce, I know you're hurting, but I have to admit, you *do* look like you're in pretty good shape. That's probably what saved you from being hurt worse than you were."

"Hey, we're friends now. How about calling me Clay?"

Allie glanced at Clay and caught him looking at her legs. Her skirt had ridden up over her knees. "Clay it is. You're a big flirt, aren't you."

"I'm big, and I'm a flirt, so I guess that makes me a big flirt, heh?"

"How tall are you anyway?"

"Six-four. I used to be six-seven, but I shrink an inch every time I'm taken to the ER. That's why I didn't want to go there."

"Oh, my God, I think you are crazy."

Clay was hurting but still managed a smile. "You know, it looks like you're in good shape too, Maryland."

"I'm okay. I'm also a runner. And I took up karate a couple of years ago."

"Karate. That's impressive. I bet you're on your way to a black belt."

She laughed. "No, I've got a ways to go before I get that. I'm a third-degree brown belt—trying to master holds and escapes, those kinds of things. I'm enjoying the challenge. You never know. My job sometimes takes me to rough areas of the city. And sometimes I have to use my training to get accident victims to agree to go to the ER. You were this close to me putting a chokehold on you." She showed him her thumb and forefinger an inch apart.

"Very funny. Another reason for me to behave myself, huh?" Clay glanced at Allie's left hand and saw she did not have a wedding ring. "Where do you live? Maybe we can run together sometime."

Allie realized Clay was hitting on her but she did not mind. "Well, I would, but *I* run in the daytime—not in the dark like some people I know. Ahem."

Clay turned defensive. "I've been running in the early mornings for years—and in all kinds of weather. It's the only time I can. If I don't run in the a.m., I'd never do it."

"You'll probably disagree, but I don't think you'll be running for the next month or so. Your crutches might slow you down a bit." Allie gave a sideways glance at Clay and added, "That assumes you'll be using your crutches."

He shrugged. "We'll see."

Allie pulled into Clay's driveway and noticed the door to his house was open. "Someone at home, Detective? Like a Mrs. Bryce?"

"It's Clay, remember? And, no, there's no Mrs. Bryce."

"Then, why is the door wide open?"

"What?" Clay immediately went into cop mode. "Stay here. I'm going to check it out." He got out of the car and hobbled to the front door on his crutches. Allie remained in her car and dug her cell phone from her purse in case she needed to call 911.

Inside, Clay saw someone had written a message in large red letters across the mirror above the foyer table.

Romans 12:19.

What the hell does that mean? Clay pulled his service revolver from the drawer, leaned his crutches against the wall, then limped through each room of his one-story house to check for intruders. He found no one and nothing appeared to be disturbed. He returned to the front door and motioned to Allie. "You can come in. No one's here."

"Is everything okay?" she asked as she entered Clay's house.

"It looks like someone has an issue with me." He pointed to the mirror. "It's a biblical reference of some sort."

Allie read aloud, "Romans 12:19. Let me look it up." She used her phone to google the passage. "Dearly beloved, avenge not yourselves, but rather give place unto wrath: for it is written, vengeance is mine; I will repay, sayeth the Lord."

Clay picked up on the key words in the passage. "Avenge, vengeance. Looks like someone wants to get even with me about something." He tried to make a joke of it. "Maybe it's from my ex-wife."

"Really?"

"No, I'm kidding. I have no clue who could have written it, except I assume it was written by the same person who ran me over."

Allie had a quizzical look. She looked at the mirror then back at Clay. "For what it's worth, do you remember this morning when you pointed to your house and said you could walk to it? Do you remember saying that to me?"

"Yes, I remember."

"Well, when I looked toward your house, I saw someone at the front door. I think it was a man." She nodded toward the mirror. "It might have been the same person who wrote this."

"A man? What was he doing?"

"Nothing that I could tell. I don't know if he was coming out of your house or going in. Frankly, I didn't think anything of it. The house was totally dark. I thought he was a neighbor or family member or someone like that. I only saw him for a second or two, but he must have seen me looking at him because he made a gesture toward me before he walked away."

"Gesture? Like how?"

"It looked like he was pointing to me." She demonstrated with her outstretched arm. "And then he jerked his arm in the air like this."

"You mean like he was pretending to shoot at you?"

"Yes, come to think of it, that's what he may have meant."

"You said the house was dark."

"Yes."

"I turned the porch lights on before going out for my run. I always do. If they were off, it means he turned them off before he came out of the house." Clay grabbed his crutches again and went to check the light switch in the foyer. "The switch is in the off position—not how I left it. I'll have it checked for prints. Can you describe the person you saw? Anything at all?"

Allie said, "Nothing I can remember, but I'll think about it. Maybe something will come to me later. If it does, I'll let you know."

He opened the foyer table drawer and pulled out his card. "Here are my work and cell numbers. Call me if you think of anything. *Any*thing. And, Allie, thanks for the lift. I owe you."

"No problem." She brushed his arm and said, "Maybe I'll check in on you again sometime."

He nodded and smiled. "I hope you do."

CHAPTER 3

Clay called his boss, Santa Fe Captain of Detectives Matthew Ellsworth. "Captain, I'm going to be late this morning. I had a little accident."

"What kind of accident?"

"I'm leaving my house now. I'll fill you in when I get there."

* * * * *

Leaning on his crutches, Clay hobbled into police headquarters. Between his bandaged and partially shaved head and his awkward use of the crutches, it was impossible for Clay to not draw attention to his injuries. He weaved his way around the labyrinth of desks and side chairs, greeting his fellow detectives as though it was just another day in the office. One detective who worked closely with Clay, Tomás Robles, burst out with, "What the hell happened to you?"

Everyone in the room looked up. Captain Ellsworth, the ramrod-straight, gray-haired, sixty-year-old Captain of Detectives was at his desk with the office door wide open. He peered over his wire-rimmed glasses when he heard Robles and exited his office. "Clay, what happened? It looks like you got hit by a truck."

"You're close, Captain. I got hit by a car this morning when I was out for a run. I just got out of the ER." Clay lowered himself gingerly onto his desk chair. He joked, "I didn't really have to go to the damned ER, but the EMTs ganged up on me. I think they were working on a quota."

"How bad is it?"

"Nothing major. I got a couple of stitches on my head and they bandaged my knees and elbows, but otherwise I'm good."

"A *couple* of stitches? I'd say a lot more than a couple judging by the size of that bandage. Don't bullshit me."

"Captain, I'm telling you, I'm good. Really, I'm good." Clay was noted for his stoic ability to withstand pain. Over his combined twenty years as patrolman and detective, the times he suffered an injury, he returned to duty in half the time the police physician said it would take him to recover. His tolerance for pain was beyond normal.

"Start from the beginning and tell me what happened."

Clay shook his head, "It happened so quick. A car came up from behind and nailed me. Never stopped. After he hit me, he left the scene. He clipped me on the back of my leg. I'm pissed my moves didn't make him miss hitting me. I must be getting old."

"Did you get the license or the make?"

"I'm not one hundred percent certain, but I think it was an SUV, maybe a light-colored Range Rover. That's all I can remember. One thing for sure, the sonofabitch hit me on purpose."

Detective Robles interjected. "Why do you say that? How can you know? Is it possible he thought he hit debris on the road or a coyote or something and kept going?"

Captain Ellsworth offered, "Maybe he was texting and realized he hit you but was afraid to stop and face the music."

"No, it was intentional. First off, I wore a reflective vest and my running shoes have reflectors too. He couldn't have missed me. A blind squirrel would have seen me! I was lit up like a Christmas tree when his headlights were on me. And when I got back home from the ER, I found this written on the mirror in my foyer. I took a shot of it." Clay pulled out his cell phone to show Ellsworth and Robles the photo he had taken.

"What does Romans 12:19 mean? Sounds like it's from the Bible."

"It is." Clay explained that the passage referred to revenge. "Someone is trying to get even with me for some reason or another."

Ellsworth passed the phone to Robles, who said, "Clay, I'm still unclear about what you said happened."

"It was about quarter to six. I was on Santa Clara on the way back from my run—almost to my house—when a car started to follow me. I looked behind and thought maybe the driver knew me, but its high beams were on and I couldn't see who it was. All of a sudden, the car accelerated, burning rubber and fish-tailing toward me. I tried to jump out of the way but the guy caught a piece of me—right behind my thigh. Sent me sailing. That's all I remember."

Robles snickered, "This proves what I've been telling you all along."

"What's that?"

"That jogging is not good for your health."

Clay busted back. "Very funny. Captain, as you probably know, that's about the only time since I've known Tomás that he's been right about something."

Ellsworth showed some irritation at the wisecracking. "Okay, boys, that's enough. Clay, do you know if there were any witnesses?"

"Not that I know of."

"None of your neighbors saw anything?"

"It was too dark to see anything. Although a neighbor, a man by the name of Alan Strickland, said he heard a car burn rubber and then the thud of me being hit. He looked out his bedroom window and saw me, but the car was gone. Strickland's the one who called 911."

"No one else saw anything?"

"I don't know right now. There was a uniform there. I'll find out from him what he learned from the people at the scene."

"What else can you tell me?"

"The paramedic who was treating me said she saw someone at the front of my house, but it was too dark for her to make him out. He made a gesture to her, like he was shooting a gun at her."

Ellsworth said, "Let's make sure she doesn't get identified to the media when the story of your hit-and-run makes the news."

"I agree. You never know what this guy might try to do."

The captain asked Clay, "Do you know who would want to target you?"

Robles answered for Clay. "Cap'n, you know how that is. We've collared a couple hundred scumbags over the years. Some of those clowns tell us what they'll to do to us when they get out of prison. It could be any one of them."

"Clay, I want you out of here. Get home. I'll stay in touch."

"I told you I'm okay. I'm not hurting even a little bit. I can do my work no problem."

Robles gave Clay a onceover. "It doesn't look like it. You could hardly make it to your desk. You need to get out of here."

Clay shook his head and grimaced at Robles. "Thanks for your support, pal. Regardless of what my buddy here says, I'm okay."

Ellsworth said, "No, you're not. Tomás is right. I don't know why you came in. Get the hell home. As of now, you're on a two-week medical leave. You return only after you get medical clearance. I'll check in with you tomorrow."

Clay insisted, "Captain, I'm not going on a leave."

Ellsworth glared at Clay. "I said get out of here." Turning to Tomás, he said, "I want you to interview all of Clay's neighbors to see if anyone can identify the driver. And get forensics to check his house for fingerprints."

Clay glanced at his watch. "I called Carton on the way in. He said he'd be at my house at three." Dan Carton was the head of forensics for the Santa Fe police.

"All right, then. Beat it. Keep me informed. I don't want to see you again until the doctor clears you. Got it?" Ellsworth liked and respected Clay. He knew Clay would always give his all to every investigation he participated in. Clay was driven and single-minded when he thought he had the bead on a suspect. He was also known to be insubordinate—not enough to get him reprimanded, but when he thought he was right he pushed the envelope to its outer limits before pulling back.

"I'll let you know if I'm not up to it, but I'll be good by tomorrow."

Ellsworth studied Clay's demeanor. "Listen to me. I know you're pissed at what happened, and I know you won't admit it, but you're hurting and tomorrow you're going to be hurting worse. Go home, get some rest, take your medicine, and wait for Carton to show up. Now get the hell out of here."

* * * * *

Dan Carton, the chief of the Santa Fe Forensics lab, and his assistant, crime scene specialist, Dick Cook, arrived at Clay's house. Carton, a gray-haired, lean, bespectacled man, seventy years of age, held a doctoral degree in forensic science and was highly regarded for his analytical skills. Forty-year-old Richard Cook was a burly former linebacker for the Arizona Cardinals who retired from football early in his career to earn a master's degree in forensic science at New Mexico State University.

The men took photos of the message on the mirror and dusted for fingerprints on Clay's front door, the foyer mirror, the light switches, and the wall alongside the mirror. The only fingerprints they found belonged to Clay.

CHAPTER 4

Seven-thirty that evening, Detective Robles went to Clay's home to report on his interviews with Clay's neighbors. "Quite a few of your neighbors up and down your street went to the scene of the accident when the ambulance was there, but no one saw anything before or after you were hit. I asked if anyone was at the scene who was not a neighbor—someone they didn't recognize. They all said no."

Clay said, "Remember I told you about the paramedic who said she saw someone at the front of my house? Did you ask if anyone else saw that same person?"

"I did, and no one saw a thing. I also asked if anyone had a security camera at the front of their house, but no one does. You must live in a safe neighborhood."

"I thought I did—until now," Clay said.

* * * * *

Alan Strickland saw the lights were on at Clay's house and called to find out how he was doing. Clay thanked him and his wife for coming to his aid but did not disclose information about the threat written on his mirror. He asked Alan again if either he or his wife had seen the car that hit him. Alan reiterated what he told the cop at the accident scene that morning and again to Detective Robles that afternoon—that he woke to the sound of tires screeching and then a thud, that the noise woke him up, but when he looked out the window, whoever had hit Clay was gone. Twice he saw a car's taillights racing down the street but he was unable to distinguish the make or model of the car.

"I had no idea it was you until I got down to the street. I called 911 and then Harriet and I waited for the ambulance to arrive."

"What about Harriet? Did she see anything?"

"She said she didn't."

"Did either of you happen to see anyone going in or out of my house?"

"Detective Robles asked us that too. But, no, we didn't see anybody at your house."

* * * * *

After Robles left, Clay lay in bed trying to recall the details of his hit-and-run. The only thing he was certain of was the color of the car, a white or silver SUV.

Then he suddenly remembered. "Oh, yeah. Sonofabitch," he said out loud. "The last number on the license plate was a '1.' It was a vanity plate. *L–G–1, G–L–1*, or something like that."

CHAPTER 5

Police Blotter

Santa Fe Detective Injured in Hit-and-Run — At approximately 5:30 Monday morning, a vehicle traveling southbound on Via Santa Clara struck and injured Santa Fe Detective Clay Bryce in what appears to be an attempt on the detective's life.

Police are looking for the driver and vehicle involved. No description has been provided of the driver, but the vehicle is a light-colored SUV with possible left front-end damage.

Captain Matthew Ellsworth of the Santa Fe detectives said, "We take very seriously any attempt on the lives of one of our own and will continue to pursue leads as they develop."

Detective Bryce has been placed on a medical leave with non-life-threatening injuries and is expected to make a full recovery. Investigators indicate there may have been one or more witnesses to the hit-and-run and have asked anyone with information to contact them at 505-222-9999.

* * * * *

On Tuesday morning, Captain Ellsworth arrived at headquarters and saw Clay at his desk in the squad room. "Bryce!" Ellsworth shouted and pointed to his office. "Now!"

Robles and the other detectives in the room looked up. They knew from experience that their captain was not one to publicly chastise his detectives, but when Ellsworth's voice thickened by fifty decibels, the normally mild-mannered captain had lost his temper—and pity the poor recipient of that rage.

Clay grabbed his crutches and followed Ellsworth into his office. The captain closed the door behind him.

"I take it you're pissed at me," Clay said.

"That's an understatement. What did I tell you yesterday?"

Clay had expected a reprimand, so he prepared what, to him, was a reasonable explanation. "You told me to stay home until I had medical clearance, Captain. I took my medications and I feel good." He was lying. He was, in fact, in pain from his injuries and the aftereffects of whiplash but would not admit to any of that. "How does this sound? To prove I'm feeling good enough to work, why don't you and I head to the parking lot and see who wins a forty-yard dash? If I win, I stay. If you win, I go on leave."

Ellsworth laughed and shook his head. "Honest to God, you are one pain in the ass. And, yes, you can probably still take me in a race even with your crutches. I'm old and out of shape and you're making me very crotchety."

"I only came in to check out a good lead. I promise I'll head home as soon as I can, if I find what I'm looking for."

Ellsworth was not happy. "*If?* You said *if* you find what you're looking for. *If* is not acceptable." He plopped himself down behind his ancient steel desk. He was tired. His inbox was stacked three inches high with case reports and files. More paperwork surrounded the PC on the credenza behind him. Paperwork was Ellsworth's enemy. He was a year away from retirement and had no interest in acclimating himself to modern information systems and applications. "I'll accept that you may have a good lead, but I don't care *if* you do, or *if* you don't. I want you out of here. Understood?"

"Yessir, I promise. In a couple of hours I'll be gone."

Ellsworth glared at Clay and took a long, deep breath. He did not answer.

Clay interpreted his boss's non-answer as a yes. "Thanks," he said.

The captain shook his head wearily. "Have you seen this?" He held up a copy of the morning's *Times Journal*. "There's news about your hit-and-run in the Police Blotter." Ellsworth was referring to the newspaper column that listed news about local crimes and the status of investigations.

Clay said, "I haven't had a chance to read the paper yet."

Ellsworth turned to the page where the Police Blotter appeared and handed the paper to Clay. "Read it now." He gave Clay a few seconds to read the column. "What is that comment about a witness? Is that referring to the paramedic? If yes, how did the reporter get that?"

"Not from me. You know how reporters are. I think it was just boilerplate language he threw in to write his column. Or it could be the cop at the scene put something in his report about the EMTs. I'll talk to him and tell him to make sure nothing else gets out."

"What's the lead you're pursuing?"

"I'm sure the car that hit me was an SUV. And I remember the license had letters followed by the number *1*. Something like *L–G–1* or *G–L–1*. I'm guessing it's a vanity plate. I'm waiting for the Motor Vehicle Division to open up so I can get a list of all New Mexico specialty plates ending in *1*."

"If the attempt on your life was premeditated, it doesn't make any sense that the guy would hit you and risk having someone recognize the plate. Seems he would've removed the plate first. On the other hand, if the car was stolen…"

"My thoughts exactly. I've also put in a call to the state police. They're working on getting me a list of all the cars that have been reported stolen in the past week. Once I have that, I'll check it against the vanity plate list. If I'm lucky, I'll find a match. I'll wait for the MVD and stolen car reports, Captain, then I'm outta here."

"Did the crime scene guys come up with anything at your house?"

"No, the only fingerprints they found were mine."

* * * * *

By midmorning, Clay had received an email listing 163 vehicles reported stolen in New Mexico in the prior seven days. Of those, four were stolen within twenty miles of Santa Fe. A half-hour later, the MVD emailed him a list of the several hundred specialized plates in New Mexico, broken down by vanity, college, military service, and other special interests.

Clay first checked the license plate numbers of the stolen vehicles. None had a vanity plate. Next, he perused the list of specialized plates and noticed one that contained the letters *J* and *G*, followed by the number *1*. The plate had been issued to a man by the name of John Grainger, of Santa Fe. *I'll be damned. Could he be one and the same?* Clay knew a John Grainger from a case he had investigated a year earlier. He checked the address. It was the same person.

Grainger had been the operations vice president of Santa Fe's Indian Bend Hotel and Casino, referred to by the locals as "the Bend." Clay had arrested Grainger for statutory rape—he had had sex with a sixteen-year-old girl which, in New Mexico, was a fourth-degree felony. The District Attorney dropped the charge upon learning the girl had been part of a conspiracy to entrap Grainger. However, the resultant negative publicity caused by the case had cost Grainger his job.

Was it possible Grainger had a motive to kill Clay?

Clay knocked on Captain Ellsworth's office door to explain what he discovered. The captain looked at Clay over the top of his reading glasses, still irritated that Clay had disobeyed his order to stay home until he received medical clearance to return. "Give it to me quick and get out of here."

"Remember John Grainger from the high desert serial murder case last year?"

Ellsworth leaned forward and nodded. "Yes, the Bend's self-important vice president, the guy who fancied himself the king of casinos. Didn't he claim he was solely responsible for making the Bend the best casino in the Southwest?"

"That's the one. The license plate I saw could belong to him. Grainger has a car with a license number *JG-1*."

"Those are not the letters you told me you saw."

"No. But it was dark and JG-1 is close to what I remember seeing."

Ellsworth leaned back in his chair. "Let's say I buy that. What motive could Grainger possibly have for trying to kill you?"

"I can't answer that now, but he lost his job at the Bend after being charged with felony sex. I'm the one who arrested him. Maybe he blames me for losing his job—a job that paid him mucho big bucks. That, right there, is motive. From the MVD's records I learned that Grainger owns an SUV—a Range Rover—and his vanity tag ends in a *1*. Those facts, plus a potential motive of revenge, tells me he could be the one who hit me."

"All right, go ahead. See if you can get Judge Wright to sign off on a warrant to examine Grainger's car, then talk to Grainger. Find out what you can."

"But, I'm on medical leave," Clay said with a smirk.

"Oh, Jesus, give me a break, Clay. You're killing me." Clay was wearing him down. Ellsworth was concerned about Clay's well-being but, by the same token, he did not want to blunt his typical doggedness. "Go ahead and talk to Grainger. Then that's it."

CHAPTER 6

An hour after he left Ellsworth's office, Clay was able to get Judge Robert Wright to sign off on a search warrant of John Grainger's car. The judge acquiesced despite the fact Clay's only evidence was a partial license plate number and Clay's own tenuous assumption of probable cause. The warrant restricted the search to the examination of Grainger's car and to whichever other articles might be "directly related to the criminal use of the car consistent with the plaintiff's injuries."

Clay asked crime scene investigators Carton and Cook to follow him in their forensics van to John Grainger's house. From the police department on Camino Entrada, Clay drove seventeen minutes through Santa Fe and up picturesque Canyon Road to East Alameda Street, overlooking the Santa Fe River. The tan adobe home, its architecture inspired by the Spanish missions in New Mexico, stretched for 150 feet along the sparsely traveled road.

Clay pulled into the driveway with the van just behind.

When Grainger answered the door and saw Clay on crutches and his head heavily bandaged he said, "What the hell happened to you?"

"Nice to see you, too," Clay said. It was nearly noon but the former executive of the Indian Bend Hotel and Casino appeared to have just awakened. Clay observed he had lost weight in the year since he had last seen him. Grainger was unshaven and dressed in sandals, a worn t-shirt, and baggy Bermuda shorts. The forty-year-old Grainger was still handsome—Hollywood handsome—with slicked-back black hair, chiseled features, and piercing blue eyes that had seduced many women at the Bend and elsewhere. In Clay's eyes, the man was a predator, a sexual addict who could not or would not control his sexual predilections.

"What do you want?" Grainger asked.

"We have a search warrant to examine your car."

Grainger snatched the warrant from Clay's outstretched hand and scanned it. "Why in the hell do you want to search my car?"

"Forensics will look for evidence that your car was used in a hit-and-run."

Grainger peered over Clay's shoulder and saw Carton and Cook standing outside the van. They waited for Clay's signal to enter the house.

"A hit-and-run? Bullshit. What do you really want?"

"I told you. We're here to examine your car. We're investigating a hit-and-run accident that occurred yesterday morning. A runner was hit by a vehicle that fled the scene."

"And you think I did it? You're kidding me, aren't you?"

"What color is your SUV?"

"White."

"I have a description of the car—a light-colored SUV—and a partial license plate number of the vehicle used in the hit-and-run. That number may match a license plate issued to you."

"That's B–S, man. Who did I supposedly hit?"

"Me."

Grainger looked Clay over from head to toe. "Listen, Bryce, don't give me any bright ideas. Trust me, if I had wanted to run you over, you wouldn't be standing here talking to me right now. I wouldn't have missed. You'd be a dead man."

Clay took a step closer. "Did you just threaten me? Please say you did."

Grainger's eyes grew as big as platters. "It's not a threat. I'm just saying, is all. Now get out of my face."

"I'll get out of your face when you back off and let us in."

"I need to call my lawyer first."

"You can call him after you let us in. Let me put it this way. If you don't let us in, like, right now, I'll haul your ass downtown, in cuffs, and book you as a suspect."

"No. I'm not letting you in. This is harassment."

"Suit yourself." Clay turned to Carton and Cook and jerked his head for them to come to the door. "I need your help." He drew his jacket back and reached to pull his handcuffs out of his front trousers pocket.

"What are you doing?" Grainger asked.

"I'm going to read you your rights and take you downtown for refusing to obey a lawful search warrant. Turn around." He handed Cook his handcuffs. "Dick, cuff him."

"My pleasure." Cook, who was built like a linebacker, latched onto Grainger and turned him around as though he were a rag doll.

"All right, all right. You don't have to handcuff me," Grainger said. "Go ahead. Examine my car. Do it and get it over with. You know, Bryce, it's not like you haven't done enough already to ruin my life. Now you're going to throw more shit at me."

"Hey, pal, I didn't ruin your life. If your life is screwed up, you did it all on your own."

"No, it was you and that asshole assistant district attorney."

"Hank Kincaid, the ADA? You're joking, right? If he hadn't agreed to drop the case against you, you'd be in state prison right now doing one to four."

"Yeah, right. The two of you had no basis to charge me with a crime. Nothing—just innuendos."

"Are you saying your confession under oath to having sex with that girl didn't count as evidence? Or don't you remember that?"

Grainger ignored Clay's question. "She set me up—she and that douchebag boyfriend of hers. Even you admitted that. You want to know the truth about what's happened to me, Bryce? The Bend was my dream job but you got me fired because of those charges, and now not one casino in New Mexico wants to hire me—not one. I've been blacklisted by every one of them thanks to you and Kincaid."

"You're not making any sense. Are you telling me you can't get a job at another casino? If you're as talented as you say you are, the casino bosses would be lined up at your door fighting each other to hire you."

Grainger stared at Clay for a moment. "How am I supposed to take that comment?"

"Any way you want. Like I said, it was *you* who lost your job—I didn't lose it for you. Now, enough! I'm not here to revisit the past."

Grainger was determined to have the last word. "Easy for you to say. I live with what you did to me every stinkin' day of my life."

Clay pulled his Miranda warning card from his coat pocket and started to read. "You have the right to remain—"

Grainger did not let him finish. "Yeah, yeah, yeah. Blah, blah, blah. I understand my rights." He turned away from Clay. "Follow me."

"For the record, you understand your Miranda rights?"

"Yes."

Grainger led Clay and the forensics team through the living room and out a door at the far end of the kitchen into a three-bay garage. A BMW Z convertible was in the first bay and a Range Rover was in the middle bay. The third bay had tools on pegboards, a workbench, and boxes neatly organized on metal shelves.

"Why didn't your maid answer the door?"

"Consuela doesn't work for me anymore. I couldn't afford her. She went to work for Simon Learner, who now has my old job at the Bend. You remember him, don't you? My loyal assistant." Grainger's sarcasm was not lost on Clay.

"You're not happy he got your job."

"No, I'm not. Would you be? I expected loyalty from him."

"I remember you once said he was the perfect candidate to replace you. What did you want him to do—turn the job down?"

"As a matter of fact, yes. If the situation were reversed, I would have refused it and backed my boss. That's what I would have done. Instead, he sacrificed me for his own personal gain. You know, Bryce, I taught him everything he knows. Loyalty. Is that too much to ask of anyone nowadays?"

"Have you had any contact with him?"

"No. But my former secretary tells me he's now married and has a daughter." Grainger added, "Actually, I doubt the kid is his."

Clay was surprised by his comment. "What do you mean by that?"

Grainger shrugged. "Listen, I was surprised that girl married him. She was gorgeous. A lot of guys would have loved to have a piece of her."

"Who'd he marry?"

"Liza Williams. From the Bend's accounting department?"

"I remember her. Why wouldn't she have married him?"

"Because he's a wimp and she's beautiful. I've run into her a few times over the past year and she's still smokin' hot." Grainger grinned. "Man, she has an ass that just don't quit. Her marrying Simon is like the eighth wonder of the world."

Clay struggled on his crutches. To his surprise, Grainger showed sympathy. "Hey, man, I'm sorry you're hurting. I want you to know I didn't mean what I said about wanting to run you over. I was only kidding. I don't go around trying to hurt people."

Clay did not acknowledge Grainger's apology. He walked behind the Range Rover to check out the license plate and confirmed it read *JG-1*. Next, he hobbled to the front of the car to look for impact damage on the left front fender. He found a dent alongside the headlight at the exact height at which he was struck. "Dan, Dick, check this out." Grainger stood with his arms folded across his chest.

Cook took photos of the dent.

Clay asked Grainger, "How did your car get banged up?"

"What do you mean banged up?" Grainger leaned in to look at the small depression. "That? You call that banged up? It's a dent. It's been like that for a while. I don't have the slightest idea when or how it happened."

"When was the last time you drove your Range Rover?"

"Yesterday afternoon. I took it to the car wash."

Clay nodded. "That was convenient. Why? To wash off evidence from the hit-and-run?"

Grainger raised his voice. "Why the hell do you think I went to a car wash? Because the car was dirty. I got it washed. Maybe you don't know it, but that's what car washes are for."

"Why yesterday?"

"Because that's when I got around to it."

"Anyone else drive it the last couple of days?"

"No."

"Anyone else have a key to your car?"

"No."

Clay noticed the keys to both the Range Rover and the Z rested on their respective dashboards. "Why are your keys in the cars?"

"I always keep them there. That way, I don't have to hunt for them."

Clay continued firing one question after another so Grainger would not have time to concoct lies. "Where were you yesterday morning between the hours of five and seven?"

"Monday? I was at a... a *friend*'s house. I spent the night."

"In other words, you were at a woman's house. Is that right? Did you drive your Range Rover there?"

"No, my Z."

"Who was the woman?"

"I'm not telling you that."

"I get it. She's married?"

Grainger did not answer.

"You look at every man's wife like they're for you to bed, don't you?"

He shrugged. "Not every wife."

Clay faced Grainger and shook his head. "You're pitiful, you know that? You need help."

"Yeah, right."

"Tell me, what did you do with the rag you used to clean my blood off the fender? Is it in the garbage?"

"What are you talking about? I didn't clean any blood from my car."

"Where are your garbage cans?"

"They're out front. Pickup is today."

Clay spoke to Cook. "Dick, check the garbage cans for paper towels, rags, anything that might have been used to scrub the fender clean. If necessary, take the cans back to the lab for testing."

Grainger argued. "You can't do that. They're my personal property."

"Of course we can. We don't need a warrant to search the trash you leave out for collection." Clay moved slowly around the inside perimeter of the garage. He kept an eye on Grainger the entire time. He knew that, during a search, suspects often looked at the location where incriminating evidence was hidden. Grainger's gaze did not waver.

Clay approached a door located on the far wall of the garage. He opened the door and saw it led into an attached shed. "Do you think someone could get into your garage through the shed without you knowing it?"

"Yeah, sure, that's possible. But I always make sure the outside shed door is locked."

The unusually clean and orderly shed was full of garden tools, bags of peat moss, and ceramic pots. Two shelves held bottles of various herbicides and pesticides. Below each was a printed label that described each bottle's intended use. Clay opened the outside shed door. A paver walkway led to a beautifully landscaped backyard. Plants and shrubs surrounded an infinity pool overlooking the Santa Fe skyline.

He looked around then reentered the shed and went back into the garage. He informed Grainger, "The shed door was unlocked. Didn't you say you always keep it locked?"

Grainger was perplexed. "I must have forgotten to lock it."

Carton continued to examine the Range Rover. Clay stood over his shoulder and looked at what he was examining. "Find anything, Dan?"

"Not yet. I've got samples to analyze back at the lab. I'll let you know what I come up with."

Grainger fumed. "This is all bullshit. Samples of what? Road dust from my car and coffee grounds from my garbage can? You've got to be shitting me. Are you setting me up?"

Clay said nothing.

Grainger continued his rant. "If you're trying to piss me off, you're doing a good job. I'm through cooperating. Why in the hell do you think I would try to kill you? That's crazy! It doesn't make sense."

"Vengeance. Revenge. You said it yourself. You believe I caused you to lose your job at the Bend. You know what Romans 12:19 is about, don't you? You wrote it on my mirror."

"What the hell are you talking about? What is Romans 12:19? It sounds like it's from the Bible."

"Yeah, you're right."

"That's it. I'm not going to answer any more questions without my lawyer here." Grainger pulled out his cell phone and called his attorney, Mark Flores.

While Grainger was on the phone, Clay spoke with Carton. "When you and Dick are through here, go ahead back to headquarters. I'll talk to you later."

CHAPTER 7

Another hour passed before Grainger's lawyer arrived. Mark Flores had defended Grainger against his felony sex charge.

Grainger seethed. "What the hell took you so long?"

"I was in court. I *do* have other clients you know." Flores looked at Clay's crutches and the bandage on his partially shaven head and asked, "What happened to you?"

Grainger answered before Clay had a chance to respond. "You remember Detective Bryce, the cop who accused me of all that shit last year. Well, he's doing it again. He's accusing me of using my Range Rover to run him over."

Flores searched his client's face for a sign of guilt or innocence.

Grainger understood his lawyer's questioning look and said, "And, no, I didn't."

Clay stood stone-faced in front of the two men, listening to Grainger berate him to Flores as if he was not there. Grainger continued to spew anger to his lawyer. "Mark, I'll tell you what—I don't appreciate the sonofabitch coming to my house to accuse me of a crime I didn't commit. In my opinion, this is a continuation of his vendetta against me. It's harassment, pure and simple." In his fury, Grainger's face turned red.

Undaunted, Clay waited until Grainger finished his verbal attack against him.

Flores looked back and forth between the two adversaries, uncertain what was happening. "Detective Bryce, what are you accusing my client of?"

"Counselor, I'm not accusing him of anything—right now. He's a person of interest, that's all. The car that hit me was a light-colored SUV, similar to the one owned by your client. And

43

it had a license plate number very similar, if not identical, to the plate on your client's car. These similarities point to him as a potential suspect. My warrant is for forensics to examine the vehicle to determine if it was the one that hit me. Does that answer your question?"

"That's a heck of a reach, Detective—a car that's a similar color and a license plate that doesn't match. That's it?"

"Yes. That, coupled with your client's stated belief that I cost him his job at the Indian Bend Casino, introduces the motive of revenge."

Grainger continued to rage. "Yeah, you cost me my job all right, but it doesn't mean I'm going to kill you," he barked.

Flores put his hand on Grainger's forearm. "Let me handle this, John."

Clay continued, "Mark, your client said he was at a friend's house at the time the hit-and-run occurred yesterday. He said he was there between five and seven a.m., but he won't divulge his friend's name, and that means I can't corroborate his alibi. I suggest you talk to him and explain—"

Grainger did not let him finish. He took Flores aside and, after a minute, Flores said, "You... have got... to be... kidding me."

Clay was leaning heavily on his crutches, waiting for their conversation to end. He thought, *I can only imagine what Grainger just told him.* A twinge of pain made Clay grimace.

Finally, after another minute of whispered conversation, Flores said to Clay, "Detective, Mr. Grainger does not wish to give you his friend's name. Divulging that information without an agreement from you to seal her name could damage the lady's reputation and quite possibly her well-being."

"I get it, Mark. He's screwing a woman, and she's married. Isn't that it, Grainger? What's news about that? You've been doing that for years."

Flores looked at Grainger, who shrugged indifferently and looked away.

"I need to know who she is and where she lives so I can corroborate his alibi. I will keep the information confidential. But, if he lies to me or she doesn't back up his alibi, all bets are off."

Flores nodded his acceptance. "My client agrees to those terms. He will disclose the name of his alibi under your stated seal of secrecy."

Grainger was still hesitant. "I can't believe I'm telling you this. As God is my witness, if you ever..." He paused for a good five seconds, still deciding if he should divulge the woman's name.

Flores said, "John, he's not going to say anything. Isn't that right, Detective?"

"You have my word."

Grainger blurted out the name of his alibi. "Arianna Arrington."

Clay was stunned. "*Mr.* Hayden Arrington's wife?" Hayden Arrington III was the fourth-generation scion of the extraordinarily wealthy and powerful Arrington family of Santa Fe.

Grainger did not answer immediately.

"You're kidding."

"No. I'm not."

"And you're saying she will corroborate your alibi?"

Grainger nodded.

"Where was Mr. Arrington at the time?"

"Traveling on business in Germany."

"Where did you meet up?"

"At her house. She lives on Coyote Ridge."

Clay was familiar with Coyote Ridge, the ultra-exclusive development of a half-dozen homes located in the foothills of the Jemez Mountains overlooking Santa Fe.

"Do you always meet at her house?"

"No. We sometimes meet here." Grainger paused then added slowly, "And sometimes other places."

"Like where?"

Flores interjected. "That's irrelevant to your investigation. I remind you of your vow to not let this out. If this information becomes public, I will take legal action against you personally and extract every penny of your current and future assets as well as sue your police department and, for good measure, the city of Santa Fe."

"I get the picture. I told you I will not disclose who he's been screwing."

Grainger turned to Clay and asked, "Are we through now?"

"Yes, for now. However, this is an ongoing investigation and I may have additional questions for you at a later date. You are advised not to leave Santa Fe without first informing me. And, Mark, please inform your client I will be interviewing Mrs. Arrington and he should refrain from contacting her."

CHAPTER 8

Ellsworth was surprised to see Clay hobbling back into the squad room. "Bryce!" he shouted and crooked his forefinger, signaling him into his office. "Close the door."

The squad room went quiet. Everyone craned their heads to look through the glass partition of Ellsworth's office, trying to read the captain's lips. "Didn't you tell me you were going to cut out after you searched Grainger's house?"

"Yessir."

"And didn't I tell you not to return until you got medical clearance?"

"Yessir. I didn't think you were serious."

"What?" Ellsworth took a deep breath, his face flush with his rising anger. "This is the second time you've disobeyed my orders." Ellsworth was, by all measures, a cop's cop, concerned about his men's welfare, willing to defend them against any criticism or fault. And he expected obedience, loyalty, and discipline in return. "You either get out of here and wait for medical clearance or I put you on unpaid suspension for a month. You see all these?" He waved his hand at the stacks of ongoing case files in front of him. "These cases would go begging. Is that what you want? A month's suspension means I'd be biting off my nose to spite my face."

"I get that you're mad. I'm mad too. Someone tried to kill me. I realize I'm pushing the envelope by coming back in this afternoon, but I thought you'd want to know what I found out about Grainger."

Ellsworth calmed down. "Here's the deal, and it's *not* subject to negotiation. Brief me on your search, then you're out of here. Got it?"

Clay avoided answering his captain directly. "I'm convinced Grainger has the motive to kill me. He blames Hank Kincaid and me for costing him his job at the Bend."

"Why Hank?"

"Because he was the ADA assigned to the case when we charged Grainger with felony underage sex. Grainger ranted how Hank and I destroyed his reputation and how we ruined any chance of him ever getting another job like the one he had at the Bend."

"What did you find out about Grainger's car?"

"His Range Rover is white and it has a dent along the left fender where it could have hit me, but we don't know what to make of it yet. It's a minor dent, but the car didn't hit me squarely either. The crime scene guys are checking it for blood and skin tissue."

"Anything else?"

"Yeah. Grainger claims he had an alibi. He was with a woman overnight Sunday into Monday morning. That's why I wanted to talk to you."

"Did he identify the woman?"

"Yes. Hold your hat. You're not going to believe it. It was Hayden Arrington's wife."

Ellsworth's mouth dropped open. "You're kidding me. Hayden Arrington's wife?" He stammered and said it again. "*Mr.* Hayden Arrington? You mean Arrington's ex-wife?"

"No, his current wife—Arianna. Now you know why I had to talk to you. Grainger had Mark Flores, his lawyer, come to his house when I was executing the search warrant. Mark agreed Grainger could give me the name of his alibi, but only if I swore I wouldn't disclose it during my investigation."

Their conversation was interrupted by a knock on the door. Dan Carton stuck his head in Ellsworth's office. "Captain, sorry to interrupt, but I have an update for Clay about John Grainger's car."

"Come in, Dan."

Carton explained, "Sorry, Clay, but we found no physical evidence to implicate your suspect. The damage to the Range Rover's left front fender occurred at two feet ten inches from the ground. Although it was almost precisely the height at which you were hit, we found nothing that pointed to it being the vehicle that hit you. The damage was slight and it was not consistent with striking a person. The car had been washed and there was no blood, skin tissue, or clothing fibers on the fender—no indication at all that it struck you or any other living thing. There are two other dings on the left side of the car, but they're most likely from car doors opening against the Rover, like in a grocery store parking lot."

"Did Dick find any evidence in the garbage cans?"

"No, nothing. If Grainger used a cloth or a sponge or something else to clean the car, it was not thrown out with the garbage. It was discarded some other way." Carton shook his head. "Sorry, Clay, but there's *nothing* to indicate his car was the one that hit you. Judging by his house, I'd say he's probably a clean freak. The damned place, including his garage, was immaculate."

"You're right about that. Thanks, Dan." Carton closed the door on his way out of Ellsworth's office. Clay resumed the conversation. "I need to visit Mrs. Arrington to corroborate Grainger's alibi."

"Did I not tell you that your medical leave was not subject to negotiation? What part of that order did you not understand? I said I want you out of here and home."

"Let me do this one last thing. I'll head home the minute my interview with her is over. I'll be an hour at most. I want to interview her before she and Grainger have a chance to rehearse their answers and blow smoke about their rendezvous."

Ellsworth looked up at the ceiling and shook his head in frustration. "Listen, Clay, I can see you're hurting. I understand you have a high tolerance for pain, but even *you* have to take time to recuperate from injuries. You look like shit. You've been going at it hard since yesterday morning. I understand this is personal and you want answers. I do, too, but don't make matters worse for yourself."

"A quick interview with Grainger's alibi, then I'm gone for the day. That's a promise."

Ellsworth eyed Clay with suspicion. He admired Clay's drive and determination, but he also wanted him to obey his order to recuperate from his injuries.

Clay continued, "Captain, I'm very close to wrapping this up. I only need another hour."

Ellsworth clearly was irritated at Clay's insubordination, but he finally relented. "I give up. Go ahead, talk to her. But I want your shield and your service weapon right here, right now." Ellsworth tapped his desk three times as he spoke. "You'll get them back when you come walking in here with a medical clearance after your two weeks leave."

CHAPTER 9

Arianna Arrington was born to Sarah and Jacob Bailey in Bernalillo, New Mexico, a small town less than an hour southwest of Santa Fe, between the Sandia Mountains to the east and the Rio Grande to the west. Jacob was a traveling salesman who earned a decent wage selling trinkets to tourist stores throughout New Mexico—knickknacks such as coffee mugs, keychains, and pens from a catalogue of hundreds of such items. His far-flung territory kept him away from home four nights a week. He would return Friday evening, usually having spent some, if not all, of his weekly earnings on women, booze, and gambling.

Every Friday, Sarah waited anxiously for Jacob's return, hoping he retained enough money to replenish her bare cupboards and pay the rent.

There seldom was enough.

Sarah worked part-time trying to make ends meet, but the sum of Jacob's and her paychecks was not enough to pay the rent or prevent the family from being evicted time and time again. They were forced to move seven times before Arianna turned sixteen. Arianna saw her mother's despair when Jacob returned home each week, often drunk and physically and verbally abusive. As an adolescent, Arianna recognized the heartache her father caused and asked her mother countless times, "Why don't you leave him? He's so mean. I hate him."

"Don't say that, Arianna. I love him. Your father will change. You'll see. He's not a bad man." Sarah gave Arianna a hug then added, "I promise you, if he doesn't change, I will leave him— one day."

The *one day* came on a Friday when, once again, Jacob returned home drunk and this time without a penny left to his paycheck. Sarah was desperate. "What's wrong with you? We don't have money to buy groceries." She stood in the kitchen and railed at him.

Jacob said, "Then why don't *you* get a job if you think you can do better?"

"I get work when I can, but we never stay long enough in any one place for me to get a full-time job. Besides, you're the man of the house," Sarah shot back. "You're the one who's supposed to provide for *us*, but you'd rather drink your way home."

Arianna had never heard her mother confront her father before. When she heard a scream, she hurried into the kitchen in time to witness Jacob snorting like a wild animal and standing over her mother with a closed fist. Jacob had knocked Sarah to the floor, shouting, "Don't you *ever* talk to me like that again!"

When Sarah rolled onto all fours and tried to stand, Jacob kicked her in the side. She fell back to the floor in agony.

Arianna yelled, "Stop it! Stop it!"

Jacob looked at his daughter, his eyes black with rage. "Stop? You want me to stop? I'll stop when I'm ready." He kicked Sarah again.

Arianna yanked open a drawer and pulled out a knife. "I told you to stop!" She advanced toward her father and screamed, "If you hit my mother again, I'll slash your face."

Jacob put up his hands and took a step back. "Okay. Put the knife down."

"You've got three seconds to get out of this house or I swear I will stick this knife in you."

"I said *okay*."

"One... two..."

Jacob did not wait for the count to reach three. He stumbled out of the house.

Arianna locked the door behind him and helped her mother to her feet.

Sarah winced with pain. "Arianna, get your things together. We're leaving now and we're not coming back. I told you one day we would. I was so wrong about your father. He's never going to change."

Sarah had been secretly saving a few dollars and had enough money to buy bus tickets for her and Arianna to get to Santa Fe where her sister, Rachel, lived with her husband, Tim, and their three children.

"Then what? Where will we go from there? What will we do?"

"I don't know yet. We'll figure it out."

Sarah left a note for Jacob on the kitchen table. "I can't bear another day living with you. I need someone to love me and hold me and take care of me. I've waited and waited for you to change. But you never do. I want more from life than you will ever be able to give me."

* * * * *

For years, Rachel had been preaching for Sarah to leave Jacob. When Sarah and Arianna showed up at Rachel's door with their scruffy suitcases in hand and Sarah's face black and blue from Jacob's punches, Rachel knew Sarah had finally left her abusive husband.

The two sisters talked late into the night. "Rachel, I should have listened to you long ago. I thought he would change. I was wrong. I'm never going back. I want to go to California and start all over again. I want to find happiness. I haven't told Arianna yet, but, I beg of you, let her stay with you and Tim for a while. She's seventeen and a beautiful young woman. She won't be a bother."

Rachel did not hesitate. "Of course she can stay with us."

Sarah said, "I'll have her find part-time work to help pay for her board. And she can babysit the children. You'll see, she'll be a big help to you."

"She'll be fine with us. Tim will clean up the room above the garage. She'll be okay there. Please, go find what you're looking for. And when you do, let us know where you are and what you're doing. Just be safe."

The next morning, Sarah sat down with Arianna. "I'm going to leave here tomorrow and go to California and try to start a new life. Aunt Rachel and Uncle Tim have agreed you can stay with them until I get settled. Then you can join me."

Arianna burst into tears. "Mom! No! I'm going with you. I'm not staying."

"You must. Sweetheart, don't make this any harder than it is right now. We can't both stay here. I'll come back for you once I've found my way. I promised Aunt Rachel you would help her anyway you can. Babysit the children. Find part-time work to help pay for your board."

Arianna sobbed uncontrollably.

Sarah hugged her tight. "Please don't hate me. This is something I have to do for both our sakes. My heart breaks."

"But, Mom—"

"Arianna, please, listen to me. You're a smart girl and so beautiful. You'll see. Everything will work out. Always remember this. Find happiness wherever the path may lead you and with whoever can take you there. Do whatever it takes to find that pot of gold." She repeated, "Remember what I'm telling you. Always follow your dreams, no matter what."

The next morning, with a loan of one hundred dollars from Tim, Sarah boarded a Greyhound bus bound for Los Angeles. No one knew if she made it to her final destination or if she got off at any of the stops along the way. She repaid Tim's loan three months later, but did not say where she was or what she was doing. She had disappeared. Was she dead or alive? Did she finally find happiness? No one would ever know.

Arianna never heard from her mother again but used her advice as a powerful mantra that would rule her life: *Follow your dreams. Do whatever it takes to find that pot of gold.*

CHAPTER 10

By the time Arianna turned eighteen, she had developed into a stunning young woman with the high cheekbones of a model and the full lips, shapely long legs, and voluptuous figure women of all ages envied—and men lusted over.

Out of feelings of obligation and gratitude, she remained with her aunt and uncle until she was nearly twenty, at which time she decided to rent a small apartment in Santa Fe and fend for herself. She took a job as a server at a popular downtown bistro where she learned quickly how to earn generous tips from men. She wore her uniform unbuttoned at the neck and leaned over to show her cleavage as she worked the tables. She bantered and flirted with the male customers, smiling to herself at how easy it was to get men to grovel over her. She was propositioned often and quickly recognized the sexual power she had over men.

After a happy two-year stint at the bistro, Arianna was recruited by the manager of the four-star Hotel Santa Fe on the iconic Santa Fe Plaza to manage the numerous private functions and cocktail parties at the hotel's luxury suites. Her salary doubled.

* * * * *

A cocktail party sponsored by the extraordinarily wealthy businessman Hayden Arrington for executives of a Japanese precious metals firm proved to be the turning point in Arianna's quest to satisfy her mother's ambition for her to follow her dreams and find her pot of gold.

The seventy-year-old, round-bellied, balding Arrington was unable to take his eyes off Arianna. Neither could the six

Japanese executives in attendance at the cocktail party. They tittered behind her back about other purposes she might serve. When the event was over, Arrington approached Arianna. "I don't mean to bother you, miss, but I was curious if you ever babysat."

Arianna had heard many creative pickup lines before, but this was a first. With a quizzical expression she said, "Excuse me? What did you say?"

"I asked if you babysat," Hayden repeated.

The hour was late and Arianna was annoyed that Hayden was keeping her from supervising cleanup duties, but she smiled and answered in a pleasant tone. "Sir, I'm not sure why you're asking, but, yes, I have done quite a bit of babysitting. I still do occasionally for my aunt."

Hayden was captivated by her. "Good. May I explain why I ask?"

"Yes. Please do."

"The babysitting job is not for me. My son and his wife are interviewing for a nanny to help care for their three daughters. And they have another child—a boy—on the way. They've been having difficulty finding someone they could trust to care for their children. I've been watching you perform your duties here and have been impressed with your diligence and personality."

Yeah, right. Diligence and personality my ass. He wants to see how far he can get with me. Arianna had caught Hayden looking at her all night. Each time, she gave him a demure smile. And each time, he smiled back.

Hayden continued, "You seem to have impressed everyone here. Might you be interested in interviewing for the nanny position? It pays well."

Arianna eyed the old man with continued suspicion. "I've never thought about working as a nanny. I make good money here. Thank you, anyway, but I really don't want to give up this job."

Hayden did not give up. He explained just how handsomely the position paid. "Whatever you make here, I will ensure your pay as a nanny will be twice that amount—plus, you'll have your own casita to live in on my son's estate. If you're interested, I will be happy to arrange for you to interview with my son and daughter-in-law tomorrow. Please think about it." Hayden reached into his pocket. "Here's my card. Call me tonight to let me know if you are interested." He handed Arianna the card then peeled five hundred-dollar bills from his money clip. "Oh, and this is for you. Thank you for taking such good care of my guests."

She took the money from Hayden and examined his card. Other than knowing he was the host of the event, she had no idea who he was. "Mr. Arrington, is it?" she asked. "This is very generous of you."

"Not at all," Hayden said. "You earned it. There's more of that in the future if you become my son's nanny."

Arianna's smile was broad and receptive. "Sir, you've convinced me to go for the interview. Will you be there too?"

"If you want me to be there."

"I do."

"Then I'll be there."

She looked directly into Hayden's eyes. "I'll look forward to seeing you again. You know, I've learned to never say no to a new opportunity." Then with a suggestive smile, repeated, "*Any* opportunity."

Hayden's mind ran wild as he speculated what Arianna might have meant. "Good. I will have my driver pick you up here at the hotel at ten o'clock tomorrow morning."

"I'll look forward to meeting your son and daughter-in-law. By the way, my name is Arianna Bailey."

He nodded. "I know."

CHAPTER 11

Hayden's driver and aide Anton Yushenko met Arianna at the hotel the following morning to drive her to Hayden's son's house for the nanny interview. Arianna was dressed in a red blouse and skin-tight white jeans that made the stoic Anton look twice.

Anton was forty-four years old and had served thirteen years in the vaunted Ukrainian special forces called the Alpha Group. Ten years earlier, Hayden had hired Anton through *Certainmente*, a Monte Carlo search firm that specialized in recruiting former military personnel to serve as bodyguards and aides for wealthy men and women. Anton was powerfully built at six feet tall, with penetrating steel-gray eyes and hands that could tear a magazine in half. His loyalty to Hayden was inviolate.

From the luxurious back seat of Hayden's Rolls-Royce, Arianna asked Anton, "What does your boss do?"

Anton peered at her from the rearview mirror, surprised by her question. "You do not know who Mr. Arrington is?" Although Anton was from Ukraine, he spoke nearly perfect English.

"Can't say I do, except that he's a *very* generous man."

"Mr. Arrington owns a number of businesses here in New Mexico, including the Indian Bend Casino. He also has copper mining businesses in Arizona and Texas and companies in Europe and the Far East. He is considered one of the most powerful men in the state—more powerful than the governor."

"No kidding," was all Arianna could say.

"Good luck today."

"Thanks. Any tips you can give me?"

"You'll do fine. Mr. Arrington's son, Hunter, is a nice gentleman, laid back. Hunter's wife's name is Harmony. She can be difficult to please, but, since Mr. Arrington has arranged for your interview, I'm sure it is a mere formality. Just be yourself. I'll be waiting outside to take you back when you're done."

Hayden greeted Arianna at the front door and escorted her in to meet Hunter and Harmony. Hunter, who was thirty-eight years old, showed his approval of the sexy Arianna by giving a thumbs up to Hayden when he thought no one was watching. He was wrong. Both Arianna and Harmony caught the gesture.

The only child of Hayden and Ruth Arrington, Hunter had struggled with ADHD all his life. With his premature loss of hair and generous belly, he resembled his father. Hunter always tried to curry his father's favor, but his inattentive, impulsive, hyperactive personality made it impossible for him to live up to the Arrington standard of success.

Hayden felt neither pride nor affection toward his son. He had intended to have Hunter, a fifth-generation Arrington, take over Arrington Industries and continue to run the family conglomerate. Over time, however, he recognized that Hunter possessed neither the drive nor the backbone needed to run the family enterprises. Most upsetting to Hayden was that Harmony dominated their marital relationship and Hunter acquiesced to Harmony's every demand.

Arianna was overwhelmed by the size and lavishness of the younger Arrington's house. She was sincere when she said, "You have a magnificent house, Mrs. Arrington."

"Thank you. I designed it," she said without humility.

Harmony was the same age as her husband and six months into another difficult pregnancy. She eschewed makeup and her thin, reddish hair lay in an unstyled mass on her head. Difficult to please, she had hired and fired three nannies since her first child was born.

"Why were they fired?" Arianna asked.

Harmony explained, "They took advantage of my kindness and good nature and did not show they were dedicated enough to care for my children."

Hunter cast an incredulous look at his father upon hearing his wife's explanation. Hayden's quick headshake told Hunter to keep his mouth shut. In truth, Harmony was demanding and highly opinionated, but Hayden did not want to scare off Arianna. He recalled private conversations with Hunter in which his son frequently referred to his wife as "Disharmony."

Arianna read Harmony well and was not going to be scared off. She recognized that working for her would present its challenges. But with the lure of her own casita and a generous compensation, she made up her mind she wanted the job.

Harmony was gracious and pleasant to Arianna, appearing to be convinced Arianna was the right person for the job. She showed Arianna the casita where she would reside if the job were offered to her—accommodations that, alone, were reason enough for Arianna to accept the position.

Harmony led Arianna back through the main house to the front door. The interview had ended. "Well, Arianna," said Harmony, "Thank you for coming. I'll be in touch with you in a day or so. We have a countless number of applicants. As you can imagine, we perform reference checks on each. I'm sure everything is fine with yours, but, you understand, of course, it does take time."

"Certainly, I understand. If you need any additional information, please let me know."

Hayden appeared from the living room as Arianna was about to leave. She smiled at him and said, "Thank you again for the opportunity, Mr. Arrington."

"You're welcome."

Anton had just lit a cigarette when Arianna walked out of the house. He quickly put the cigarette out by crushing it between his thumb and forefinger, then put the unsmoked butt in the pack to finish later. He held the door of the Rolls-Royce open for Arianna and asked, "How did it go?"

"Mrs. Arrington will be tough to work for, but I'll be able to handle it. They're going to let me know in a day or so. I'm positive they'll offer me the job if your boss, the old rich guy, has anything to do with it." *There's no question he likes me. This is going to work out just fine.* Arianna sat back in the Rolls and smiled.

Anton disapproved of the way she referred to his boss as "the old rich guy." He looked at her in the mirror, suspicious of her intentions.

* * * * *

No sooner did the door close behind Arianna than Harmony turned to her husband and said, "I don't like her. She won't last a month taking care of the kids. She'll leave and go back to being a waitress or whatever she's been doing. I know the type. She needs men to ogle her. She wouldn't be happy here."

Hunter was surprised. "The way you acted toward her I thought you were going to hire her on the spot! Now you say you didn't like her? That's disappointing. I thought she was delightful and I'm sure the children would have liked her."

Hunter was servile to his wife on all matters domestic. "But, whatever you decide."

Hayden finally spoke. He pressed for Arianna to be hired. "I recommend you give her a try. Personally, I think she'll be wonderful with the children. I saw how she worked my event last night and I was very impressed. She's a bright young woman, and she said she's done a lot of babysitting. What's the worst that can happen? If she doesn't work out, you can let her go—like you've done so many times before." Harmony raised her eyebrows at Hayden's last comment and looked away. He said, "I think she'll be excellent for you. Besides, you haven't liked any of the other eight nanny candidates Hunter tells me you've already interviewed."

Harmony looked cross-eyed at Hunter for disclosing how many interviews she had conducted. She was reluctant to agree with her father-in-law, but she caved. "As usual, Dad, you make valid points." She rubbed her belly and added, "My time to hire and train a suitable applicant is limited. Hunter, let's go ahead and offer her the job."

"Whatever you say, dear."

CHAPTER 12

Arianna's job as nanny to Hunter and Harmony's children began the following Monday. From the first day, Harmony was as cold as Arianna expected her to be, often requiring her to do chores outside the normal responsibilities of a nanny. Harmony's attitude toward her new nanny, however, had nothing to do with ensuring Arianna knew her place in the household hierarchy. Rather, Harmony was intimidated by Arianna's beauty and sexuality and took her insecurities out on Arianna the only way she could—by being critical and haughty.

"I told you we shouldn't have hired her," Harmony said to Hunter. "She's never going to work out. Look how she dresses and how she struts around in front of your father like she's God's gift to men."

"I don't see anything wrong with the way she *walks* around," Hunter said with an impish grin.

"Of course you don't. And your father doesn't either. He fawns all over her. Who knows why a girl like that would take a nanny job. Mark my word, she's angling for something. She'll probably end up suing us for something or other."

In spite of Harmony's attitude and treatment of her, Arianna did her job well. She proved to be a good caretaker for the children, sweet and gentle, yet strict when she had to be.

* * * * *

Three months after Arianna started working for the Arringtons, Harmony gave birth to a baby boy. Hayden was so thrilled that a boy had been born to the Arrington family—"to keep the bloodline alive"—that he visited the child often. And, of course, he always took the time to chat with Arianna to ensure she was happy in her nanny role.

Arianna could tell Hayden lusted for her. She had been right about him all along. She knew men and what they wanted from her. It was always the same thing and she did not object. *What did Mom say? I should follow my dreams? Does that mean I lower myself to be with a rich old man? Of course it does. He's a billionaire for God's sake. I could have everything I've ever wanted—money, jewelry, clothes. Why the hell not? Can I live with myself if I have sex with him? Better yet, can I get him to leave his wife and marry me? Damned right I can. Mom said it. Do whatever it takes.*

Harmony observed her father-in-law's starry-eyed behavior toward Arianna. She said to Hunter, "Something's going on with the two of them."

Hunter shrugged the matter off. "For God's sake, Harmony, he and Mom have been married for forty-five years. He's not going to do anything."

One day, Hayden visited when Arianna was alone with the children. She greeted him with a kiss on both cheeks and a hug that lasted long enough for him to feel the contours of her breasts against his chest

"Mr. Arrington, I wish you would visit more often. I do miss seeing you."

"I have to confess, Arianna, you bring light into my life each time I'm with you."

Arianna feigned embarrassment with a shy smile.

He said, "That's silly of me to say. I apologize."

"No, please don't apologize. Frankly I'm having a… a difficult time too, and…" She did not finish but instead brushed his arm tenderly.

"That's very nice for an old man to hear." Hayden's heart beat faster.

"Oh, Mr. Arrington, you're not an old man. Why, you don't even look fifty!"

"Thank you for saying that. That's very sweet, Arianna."

"Well, I mean it."

"Oh, before I forget, I want to give you something. Now, please, keep this to yourself." Arianna nodded her agreement. "I want you to know how much I appreciate that you're able to withstand the rigors of working for my daughter-in-law." He peeled off ten hundred-dollar bills.

"Oh, my God, Mr. Arrington. You are *so* generous."

"I enjoy being generous with such a charming woman. And, dare I say, I trust there will be more to come for you."

From then on, anytime Hayden visited while Harmony was not home, Arianna greeted him with effusive displays of affection. During one visit, she kissed him softly on his lips, a move that drew a gasp from Hayden. He could not control himself and pulled Arianna awkwardly to him, kissing her hard. She pretended to swoon over his tight-lipped kiss.

In that instant, she knew. *I have him. He's mine.*

Days later, Harmony and Hunter were attending a gala and not expected back until late that night. Arianna called Hayden to tell him she had something to discuss with him privately. "The children will be asleep by nine. Can you come then?"

"Of course." At nine o'clock sharp, Hayden entered his son's home. Arianna greeted him in the foyer dressed in a sheer nightgown that hid nothing. The old man stood with his mouth agape, silent, except for the sound of his rapid breathing. Arianna reached for his hand and led him to her casita.

After many such rendezvous, Hayden confessed to Arianna that he had fallen hopelessly in love with her. "Will you marry me?"

Follow your dreams. Whatever it takes!

* * * * *

Hayden and Arianna met with Hunter and Harmony to announce their intentions. Son and daughter-in-law were speechless—shocked and disbelieving. Finally, Harmony spoke in as calm a voice as she could muster to suggest that their age difference might be a problem. Hayden brushed off her arguments and spoke of happiness, love, and affection. A smiling Arianna held Hayden's hand and looked adoringly at her billionaire lover the entire time.

When Hayden dismissed Harmony's argument with a wave of his hand, Harmony jumped up from her chair, looked at the mismatched lovers, and glared at Hunter. "Say something." Hunter simply shrugged and looked away. Harmony stood over him and shouted, "You're pitiful. You know that? You're pitiful." She stormed off and said loud enough for everyone to hear, "I can't believe it. That old fool wants to marry a slut. She's nothing but a gold-digging whore and my husband sits there with his mouth open."

* * * * *

After forty-five years of marriage to Ruth, Hayden ingloriously filed for divorce. What followed was a bitter and very public proceeding that lasted over three years and was the subject of Santa Fe high society gossip and national media coverage. In typical tabloid fashion, the *National Enquirer* characterized the divorce as a boxing match and published images of Ruth and Arianna in a boxing ring—Ruth wearing boxing gloves and Arianna surrounded by a halo of hundred-dollar bills. Nevertheless, Arianna argued to anyone who would listen that she loved Hayden and their forty-plus-year age difference was not important to the success of their relationship.

When Hayden's divorce became final, the billionaire married the twenty-seven-year-old beauty in a private ceremony in Taos. Hayden's long-time lawyer and only friend, Wallace Sanderson, served as best man and witness. Hunter and Harmony were not invited to the wedding.

CHAPTER 13

One marketing strategy John Grainger used often at the Indian Bend Casino was to host events and galas for various charities. At one such event—a charity gala for the internationally renowned Santa Fe Opera—Grainger met the recently married Arianna Arrington. The gala was Hayden and Arianna's first appearance in public as a married couple. John had seen photos of Arianna in the newspaper during Hayden's divorce battle, but, when he saw her in person, dressed stunningly in a head-turning red satin dress that accentuated her slender waist and bountiful cleavage, his antennae were immediately raised. The disparity between Arianna and Hayden was striking. She was tall and elegant while her seventy-three-year-old husband was shorter by four inches and, although he wore an expensive, custom-made tuxedo, he appeared to be precisely what he was—a rich old man with a trophy wife. Hayden beamed ear to ear as he paraded his new wife for all to meet and greet.

When introduced to Arianna, John Grainger kissed the back of her hand and remarked, "Mrs. Arrington, you are the belle of the ball. It is my great pleasure to meet you." He turned to Hayden. "Mr. Arrington, I wish you and Mrs. Arrington heartfelt congratulations and best wishes on your marriage."

As Grainger walked off Arianna said to Hayden, "He seems like a nice fellow—and handsome, too."

Hayden looked at her suspiciously.

Arianna spotted his look and kissed him on the cheek. "But, Hayden, sweetheart, I only have eyes for you." Her faithfulness did not last long. Within a year John Grainger and Arianna Arrington had had their first rendezvous.

* * * * *

Clay called Arianna and asked to meet with her privately to discuss a confidential police matter. "We can meet at police headquarters or at your home. Your choice."

"What's it about?"

"I'll explain when I see you."

"Sounds mysterious and exciting, like in the movies," she said. "Let's meet at my home at five-thirty this evening. Mr. Arrington is out of the country on business and my maid will be gone for the day at that time. I assume you know where I live—2019 Coyote Ridge."

Named for the coyotes that abounded in the foothills of the Jemez Mountains, Coyote Ridge was the site of the Arrington's ten-thousand-square-foot mansion built on the mountainside among prehistoric boulder formations. Clay took in the scenery and let out a low whistle as he pulled into the entrance of the Arrington's gated property. "Not too shabby," he said aloud.

He announced himself to Arianna through the intercom embedded in the stone wall at the driveway entrance. Seconds later the gate swung open. Driving up the steep, winding drive, he marveled that the boulders perched above the mansion remained in place despite the contraction and expansion of the granite cliffs. *I wonder if the Arringtons ever fear one of these monster boulders crashing down on their home.*

With difficulty, Clay exited his vehicle and used his crutches to hobble to the front door where Arianna stood ready to greet him. He was instantly struck by her looks—blonde hair flowing to below her shoulders and azure, almond-shaped eyes. She wore white short-shorts and a tight pink t-shirt that left little to the imagination.

"Hello, Detective Bryce. What happened to you?"

"I was hit by a car."

Arianna twisted her face. "Seriously? Well, gee, I know I'm not the best of drivers, but I hope you don't think I did it."

"No, I don't think that, but I want to ask you about someone you know who may have. It was a hit-and-run. The driver never stopped."

"Who's that?"

"John Grainger. I understand you two are friends." Clay did not imply he knew the extent of their relationship.

She delayed answering. "I've met him, yes."

Clay noticed her hesitation. "Mrs. Arrington, may I come in or would you prefer to answer my questions out here on the front landing?"

Arianna looked nervously over Clay's shoulders.

"Are you expecting someone?"

"No, I'm not. You're right. How rude of me. Certainly it's better if you come inside."

Clay followed Arianna into the large living room. "You have magnificent views through every window."

"Yes, Hayden says we sit at about four thousand feet, so we can see forever."

"Your home is beautiful."

"Thank you. Hayden has good taste in beautiful things."

Clay realized Arianna's comment was meant to include herself and smiled to let her know he agreed.

"So, Detective, what do you want to ask me? You've got me on pins and needles." She flashed a fake smile. "Would you like to sit?"

"No, I'm better off standing. I won't be long. What can you tell me about John Grainger?"

"Not much. I mean, I know him, but not that well. He's an acquaintance."

"Mrs. Arrington, please. I've spoken with Mr. Grainger and he's already told me the nature of your relationship. In fact, he told me he was here with you from Sunday night to yesterday morning. I'm asking you to confirm his statement. Was he here?"

"I don't know what you're talking about."

Clay's disposition turned sour in a flash. He leaned in toward Arianna on his crutches, towering over her. "As you can imagine, I'm not exactly in a mood to be playing games with you."

She ran her fingers through her hair. "What kind of mood do you need to be in to play games with me?"

Clay showed his impatience. "Listen to me, Mrs. Arrington. You can either answer my questions here and now or you can answer them at police headquarters. I suggest, however, that you really don't want to go downtown." His voice had an angry edge to it as he exaggerated what could occur. "I'm sure the television reporters assigned there would love nothing more than to report that the wife of the powerful Hayden Arrington was dragged into police headquarters in cuffs as a suspect in an assault case."

Arianna became immediately defiant. "Detective Bryce, you are not my father. I didn't appreciate him shouting at my mother and me, and I certainly don't appreciate you raising your voice at me either."

Clay took a deep breath. "I'm sure you can understand that I'm not happy someone tried to kill me. I suspect your boyfriend may have been involved. You can help me by answering my questions about his whereabouts yesterday morning. I'll ask you again. Was John Grainger here with you Sunday night into Monday morning as he claims?"

Arianna looked away and responded with a flip, "Perhaps."

Clay struggled to maintain his temper which could become volcanic if pushed. "What do you mean *perhaps*? Were you with John Grainger yesterday morning? That's a yes or no question. I don't care to know what he was doing here and I don't care if you're having an affair with him or just telling each other bedtime stories."

"Detective, puh-*leeze*. If you already know the answer to your own question, why are you asking me?"

She's pissing me off. "It's very simple, Mrs. Arrington. I need you to either confirm or deny what Grainger has told me. Was... he... here?"

Arianna tilted her head, deciding whether to answer or not.

"And understand this. If I find out you lie to me, I'll be forced to discuss this matter with your husband to learn what he might know about your relationship with Grainger. Tell the truth and this stays between us."

"You know, I could get Hayden to talk to the chief of police about you and your strong-arm tactics. You don't want that, now, do you?"

Clay knew Arianna was bluffing. She would never risk giving up her luxurious lifestyle by telling her husband what was going on. "Are you threatening me, Mrs. Arrington?"

Her cavalier air continued. With eyes tilted toward the ceiling, she put the tip of her finger to her lips as though in thought. "Well, now. Let me think." She tapped her lips then smiled sweetly. "Why, yes. Yes, I am. I guess you have no idea how powerful my husband is. But we don't really have to go that route, do we? Why don't you ask me again what it is you want to know—but ask nice this time."

Resigned to play it her way, Clay asked, "Mrs. Arrington, was John Grainger here with you Monday morning?"

Arianna was still not prepared to answer directly. It was now her turn to fume. "I have no idea why John told you such a thing! How idiotic of him. If Hayden learned about us, he'd divorce me and take me out of his will."

"Listen to me. I told you before I would not divulge your affair. I just need to know the truth."

"Since you swore this will not go any further, I guess I can tell you. Yes, John was here," she said at last.

"When did he get here and when did he leave?"

She bit her lip, showing signs of nervousness for the first time. "He got here Sunday night at about ten. He parked his car in our garage and didn't leave until the next morning. He always leaves before nine—before my maid, Imelda, comes to work."

"Do you know if he left during the night?"

Arianna shook her head. "No. I don't think so."

"You don't *think* so? I'm unclear what you mean by that. Could he have left for an hour while you were asleep and then come back?"

She reverted to her defiant self. "Detective, when John's here overnight, we don't sleep much. You can imagine why, can't you?" Her sarcasm made Clay uncomfortable. "He's not here, as you suggested, to tell me bedtime stories. I can explain it to you if you wish."

Clay felt his face heat up, but he continued. "You said Mr. Grainger left before nine. Exactly what time did he leave?"

75

"I'm not one hundred percent sure, but probably close to nine. I don't remember precisely when it was. Actually, I was dead to the world. But I woke up at about eight-thirty and panicked because he was still here. I had to rush him out the door before Imelda arrived."

"What car did he drive here Sunday night?"

"His sports car."

"You mean his Range Rover?" He tried to lead her into saying Grainger had driven his SUV.

"No, I know what a Range Rover is and it's not a sports car. John's car is a two-seater convertible—a BMW Z."

"Where was your husband yesterday morning?"

"Hayden left for Germany on Sunday morning from his hanger at the Santa Fe airport." She wanted to impress Clay further. "That's where he keeps his jet."

"It must be nice having your own jet," Clay said.

"It is. We use it to fly everywhere."

"Well, good for you," Clay said with his own touch of sarcasm back at her. "So, then, your husband left Sunday morning through the front door and John Grainger came in through the back door?"

"That's a mean thing to say."

"It's true, isn't it? Here's what boggles the mind. Why jeopardize all this by having an affair?"

Clay's comment put Arianna on the defensive. She grimaced. "I know it's stupid. You wouldn't understand."

"Try me."

"Hayden isn't that great in bed. I mean, he... he just isn't... He's older. He can't always get it, ahh... You know what I mean, don't you?"

Clay stared at her and shook his head slightly, continuing to make her feel uncomfortable.

"Maybe you don't understand. You see, I have a *very* high libido which Hayden can't satisfy. I always have. I bet you do, too, don't you?"

"I do too *what*?"

"Have a high libido. Don't you? A big rugged guy like you?" Arianna looked Clay straight in the eyes and added, "No matter what you think of me, I *do* love my husband."

Clay tried unsuccessfully to conceal a smirk.

Arianna shrugged. "I see how you look at me. But it's true— I do love him. And I like that he spoils me. He treats me like a princess." She tilted her head and posed pretentiously. "And, as the commercial says, I'm worth it. Don't you agree?"

"I'm sure you are worth it."

Arianna acknowledged Clay's comment with a smile.

"Does your husband have any reason to suspect you're having an affair with John Grainger?"

"No! God no. Besides, what would that have to do with you being hit by a car? I don't know why you're so interested in my husband. You said you were here to discuss John, not Hayden."

"You're right. I was just curious."

"Actually, I *will* answer your question. No, Hayden does not know about John and me. We've been extremely careful." She swept her hand to encompass her luxurious house. "You see all this? I don't want to lose it. If I thought Hayden suspected I was having an affair, I'd put an end to it in a heartbeat."

Clay shook his head at Arianna's brazenness. With what he knew about Hayden's reputation, she would have hell to pay if he ever found out about her affair with Grainger. "Why don't you divorce your husband, get what you can in the deal, then marry John so the two of you can live happily ever after?" His comment stung with sarcasm.

"John would never be able to provide me the lifestyle Hayden does."

"Does John know you feel that way?"

"Truth be told, my attraction toward John is fading, if you know what I mean. I've been thinking about breaking it off anyway. I mean, he's good in bed, but..." She let her words trail off.

"But what?"

"He's been getting needy. I hate being smothered." She stopped abruptly and waved her hand to end their conversation. "That's it. That's all I'm going to tell you about my sex life. I've told you what you came here to find out—that John was here Monday morning. And you've agreed to not say anything to Hayden. Can we end this discussion now?"

"I have one final question."

"What's that?"

"Did John tell you I planned on questioning you?"

She hesitated. "No. I mean, uh... yes."

"Which is it—yes or no?"

Arianna looked away from Clay briefly then turned back. "The truth is yes. He didn't want me to be surprised by your visit."

"So he told you about the hit-and-run and you've pretended all along that you didn't know anything about it?"

"Yes, but I've been truthful about everything else. Trust me. I'm not happy that John told you about us."

"Did he tell you that I arrested him a year ago for having sex with an underage employee at the Indian Bend casino?"

"Yes. And he said the charges were thrown out. He said the publicity about his arrest is why he was fired from the Bend. It's true, isn't it?"

"John must've also told you he has it out for me, right? Revenge on his mind? Maybe get even with me by running me over?"

"No, he never told me any such thing."

Clay nodded. "When does your husband return?"

"The day after tomorrow. Thursday." Her eyes flashed concern. "Why are you asking?"

"As I've said, if I find out you've lied to me, I'll meet your husband on the tarmac when his plane lands and disclose your affair. Then you and he can hash it out. Understood?"

Arianna remained silent.

"And for the record, Mrs. Arrington, if you're giving John Grainger a false alibi, you'll be looking at five years in prison for obstruction of justice. That's no exaggeration—it's a fact. With that in mind, have you told me the truth about John Grainger?"

"You decide, Detective."

CHAPTER 14

Immediately after Clay drove off, Arianna called Grainger. "That detective you said was going to question me just left my house."

"How did it go? Did you cover for me?"

"Yes, of course I did. What choice did I have?"

"Listen, I need to talk to you. Is the coast clear? I'm coming over."

"No one is here. I'll open the garage on the far left. Anton has one of the cars out for servicing."

"I'll be there in fifteen minutes. Open the gate for me."

The Arringtons had four garage bays—one each for their Lamborghini, BMW, Rolls-Royce, and Suburban SUV. When Arianna saw Grainger's Z come up the driveway, she pushed the garage door opener at the kitchen entrance and watched as Grainger pulled into the vacant bay. She hit the button again to close the door.

Grainger embraced Arianna but she reacted stiffly. "What's the matter?" he asked. She pulled back from him and walked into the kitchen.

Arianna could not control her anger. "Why in hell did you tell him you were here? And, why on earth would you admit we were having an affair? Who else have you told?"

"No one. I told you why I had to tell him. I had no choice. He thought I tried to kill him! He was going to charge me with attempted murder. I *had* to tell him I was with you. You were my alibi."

"Good God! What happens if he tells Hayden?"

"He's not going to. He swore he would keep your name out of the investigation. My lawyer was present when he promised me. We could sue him for all he's worth if he told anyone."

"Sue him? Ha. For all the good that would do me."

"Tell me exactly what you told him."

"He threatened to tell Hayden and have me arrested for obstruction of justice or some such thing if I didn't tell him the truth. So that's what I did. I told him you were here."

"Good."

"I need to ask you, John—and don't you lie to me—did you try to kill him?"

Grainger looked away momentarily then turned back to look Arianna in the eyes. "No, of course not. I was with you. How could I have tried to kill him?"

"That's what I told him. I said it couldn't have been you, that I had to rush you out before Imelda showed up. But, honest to God, John—and I didn't say this to him—I can't say for sure you were asleep the whole time you were with me. Did you leave at any time?"

"What? Is that what you think I did? After making love, I waited for you to fall asleep, then got dressed, snuck out of the house, got into my car, found out where Bryce was jogging, ran over him, then drove back here, pulled my car back into the garage, snuck upstairs, and jumped back into bed without waking you? I'd have to be Houdini to have done all that."

"John, I just don't know." Arianna stood with her hands on her hips. "If you wanted to kill him bad enough, I'd say it's *all* possible. I don't know."

Grainger responded angrily, "I'm going to say this one last time. I did not run him over. Now get off that subject."

81

"Don't you dare raise your voice to me. This is all your fault. You were dumb to tell the detective about us to begin with." Arianna studied Grainger closely. "You know what, John? No matter how many times you deny it, I'm still not sure you're being honest with me."

Grainger looked deep into Arianna's eyes. "I have never lied to you—about *any*thing."

She was not convinced. "After he left, I got to thinking that we should stop seeing each other."

"What are you saying?" Grainger asked.

"If we don't, sooner or later we're going to get caught and I could lose everything."

"Bryce told you he wasn't going to say anything to Hayden, right? Look, we're safe. Your imagination is running wild. He won't talk."

"Well, here's something a little unnerving. As soon as I hung up from talking with you, Hayden called me from Germany. It's almost like he knew the detective had been here."

"Arianna, come on. I'm sure it was a coincidence. How could he have known?"

"I don't know. Maybe Anton said something. I don't trust him. He's always in my face. Hanging around. He probably reports to Hayden what I do every day. I have to shoo him away sometimes when I want some alone time."

"You mean alone time with me."

"Yeah, whatever.

I just thought it was strange that Hayden would call me at that exact moment."

"What did he say?"

"He said he's flying back on Thursday and that he misses me."

"I'll bet—but not as much as I've missed you."

Arianna softened her tone. "Silly boy, it's only been since yesterday morning."

Grainger pulled Arianna close and kissed her on the forehead. He moved to her lips then slid his hands down her back to her firm behind.

Arianna responded to his touch. She ground her hips against his body, pleased to feel his arousal grow—a far cry from her foreplay with Hayden, who needed help from a pill.

Grainger had had sex with many women, but not one who wantonly craved sex as much as Arianna. "I can't keep my hands off you," he breathed as she continued to grind against him. He shook his head at this gorgeous woman. "You are, by far, the most exquisite woman I have ever known."

Though she did not doubt her beauty, Arianna responded with unusual humility. "I'm all right, I guess."

Grainger tilted his head toward the staircase. "Let's go upstairs. If we're going to end this, we should do it in style."

"Let's see what you can do, big boy. If you're good, I might have to reconsider."

They climbed the stairs to the second floor and entered the master bedroom. The massive room featured an extravagant Italian marble bathroom with a whirlpool tub, six-jet shower, and wine cooler filled with expensive French wine. Arianna locked the door behind them as an extra precaution. "I keep thinking about Detective Bryce. If he tells anyone about us—"

Grainger cut her off. "If keeping him quiet means I have to get rid of him, I will."

"What do you mean 'get rid of him'? You don't mean *kill him*, do you?"

"No, no. Of course not."

Arianna kicked off her sandals as John opened a bottle of Chardonnay. They clinked glasses. Arianna followed her first sip with a suggestive roll of her tongue over her lips. Grainger's eyes were glued to her. She set her wine glass on the bedside table then slowly, deliberately, removed her t-shirt. Grainger exhaled with an exaggerated, "Whew." He set his glass aside and eagerly fondled Arianna's breasts as she unbuckled his belt and moved to unzip his pants.

Arianna delighted in Grainger's reaction to her foreplay. *Men are fun to watch when they lose control.* She sat on the edge of the bed and smiled with satisfaction when Grainger, fully aroused, tore off his clothes and stood over her. Arianna fell back and lifted her legs for him to pull off her shorts, then reached up and wrapped her arms around his neck to gently draw him down to the bed. He kissed her breasts, her stomach, her thighs. She arched her body to signal her desire—she wanted him in her. Her head twisted back and forth in ecstasy. At first, they moved slowly, rhythmically. Arianna dug her fingernails into his back and restrained him with "Not yet! Not yet," to make her pleasure last. Then she moaned, "Faster, faster, faster. Yes! Yes! Yes!" until their passion exploded.

CHAPTER 15

John Grainger woke when a sliver of sunlight angled its way through a crack in the drawn curtains and cast a line of light directly into his eyes. He tilted his head to avoid the light then interlocked his fingers behind his head and looked over to Arianna. She had slept the night with her arm resting on his chest. He was in love with her, or so he thought, and had been wondering where their relationship was heading. In reality, his relationship with Arianna was no different from all his other relationships with women—relationships built on lust, an emotion that blinded reason.

Arianna woke a minute later and looked up at her lover. She ran her hand over his chest. "Good morning, big boy. Have you been awake long?"

"Only a minute," he replied.

She teased him. "You look lost in thought. Probably waiting for more sex, right?" She propped herself up by her elbows to kiss him on the cheek.

"No I know it's hard to believe, but I wasn't. I was thinking about what you said last night, about how we should stop seeing each other. Did you really mean it?"

She smiled, "We'll see."

"I was... you know... wondering about you and me. I mean..." Grainger struggled to find the right words.

"What about you and me? Just say it, John."

"Have you ever thought about leaving Hayden?"

Arianna was startled by his question and quickly removed her hand from his chest. "What are you talking about? Why on earth would I leave him?" She got out of bed and put on a robe.

He watched her move across the room. "Because you don't love him. And because you and I are the same in so many ways."

"You mean because we're addicted to sex."

"Yes."

"What would happen to us if we got tired of having sex with each other?"

"Arianna, *you*? Get tired of sex?"

"No, I mean tired of sex with each other."

With a smirk of incredulity, Grainger said, "That ain't *never* gonna happen on my end."

"Maybe not, but I don't want to talk about it anymore." Without an ounce of shame or embarrassment, Arianna added, "Hayden gives me everything I've ever wanted—money jewels, cars, things. I'm not going to give all that up—even for sex with you." She stood by the bed, looked down at Grainger and said, "You've got to think about leaving before Imelda shows up."

Grainger did not move. He was stunned at how abruptly Arianna dismissed the thought of leaving Hayden. "If I was still at the Bend, making the bucks I was making back then, would it make a difference to you?"

She had a look of disdain. "The answer is no. I'm not leaving Hayden." She wanted to end the conversation. "Come on, you've got to leave. I need to make the bed."

"What if I don't? What happens if I decide to talk to Hayden and tell him about us?"

"What are you, crazy? You're starting to worry me. Now, come on, get out of bed."

Deflated, he rolled out of bed and dressed as she tidied up the bedroom. She dumped the remaining Chardonnay, picked up the bath towels, and pulled the linens off the bed. They avoided looking at each other until Grainger finally broke the ice. "And if Hayden were dead? What would your answer be?"

"What are you talking about? First you talk about killing that detective and now Hayden? Don't talk like that."

"Why not? I mean, what if he happens to die?"

Arianna could not believe her ears. "What is wrong with you? I said to stop talking like that."

"Why? Don't you stand to inherit a mother lode if he dies?"

"I don't want to get into that."

Grainger said, "Even the great Hayden Arrington is going to die one day. You do realize that, right?"

"Don't be ridiculous. Of course he's going to die. But not now. He's got to stay alive or—"

"Or what?" Grainger pressed.

"Or else I don't get anything."

He was stunned. "Arianna, your husband is, what, forty years older than you? You can't possibly have anything in common with him. You're on cloud nine right now because of all the stuff he gives you, but when you've been married a half-dozen years and he's feeble and you've got to take care of him, nurse him, and he can't get it up for you even with a pill to help him, what then? How are you going to feel then?"

Arianna knew Grainger was right, but the pull of all things material that Hayden lavished on her was a way of life she was not willing to give up. Not for Grainger. Not for anyone. Grainger served the purpose of satisfying her sexual needs, but she was certainly not in love with him. "I realize I'm not the smartest person in the world. But I got lucky because I happen to be pretty and I don't mind having sex with one of the richest men in the country. Yes, he's old, but so what? He gives me things and makes me realize that being rich is better than being poor." She paused and turned introspective. "I believe one talent I *do* have is knowing how to make Hayden happy."

"You make me happy too." Grainger was serious.

"I know I do. I can make any man happy. Men are easy," she said. "But when Hayden's happy, I'm happy. So, yeah, okay, that's my talent—making Hayden happy. And sometimes it scares me to know how stupid I am by being with you."

Grainger grew defensive. "Stupid? By being with me?"

"You know what I mean. I know we've been careful. But when you told the detective about us, that changed everything. Now I'm scared to death it'll leak out and Hayden will find out about us."

"It won't—"

"John, stop. I've made up my mind. We can't see each other anymore. I'm not going to risk all this. I'm done talking about it. The fact is, I don't plan to ever leave Hayden."

"This is it? I can't believe it. I don't believe you really mean what you're saying."

"You're not listening to me. I *do* mean it. As of right now, we're not going to see each other anymore." Arianna's back was up.

Grainger sounded desperate. "Why don't we meet at my house instead? That's safer, isn't it?"

"John! No! We've got to stop. I've loved being with you. I need... I mean, I love Hayden and all, but—"

"But what? You can't love him. I don't believe it."

"We have to stop. I'll find another way to satisfy my... " Her voice trailed off.

Grainger was crestfallen.

Arianna saw his reaction and embraced him. "Don't go making me feel worse than I already do. Who knows? Maybe, if

I'm *totally* certain Hayden wouldn't find out about us, we could still get together once in a while. But, for now, he can't know about us. He'd divorce me in a split second. I can't let that happen. We need to stay married for twenty years or I don't get a thing. Okay? Now you know."

"So that's it. Now I get it."

"You tell me you're bored to tears without a job. Why don't you try to go back to the Bend? You keep saying you made a lot of money there. Why not go back to your old job? It doesn't have to be there. What about working at a different casino?"

Grainger shook his head. "I wish I could, but I can't. Bryce destroyed my reputation. No one's going to hire me because of what he did to me."

Arianna recalled something Hayden had told her recently. "I don't know if you know this, John—and I don't really know why Hayden told me, because he never talks business with me—but he said that the Bend might go bankrupt if they don't turn it around soon. Apparently, the guy who replaced you is not doing a very good job."

"Simon Learner?"

"Yes, that's him. I met him a couple of times at Bend functions. He seems like a nice person, but Hayden has been awful with him. He called him an Ivy-League know-it-all who didn't know anything-at-all. And one time he said—in front of Simon's wife—that if Simon didn't straighten things up, he would be out on his ass. I actually was embarrassed at how mean Hayden was to him. You can imagine how Simon must have felt, especially with his wife there."

"I guess. But it's part of the territory working for your husband."

A year earlier, the Indian Bend Hotel and Casino had been the most successful casino in New Mexico, thanks to John Grainger's leadership. Grainger knew that the murders of several casino employees as well as his own firing had caused attendance at the Bend to spiral downward and revenues to plummet, in spite of Simon's best efforts.

"Sounds like you have a thing for Simon."

Arianna sensed Grainger's jealousy, "Oh, for crying out loud. I haven't had sex with him, if that's what you mean. You're jealous, aren't you?"

"Jealous of that weasel? Not a chance. If anything, he was jealous of me. His wife was all over me when I was at the Bend."

"From what I understand, every woman there was all over you."

He smiled. "Well, maybe not *every* woman—but yeah, most of them."

Arianna continued, "Why don't you talk to Hayden about going back to the Bend? You told me more than once that you were the one who made the Bend successful in the first place. Now that the casino is not doing as well, maybe he'll take you back."

"Your husband's the one who fired me over the sex crime charge. He's not going to rehire me."

"He might," she smiled. "You never know."

CHAPTER 16

Thursday evening, after a twelve-hour flight from Frankfurt, Hayden Arrington's Gulfstream V jet arrived at the Santa Fe Regional Airport. Anton Yushenko was waiting on the tarmac to drive Hayden home. Anton had been Hayden's driver, aide, bodyguard, and personal attendant for ten years and was always on call for Hayden and Arianna regardless of the hour. Although tired from his long trip, Hayden was unusually cheerful to be getting back home. His negotiations had been successful and he was eager to see his young wife.

Hayden was the sole owner of the privately held Arrington Companies. Founded in 1834 by Hayden's great-grandfather, the company was formed as a metals and mercantile firm producing copper kettles and wire. Over four generations of Arrington ownership, the company evolved into a global conglomerate headquartered in its founding city of Santa Fe. Hayden was respected for his financial acumen, political influence, and civic and philanthropic contributions. He was regularly listed in the *Forbes List of the 400 Richest Americans*. But he did not suffer fools gladly and used hard methods to achieve success. He had earned a reputation for being litigious and aggressive, rude, intimidating, and extraordinarily egocentric. Publicly and privately, he insisted on being addressed as *Mr. Arrington*, even though, with the exception of family, his lawyer, and his personal body guard, he called everyone he knew by their last name

"How was your trip, Mr. Arrington?" Anton asked. The two men had a surprisingly warm relationship.

Hayden answered, "It was good, Anton. It took until yesterday, but we reached agreement on the terms of my acquisition. I'll have to fly back next week to tie up some loose ends, but I'm very pleased with how the negotiations went. How has everything been here?"

"Good, sir."

"And Mrs. Arrington?"

"She is fine, sir. I've driven her shopping several times and to the country club for lunches with her friends. She has been keeping herself busy."

"Shopping always keeps her busy, doesn't it, Anton?"

"Yes, sir." Anton nodded and showed a smile to Hayden in the rearview mirror. "And, as you asked, I have maintained a diary of her schedule for you to review at your leisure."

"Good. I'd like to look at it tomorrow."

Anton had been suspicious of Arianna from the first day he met her. He never spoke of his belief that Arianna had married only for money. It was not his place to offer Hayden an opinion about her spending habits, but he recognized that nothing escaped her desires. To Anton, Arianna was governed by neither budget nor any sense of self-denial. She shopped at high-end clothing boutiques and jewelers and spent hours on a regular basis at an exclusive spa enjoying massages and other beauty treatments.

Anton also questioned Arianna's faithfulness to Hayden. On more than one occasion, he had walked into the house to hear Arianna whispering on the phone then abruptly hanging up when he entered the room. Each time, she had laughed the call off as a wrong number. Anton suspected that, when Hayden was away, Arianna was having secretive, late-night visitors at the mansion.

Hayden called Arianna to tell her he had just landed and to expect him within thirty minutes.

"I've missed you, Hayden. I can't wait to see you."

"I also."

"I have something planned for us. I hope you're not too tired."

"I'm never too tired for you, my darling. Is it what I think it is?"

She giggled. "Well, hurry home and you'll see."

Anton pulled up to the front entrance of the Arrington home and walked briskly around the car to open the door for Hayden. "Sir, I shall inform Mrs. Arrington you have arrived and carry your bags to your bedroom."

"Thank you, Anton."

Arianna stood at the living room window to watch her husband's arrival. She composed herself with a deep inhale, put on a wide smile, then opened the front door and stepped outside with a flourish. She brushed past Anton and into the arms of her husband who welcomed her embrace and kiss. "I've been lonely without you here, Hayden—so , so much!"

"I've been lonely too, dear," Hayden replied, showing his perfect dentures.

Anton observed the interaction, shook his head imperceptibly, and carried Hayden's suitcases up to their bedroom.

Arianna took her husband's hand and led him into the house. "Have you eaten?" she asked.

"Yes. As usual, Rose and Ann prepared a wonderful dinner on board." The women were Hayden's longtime personal flight attendants. "You must travel with me to Frankfurt the next time."

"I'd love to." Arianna stepped in close to her husband and whispered in his ear, "Come now. I want to show you what I've got planned."

Hayden smiled with anticipation. Arianna continued to hold her husband's hand as they climbed the stairs to their bedroom.

Anton stood by after he deposited Hayden's suitcases in the master suite. "Sir, is there anything else I may do for you?"

"No. Thank you, Anton. You may leave for the night. I'll be in touch with you tomorrow." Hayden turned to Arianna and said, "Sweetheart, I picked something up for you in Germany."

Arianna smiled knowingly. He always brought her an expensive gift from his travels. Hayden unzipped his carry-on bag and extracted a small box. The box was wrapped in gold foil and tied with a black ribbon. Arianna ripped off the paper and opened the box to find an oval and cable link gold chain necklace. She squealed in delight and turned her back to him. "It's beautiful! Put it on for me."

Hayden attached the clasp.

Arianna went to the bedroom mirror to admire the necklace. "Oh, it's so pretty."

"Do you like it?"

"I love it. You are always so sweet to me, Hayden. I love you"

"And I love you too."

"Now, I have something for you."

"What?"

"Well, I thought first you might want to shower after your long flight."

Hayden nodded. "Good idea."

"Well, here. Let me help you." Arianna loosened his tie and helped him take off his suit jacket. "Let's drink to us first." She led him into the cavernous marble bathroom where an ice cooler holding a bottle of Perrier-Jouët champagne sat on the vanity. "This is my favorite. It's yours too, isn't it, Hayden?"

"Sweetheart, anything I drink when I'm with you is my favorite." He uncorked the bottle, letting the cork explode across the bathroom. Arianna giggled. He gave a toast as they clinked glasses. "To us. Thank you, my dear, for making my life exciting again."

"Did you take anything?" She reached down to feel. "Oh, good, you did." He was erect with the help of a blue pill. Within a minute she had artfully removed her husband's clothes. His arousal grew as he watched her remove her blouse and shorts. She stood naked, except for her new gold necklace. He reached for her breasts and fondled them awkwardly.

"I cannot believe how magnificent you are," he said.

Arianna turned on the steam, then coaxed Hayden to sit on the heated marble bench in the shower. Having Hayden partially obscured through the fog of steam made it easier for her to have sex with him. She let him continue to fondle her.

His face turned redder and his chest rose and fell rapidly. "I'm ready. I'm ready," he moaned. She turned her back to him and sat on his lap. With hardly any movement on her part, he erupted in seconds. "I'm ready. I'm ready," he said over and over, even after climaxing.

Arianna shut her eyes tight and grimaced.

CHAPTER 17

Friday afternoon, the day after his return from Germany, Hayden had Anton drive him to John Grainger's home. Anton knocked on the front door, but Grainger did not answer. Hayden then stepped forward and leaned on the doorbell.

Grainger cursed to himself. *Who the hell is that?* He peered through the lace curtain on the door's side window and saw it was Hayden. *Oh, my God. He found out about Arianna and me. The other man is probably his bodyguard.* Grainger cowered behind the door and tried to control his breathing which had quickened nearly to the point of hyperventilation. He heard Hayden say, "Check around back. I'll wait here."

Grainger quickly calmed himself then opened the door as Anton started toward the back of the house. He greeted Hayden with a false smile of welcome. "Hello, Mr. Arrington. What brings you here?"

Hayden uttered, "We need to talk."

Grainger did not respond. He was enfeebled by Anton's cold stare.

"Well?" Hayden said.

Well what? Grainger's mind was racing. He did not know what Arrington wanted. *Does he want me to confess? Right here, right now?* Grainger visualized an escape route through the house and out the back door. *I can make a run for it. No! I can't do that. Anton would catch me.* He stood mute and terrified.

Hayden asked, "Are you going to let me in or not?"

"Oh. Yeah, sure," Grainger stammered. "Come in."

Arrington brushed by him to enter the living room.

Grainger assumed Hayden's bodyguard would wait outside. He started to close the door, but Anton used his foot to block the door from closing. Grainger looked at Anton's emotionless face and then down at his foot. *I'm dead.* "Mr. Arrington, do you want him to come in too?"

"What do you think?"

I guess that means yes. Grainger stepped away from the door to let Anton pass.

The bodyguard continued to glare at Grainger who stood ill at ease dressed in shorts and a worn t-shirt. "Pardon the way I look, Mr. Arrington. I've been working out."

"Do I care?" Hayden huffed.

"No, I guess not."

"I have a personal matter to discuss with you."

Grainger was certain Hayden could see his heart beating through his t-shirt.

"What do you mean a *personal matter*, Mr. Arrington?"

"It is not in my DNA to accept embarrassment, insult, or offense without taking drastic action in return—when necessary. Is that not true, Anton?"

Anton nodded once.

"You are aware of my financial interest in the Indian Bend."

"Of course, sir."

"The Bend today is on the verge of collapse, of financial ruin. Are you aware of that too?"

"I have heard rumors, yes, sir."

"Rumors, eh? The Bend's losses due to falling attendance is not rumor—it's reality. And it's an embarrassment. I don't like to fail at anything. *Comprendez vous*?"

Grainger did not know what to say. "I do, yes, sir." Every few seconds, he peeked at Anton and noticed the muscles in the bodyguard's jaw clenching and unclenching. He recalled Arianna telling him of Anton's military background in Ukraine and it struck him that the bulge underneath Anton's breast coat pocket was probably from a pistol.

"Perhaps you are aware I hold you personally responsible for the Bend's near total collapse—all because you can't keep your dick in your pants."

Inexplicably, Grainger smirked.

"You think that's funny?"

Grainger's eyes darted to Anton and the bulge in his pocket. With the knuckles of his right hand, Grainger casually wiped away the perspiration that had developed above his lip. "Sir, I thought you were being funny. My mistake. Yes, I know I'm somewhat to blame for what has happened, but there's nothing I can do about the past."

"Somewhat? Did you say *somewhat* to blame?"

Grainger shook his head rapidly and took on the role of self-defender. "It's not strictly my fault, Mr. Arrington. You understand, of course, that there was a serial killer on the loose murdering our employees. And that damned Detective Bryce let the case drag on for weeks. People simply went to other casinos rather than risk falling victim themselves."

"I don't accept that excuse. Yes, the case was dragged out ad infinitum, but you were in charge. You could have facilitated the police investigation and helped to put an end to it sooner. Apparently you were too busy screwing every woman who shook her tail at you. You enjoy taking risks, don't you, like going to bed with underage women. And married women."

Here it comes. Here comes the hammer. He felt himself turn red, as if he were an adolescent caught in an apologetic act. "Mr. Arrington, I'm aware you are upset with me, but the reputation of my womanizing is greatly exaggerated. For whatever it's worth, I can honestly say I've learned my lesson."

Hayden did not buy Grainger's false contrition. "I *don't* think you've learned your lesson. You are what you are. However, after I explain why I'm here, I do not want to broach this subject again."

"I understand."

"You *understand*? I like that word. You know why I like that word?" Hayden did not wait for Grainger to answer. "It means people see my point of view. And if they see my point of view, that pleases me."

Grainger nodded as if he followed Hayden's line of conversation, but thought to himself, *What the hell is he talking about?*

"I typically remove myself from the hands-on operations of any company I own. But in this instance, I feel it is imperative to take strong action to keep the Bend from collapsing. I can no longer stand idly by and watch it crumble. I have put a great deal of money into keeping the Bend afloat, but I have reached my limit. In the scheme of things, if the Bend outright collapsed, it would be a huge embarrassment to me. Do you understand, John?"

John? He called me John? He's never called me by my first name. What's that about? "I'm really sorry about what's happening at the Bend, Mr. Arrington, but I don't know what you want from me."

"I will explain. You should know that Simon Learner has not been able to handle the challenges the Bend has faced. Attendance is down fifty percent year to date and revenue continues to plummet at a similar rate. Learner is a well-educated man, but he's not cut out to turn around a business of this size and scope."

"I'm surprised, sir. I thought he would have been able to cut it."

"Well, he hasn't. Now, what I'm telling you is confidential. Do you understand?"

"Yes, sir."

"Not a word to anyone. Three months ago, I spoke with Learner personally and placed him on warning. I told him he would be let go at the end of the three months if the Bend's bottom line did not improve significantly."

"Has it?"

Hayden looked at Grainger quizzically. "For Christ's sake, I just told you that. Are you listening to me or do you think I came here on a social visit?"

"I'm listening, of course. But, what do you want from me?"

"Where are you working now?"

"I'm not. I'm between jobs."

"Good, because when I put Learner on notice I also told him I was going to hire you back to replace him if he didn't turn things around."

Grainger was stunned. "Me? Did you say me?"

Hayden looked at Anton, shook his head, then looked back at Grainger. "Yes, you. I said you. What part of 'I was going to hire you back' do you not understand?"

Grainger's excitement at being rehired was palpable. "I understand. I do. And I'm very pleased. In all honesty, sir, I'm surprised Simon hasn't been able to hack it. I'm sure he's worked hard this past year trying to turn things around, but I think he lacks a flair for marketing, which is what the Bend needs. As you know, I have those skills."

"You do, huh?"

"Yes, sir, I do. New Mexico has more casinos than ever before, and the business has become cutthroat competitive. The Bend needs to stand out from the others."

Hayden tilted his head and squinted, clearly interested in hearing Grainger's perspective on solving the Bend's financial woes. "What would you do differently?" he asked.

"Well, off the top of my head, a good starting point would be to make the Bend more fun than the other casinos. Offer more variety."

"More fun and variety?"

"Absolutely. More comps, low bet tables, slots with winnable odds, good entertainment. I've driven by the Bend a few times and I can tell it's not the same as when I left it. The parking lot is only half full. There's no excuse for that. I would change things to make the Bend the exciting and popular casino it once was."

"You think you have the magic touch to bring gamblers back?"

"No question I do."

Hayden stared at Grainger and spoke after several seconds. "You know, John? I believe you do. I'm rehiring you to take over as operations vice president beginning a week Monday. By now, the negative news about your egregious sexual exploits and the serial killings have faded from people's minds. You should be able to slip back into your former role at the Bend without the media making it a major event."

"I certainly hope so."

"One other thing. You must keep this news confidential until I tell you it's okay to discuss it. No one should know of this plan until I'm able to review it with my board of directors.

For now, you and Simon will be the only ones to know my plans."

Grainger asked, "Sir, so, Simon knows for a fact that you are terminating him and rehiring me?"

Exasperated, Hayden took a deep breath. "Yes. I informed him last week."

"You mentioned the board of directors. They didn't care much for me after I was arrested. How will they react to me being rehired?"

"The board be damned. I own the Bend. The directors serve at my bidding. I will inform them of my decision a week from today, at next Friday's board meeting. I informed Learner that I would be discussing this with you today and told him I wanted him to contact you next week to arrange for an orderly transition. His severance will depend on that."

Grainger's initial feeling of dread at seeing Hayden at his front door had turned to elation. "Frankly, Mr. Arrington, I'm both surprised and ecstatic." Grainger wondered if Arianna had anything to do with the plan to rehire him, but asking Hayden was out of the question. *I'll ask her directly.* He extended his hand to Hayden. "Thank you, sir. This is wonderful news. I'm thrilled to be going back to the Bend. I won't let you down."

Hayden did not offer his hand in return, forcing Grainger to quickly withdraw his. "I will add one caveat, John."

"Sir?"

"I demand that you avoid, *totally*, the type of affairs that caused all the problems we face now."

"I will... For sure, I will," Grainger stammered.

"I mean *all* such affairs. If you don't, I can assure you that future generations of Graingers will never emerge from any woman's womb."

"I understand."

Hayden glowered at Grainger. "As I said at the outset, it is not in my DNA to accept embarrassment of any kind. Do not embarrass me—ever again."

Grainger nodded vigorously. "I will not. I promise I will not." *He knows. So does Anton. They know about Arianna and me. I don't know how they know, but they know.*

CHAPTER 18

As ordered by Captain Ellsworth, Clay was forced to go on a two-week medical leave. He was recovering quickly from his wounds. By the first Saturday, he no longer needed crutches and took only an occasional aspirin. That afternoon, he received a call from Allie Marland.

"Hi, Clay. This is Allie, your favorite paramedic. Remember me? I was calling to see how you were doing."

"Who? Oh, yeah. Maryland. I remember. You want to know how I'm doing? I'll tell you how I'm doing." Clay spoke in an angry tone. "First off, you forced me to go to the ER. Then, to make matters worse, my captain puts me on medical leave for two weeks. I've been sitting in my house like a caged tiger, not getting any closer to finding out who tried to kill me. And, I still have another week before I can get medical clearance to return to active duty. Does that answer how I'm doing?"

Allie did not know how to respond. "I... I'm sorry, but I had nothing to do with you being put on medical leave."

Clay paused for effect, then guffawed. "I'm only kidding. I really am good with how well you and your partner treated me."

"Really?" Allie was relieved. "You were joking? You devil. You had me going for a second. You are so bad."

"But, Maryland, I have a bone to pick with you. You out-and-out lied to me when you promised I would be out of the ER in half an hour—yeah, half an hour—and pigs can fly."

"Sorry about that. You were being stubborn and I thought you needed to be checked out by the ER docs. How are you really doing?"

"Actually, I feel good. I'm ready to get back to work now, but my captain threatened me with a month's suspension if I set foot in headquarters without a doctor's clearance."

"I only just met you, but I get the impression you're a bit on the hyper side. You're not going to relax and enjoy your time off, are you?"

"Not likely."

"I've been thinking about the hit-and-run and I'm curious to know if you have anything more on who might have run you over? Or why?"

"Nothing solid yet, but I will find the guy. And when I do, I'll rip him another you-know-what. "

"You're definitely feeling better."

"Let me ask you a question."

"About?"

"You."

"Me?"

"Yes, you. Do you normally check on everyone you transport to the ER? You checked in on me that day and now again."

She laughed. "No, not everyone." Then, surprising even herself, she added, "Only the handsome ones."

"You put me in the handsome category? Good God, for a pretty girl like you, I'm shocked you have such poor taste."

"I think that's what you call a backhanded compliment."

"You *are* pretty, but calling me handsome—especially with my nose bending in two different directions—makes me question your judgement."

Allie laughed again. "How *did* you break your nose, anyway—in the line of duty?"

"No, playing Aggie football."

"Really? What position?"

"Tight end. Do you know what that is?"

"Yes."

"Then you know it has nothing to do with my butt."

"You're funny, but I've heard that one before. Actually, I know quite a bit about football. Jordan, my ex-husband, was the quarterback of our high school team."

"If Jordan was the quarterback, that means you were probably a cheerleader."

She laughed again. "I was. But I don't know why you would assume that."

"C'mon. Quarterbacks and cheerleaders. That's as American as apple pie. Besides, you're perky. You fit the role."

"Okay, that's it," Allie said. It was now her turn to pretend she was mad. "I accept that you insist on calling me Maryland, but if you call me perky again, I'll be the next one who runs you over."

Clay laughed. "Touché. You've got yourself a deal. No more perky, but tell me more about yourself."

Allie said she was thirty-two years old and added, "I've been married one time—to my high school sweetheart."

"Right. The quarterback."

"He was the big man on campus. I fell for him hook, line, and sinker. We eloped a week after graduation but, within a month, I realized I was too young and immature to be married. I went back home and my folks were more than happy to help me get the marriage annulled."

"When did you become a paramedic?"

"Not for a while. I had to get my life in order first. I thought about going to nursing school, but I didn't have the money, so I bounced around for five or six years working in different retail shops in the city—in those tourist stores. I was trying to earn enough money to pay for nursing school, but there were always other bills to pay."

"So you became a paramedic."

"It wasn't quite that easy. They don't just hand you a paramedic certificate. First, I had to go through a hundred hours of basic EMT training. After I finished that, I thought maybe I'd found my niche. So I went through advanced training. After that, since I'd gone that far, I decided to work toward becoming a paramedic. I took a concentrated two-year course load at UNM to earn my Paramedic Associate of Applied Science degree. That's a mouthful, isn't it? I bet you're sorry you asked!"

"Not at all. That's very interesting. Good for you to pull yourself up like you did."

"Thanks. And guess what? I got some good news today."

"What?"

"I've been working seven to seven on night shift since I became a paramedic, three days on three days off. I haven't minded the hours, but you're the first to know that, several months ago, I submitted a request to transfer to the day shift and it was approved today. It's still three days on three days off, but it's during daylight hours for a change. In fact, I start my new shift the same day your medical leave ends. Nice coincidence, huh?"

"Obviously, I must be your good luck charm."

"Maybe so. I'm excited about my new shift. It will be a whole new routine for me. Okay, Clay, now it's your turn. Tell me more about you. After all, what's fair is fair."

"What do you want to know?"

"How and why did you become a cop?"

"It was no big deal. I mean, I wasn't struck by a bolt of lightning or anything. No super-hero ambition."

"You're big enough to try out for the super-hero role."

"Yeah, well, that ain't gonna happen. Remember about my nose?"

"I like your nose. But go on."

"Being a cop was something I always wanted to do. I majored in criminal justice at State and joined the department as a uniformed cop right after graduation. I made detective five years later. My wife and I married a year after that but, like you and your ex, it didn't last long. Everything was good at first till she thought I loved being a cop more than I loved her. The long and short of it is we fell out of love and got divorced after three years. That was fifteen years ago. She's remarried and has a couple of kids. I'm happy for her."

"You never had kids with her?"

"No, although I think I would be a good father."

"I bet you would be."

"You do know, Maryland, that people are going to talk about us, right? Both of us working the same shift and all."

"People will talk about us? You're crazy, aren't you? Are you ever serious?"

"Of course, like right now," Clay responded. "Like inviting you to come over for dinner tonight? We'll celebrate your transfer."

"Hmm. If I say yes to dinner with you, I won't have to fight off your ex-wife, will I?"

"No, you may have to answer to all my girlfriends, but not my wife."

"Really?"

"No, I'm kidding. I'm not in any serious relationship."

"That's good."

Allie and Clay had been chatting for nearly an hour. Finally, Clay asked again, "Is your answer about dinner a yes or no? If it's a yes, I'll order Chinese. And I've got a bottle of wine we can open to celebrate."

Allie let a number of seconds pass in silence. Clay heard her breathing but wondered why she did not answer his invitation. "Hello? Are you still there?"

"Yes. Sorry."

"Sorry? Is it yes to dinner?"

"Well, you know, I *do* lead a busy social life. I'm trying to figure out how to squeeze you in tonight."

Clay was deflated. "Oh."

"I'm kidding."

"What?"

"I was looking for my Chinese take-out menu. I'll pick up the food and see you at seven. Does that work for you?"

CHAPTER 19

Allie rang Clay's doorbell. In one hand she held a plastic bag filled with Chinese takeout food and in the other she clutched her black leather trauma bag. She was dressed in white slacks and a teal-colored tunic top. She wore only enough makeup to accent her lovely features and bright smile.

Clay was impressed. "You look very pretty, Maryland."

"Thanks. You don't look so bad yourself. I see you're not on crutches anymore and your hair is growing back."

Clay was wearing Bermuda shorts and an oversized black swoosh t-shirt. "Yeah. I'm making progress. I'm not quite there yet. Still a little gimpy, but I'll be ready in another week. Excuse my clothes. This is the most comfortable stuff I can wear right now because of my knees. They're still a little raw."

"That doesn't surprise me." Allie handed Clay the bag of Chinese food and set her trauma bag on the foyer table. She nodded toward the mirror. "I see you cleaned off that message."

"Yeah, I kept it there a couple of days hoping to make sense of it, but finally scrubbed it off. What's in the leather bag?" he asked. "Your EMT stuff?"

"Yes. It's my trauma bag and first aid kit, and, why do I have it with me on a Chinese dinner date night?"

Clay shrugged.

"Because I knew you wouldn't have changed your bandages since the ER and they'd be all skunky. By the looks of things, I believe I'm right."

"You think you know me, huh?" Clay pretended to be hurt by Allie's scold. "For your information, I have an appointment in a week with the police department doctor."

Allie rolled her eyes. "Nice try, but you don't have a choice if you want medical clearance, do you?" She picked up her bag and said, "Come on. Let's go into the kitchen."

"Are you ready to eat? You just got here."

"No, I want you to sit down so I can change your bandages." Clay laughed.

"What's so funny?"

"Nothing. I'm tickled you're making a fuss over me—like my mom used to."

Clay's observation drew a swift reaction from Allie. "Your mom? Oh, gawd. If you don't want me to do anything, say so. If you haven't noticed, I'm not your mom."

"Oh, I've noticed all right. No, no, make a fuss. Please. Make a fuss." Clay had a warm feeling about her. No woman had shown such concern for him in some time.

Allie, on the other hand, was unsure how Clay felt about her. "Seriously, I hope you don't think I'm a pain in the butt."

"A little bossy maybe, but no."

"Bossy? Really?"

"Not at all. I've been looking forward to seeing you. I'm tickled you called."

"I've been looking forward to seeing you too," she said. "To reiterate, I don't make house calls with anyone else."

"Thanks for taking such good care of me. I really do appreciate it."

"Okay, let's check you out. We'll start with your knees and elbows." Allie was all business—cleaning wounds, applying ointments, and rebandaging each still-raw scrape and cut. She was impressed with Clay's muscular legs and bulging biceps.

"Everything's healing nicely, but you're still hurting, aren't you?" she asked. "You probably overdid it the first couple of days."

"Nah, I didn't overdo anything and I'm not hurting."

"You're lying. If there is one thing I've learned about you, it's that you're a terrible liar. I see how you move. You can barely turn your hips. And when I removed the bandage from your head, your eyes teared."

"That's because I'm allergic to your perfume."

"Really?"

"No. I love the smell of your perfume."

Allie looked at Clay and shook her head. "I don't know when to believe you and when not to."

"I'm really as honest as the day is long. I promise from this day forward I will never lie to you again."

She squinted at him. "Now I really don't believe you."

"I wouldn't either if I were you." He laughed. "Say, how about I open that bottle of wine?"

"I don't think so, Clay. As much as I'd like to stay, you should be resting, not socializing. I think it's best I leave. I probably shouldn't have come after all."

Clay squinted at Allie, "Man that's the fastest brush-off I've ever had."

"Oh, stop it. It's not a brush-off. When you're well enough, we'll open the wine, all right? I'm going to leave so you can get back to resting. Rest is really the most important thing you can do for yourself if you want to get your medical clearance."

"I don't agree that I need more rest. That's all I've been doing since Tuesday. Why don't you at least stay for dinner? After all, you bought it."

Allie did not argue. "Okay. It *does* smell good, doesn't it?"

They ate at the kitchen table and chatted for another half hour, keeping the conversation light and fun. At one point, Clay asked Allie if she remembered anything else about the person she saw standing in front of his house on Monday morning.

She shook her head, "No. Sorry. I only saw him for a second and didn't think twice about him till you asked." She paused for a second. "You know, come to think of it, I remember he was wearing a baseball cap."

"You never told me he was wearing a hat."

"I didn't think it was important enough to mention. But, yes, he was wearing a baseball cap."

"That's good. That's good. Anything else?"

"That's it. I'll keep thinking about it, though. I promise I will. But, for now, I've got to get going."

"You're sure you won't stay a little longer?"

"Clay, I really do hate to leave, but I think it's best."

"When will I see you again?"

"How about I come by to change your bandages again next week?"

"That's a deal."

Allie gave him a kiss on the cheek. "Now, be good and take care of yourself."

Clay walked Allie out and watched her get into her Jeep Cherokee. He liked her—a lot.

* * * * *

Neither Clay nor Allie noticed an SUV parked along the curb a hundred yards up the street from Clay's house. The driver watched as Allie drove away.

113

CHAPTER 20

By the end of the second week of his medical leave, Clay was nearly totally recovered from his injuries. Allie's promise to return the following week to change his bandages turned, instead, into a daily visit. At first they simply enjoyed each other's company. However, what had started out with a kiss on the cheek on Allie's first visit was developing into a physical and emotional attraction—one Clay hoped was heading toward intimacy.

Allie, however, was not yet ready to commit. Saturday evening, when she felt their emotions were heating up to the point of no return, she pulled back and uttered, "Whoa, I've got to go. It's getting too hot in here."

Clay tried to get her to stay. "Don't leave. I'll behave."

"I don't think you can, and I'm not sure I can either."

"That means you'll have to come back tomorrow night."

"And why is that?"

Clay thought quickly, "Let me see. It'll be Sunday. Among other things you need to change my bandages before I see the doctor on Monday. You don't want me to fail my medical exam, do you?"

Allie looked at him and smiled. "I just changed them today. You'll be fine until Monday."

"I'm not so sure about that."

"You know how to get to me, don't you? Okay, I'll be back again tomorrow. But only if you're a good boy."

"I'll be good."

Allie understood Clay's double meaning and smiled. "We'll see. I'll be the judge of that."

"Seriously. I'll be good. I'll order us a pizza and we'll have a quiet evening."

"All right, that's a deal. Tomorrow night. Seven thirty." After Allie left Clay's house she drove to CVS to pick up some items. She paid no attention to the SUV that followed her into the parking lot.

The driver—a bearded man in a baseball cap—pulled into a spot in the opposite corner from where Allie had parked. He slumped low in his seat as he watched her go into the store. Five minutes later, Allie came out with her purchase and climbed into her Jeep. The SUV driver backed slowly out of his parking space and fell in line behind her as she drove to her condominium complex.

Allie noticed the SUV as it mirrored her every turn and then pulled to within a few feet of her bumper. The SUV driver flicked on the high beams. Allie positioned her rearview mirror so the headlights would not blind her, then put on her signal and pulled over to the curb. She stuck her arm out the window, motioning for the SUV to pass, but instead the vehicle slowed to a crawl and stopped twenty-five yards behind her. She wondered if it was a cop. *No, it can't be. He would have his flashers on.*

Allie knew better than to step out of her car to confront the driver. She drove away, slowly at first, then accelerated to see what her pursuer would do.

The SUV pulled away from the curb and sped up to drive close behind her again.

Allie checked her rearview mirror every few seconds. At one point, she threw her hands up in irritation, hoping the driver of the SUV would see the gesture. Instead, he tapped her bumper then backed off when a car approached from the opposite direction.

What the hell is he doing? She was scared. She clicked the control button to lock all the doors then used her Bluetooth to call Clay.

Clay read the number on his screen. "Hi, Allie. Miss me already?"

"Clay! I need your help! A car has been tailgating me. He hit my bumper a minute ago and just hit me again. I'm scared."

"Where are you?"

"Approaching the intersection of Vista Chiara and San Raphael."

"Turn onto Vista Chiara. There's a 7-Eleven gas station not far from where you are. Pull in and call 911. Tell them what's going on and wait for the cops to get there. If the guy follows you there and approaches your car, lean on the horn and don't let up. I'll be right there. And when the cops *do* show up, do *not* open your door or get out of the car until I get there. Crack your window and talk to them through the opening. Got me? You need to be sure they're real cops."

"Okay."

"And lock your doors."

"I already have."

Allie turned sharply onto Vista Chiara and a quarter of a mile later pulled into the brightly lit 7-Eleven. She backed her car into a parking space at the front of the store to have a clear field of view to spot the tailgater. She then called 911.

Clay arrived ten minutes later in his unmarked Crown Victoria, its lights flashing. Allie was talking to a cop through her half-open window. Clay pulled in front of Allie's car, identified himself to the cop, and said he was her friend. "You okay, Maryland? Have you seen the guy since you called me?"

Allie stepped out of her car. "No one followed me into the gas station. He might have driven by or maybe turned around when he saw me pull in here. I've got to admit, he scared the heck out of me."

Clay looked around at what seemed like normal activity—people pumping gas, others walking in and out of the store, all of whom were staring at the scene of the two cop cars up against Allie's car. "Do any of the vehicles here look like the one that followed you?"

"No. He's probably gone by now. The car was probably an SUV or a pickup. It was hard to tell with the lights up high."

The cop asked, "Were you able to get the license plate?"

"No, I couldn't see anything. He was blinding me with his high beams. I mean, he was literally inches from me the whole time and hit my back bumper twice."

Clay walked to the back of the Jeep to check for damage. There was none. "Your bumper is not damaged."

"He tapped it. It wasn't a hard bump."

Clay said, "Officer, I can take it from here. I'll escort her home." The cop wrote some additional notes about the incident and left with Allie's thanks.

"What could this all be about?" Allie asked.

"Most likely it was kids out joyriding—probably Saturday night drinking and trouble-making. Let me follow you home to make sure you're okay."

"I'd appreciate that. I'm still shaking."

Clay followed Allie into her sprawling development of single family homes and condominiums surrounding a semiprivate golf course. He parked his car in a visitor parking space and waited as Allie parked in her detached single-car garage.

"Let me walk you to your condo. I'd like to make sure everything's okay."

"Clay, there's no reason for that. I have a security system, so I'm sure I'll be fine."

"It won't hurt to check."

When they entered the condo Clay noticed the light on the security system showed green, which meant it was not activated.

"Your security system wasn't on."

"Oops. I don't always set it if I'm in a hurry."

"Okay if I walk through?"

"I don't think there's any need to. But, what the heck, yes, of course. It's a mess though," she apologized.

Clay looked around. He checked that the windows in the kitchen and bedrooms were locked then went to the sliding glass door in the living room. "That's your patio?" he asked.

"Yes. It overlooks the cart path along the seventeenth hole on our golf course."

Clay pulled on the handle and slid the door open. "It's unlocked. Don't you lock it when you leave?"

"No, not usually. I've never had a problem."

"Do you at least lock it when you go to bed?"

She shrugged no.

"Seriously, Maryland, I don't want to lecture, but you've got to—"

"I know what you're going to say. I'll lock it from now on."

"Please do, especially after what happened tonight. In fact, it should be locked all the time—even when you're home."

"In my defense, there's no crime out here. Security drives through every hour, so I don't always set the alarm or lock the slider. But I will now. Besides, I keep a gun in my bedroom."

"You do? Have you ever used it?"

"Do you mean have I shot it? Of course. I go to the target range every once in a while."

"That's good. One last question. Did you tell anyone you were going to visit me tonight?"

"No. I had no reason to," Allie responded. Then, just as quickly, she recalled, "Oh, wait a second. I did. I told my partner I had a date tonight, but I never told him who with."

"Any reason to suspect he would harm you?"

"No. I can't imagine why he'd want to. He's a nice guy. We get along well."

"It's Evan, right?"

"Yes, Evan Evanysham. Listen, Clay, I know you're worried about me, but I'll be fine."

"I know you will—as long as you lock your doors and set your security system."

Allie kissed Clay goodnight. "Thank you, Mr. Knight in Shining Armor, for coming to my rescue. I'll see you tomorrow night."

CHAPTER 21

Clay pulled two stem glasses from the cupboard. He was about to rinse them out when the doorbell rang. He glanced at his watch. *It's only six thirty. It's too early for the pizza delivery, and Allie's not due for an hour.* He opened the door and was surprised to see Arianna Arrington standing on his porch. She was dressed in a short pink skirt, white tank top, and open denim jacket.

"Mrs. Arrington, what are you doing here?"

"I need to talk to you."

"Is everything okay?"

"Yes, fine. May I come in?"

Clay looked over Arianna's shoulders to see if anyone was in sight. Her BMW was parked in his driveway. "I'm expecting company."

"I'll only be a minute."

"Okay, come in."

Arianna entered the house and glanced around Clay's sparsely furnished living room.

"You're not married, are you?"

"No. How can you tell?"

She smiled. "There's not a whole lot of furniture here."

"I haven't gotten around to it. Mrs. Arrington, as I said, I'm expecting company, so please tell me what you want."

"Are you going to offer me a glass of wine?"

"I'll say it again. I'm expecting someone, so I don't have a lot of time to give you."

"When will your company be here?"

"In an hour."

"Then we have time. Chardonnay, if you have it."

Arianna sat on the couch and crossed her legs. Her skirt rode up her thighs to expose more of her long, shapely legs. She smiled to herself when she saw Clay glimpsing at them.

Clay was irritated by Arianna's brashness but she had piqued his interest. *Has to be about Grainger.* He went to his kitchen for the wine. He pulled a half-empty bottle of Chardonnay from the refrigerator. He recalled opening the bottle a month earlier. A sniff of the wine told Clay it had nearly turned to vinegar. He poured a glass anyway and took it to Arianna in the living room.

"Thanks," she said.

Clay sat on an armchair opposite the couch. He leaned forward with his forearms on his knees. "Okay, what do you want to talk about?"

Arianna was in no hurry to explain herself. She took a sip of wine and twitched her nose.

"Not very good, is it?"

"No, this is fine. Aren't you going to join me?"

"No, Mrs. Arrington, I'm not. Please, tell me why you're here. You've got five minutes." Clay's tone had turned harsh.

"First things first. Please, call me Arianna. May I call you Clay?"

Clay inhaled deeply to show his exasperation. "Okay... Arianna...What do you want to talk to me about?"

"I wanted to clarify something about your accident."

Clay was irritated but also curious. "Was Grainger at your house that Monday morning or not?"

"He was there, for sure."

"So what needs clarifying?"

"Well, at first I thought John couldn't have been the one who tried to run you over, but now I'm not so sure."

"What made you change your mind?"

"He doesn't like you very much, you know."

"What are you saying?"

"I'm saying I can't be one hundred percent sure he never left. I've been thinking about it and I suppose it's possible he could have left while I was asleep. I had a little too much wine the night before and I slept hard. So, yes, it's possible he left and returned before I woke up."

"Why are you telling me this now?"

"I wanted to make sure you knew I wasn't lying. I'm very upset he told you about me—us. He *obviously* is only concerned about himself. He really doesn't care what happens to me. And now, because of him, I could lose everything if Hayden finds out."

"Thank you for telling me that. As I already promised you, your husband won't hear about your affair from me. Of course, if Grainger gets charged with attempted murder, his lawyer will defend him by claiming you are his alibi. In that case, your husband will learn you were cheating on him."

Arianna bit her upper lip. "I wish you wouldn't say *cheating*. I mean, that sounds so wicked. I much prefer the word tryst. Don't you think that's more dignified?"

"I've never given any thought to it."

"The way I look at it, Hayden was unfaithful to his wife when he had an affair with me, so why can't I do the same? I mean, I'm not going to publicize that I'm having an affair, but I think it's an unfair double standard. Besides, remember? I have a huge libido that Hayden can't possibly satisfy."

"Does your husband know that? Does he expect you to look for sex elsewhere?"

"No, I let him think he satisfies my needs."

122

"Okay, Mrs. Arrington. You've clarified your comments about your boyfriend so now it's time you leave."

Arianna set her glass on the coffee table and uncrossed her legs, exposing more of her thighs. She made a show that she was struggling to get up from the couch. "Help me get up, please. This couch is so low." She held out her hand to Clay.

Clay tried to look away but his eyes were once again drawn to her legs. He exhaled and extended his hands. Arianna latched onto them and then, without warning, put her arms around him and kissed him with an open mouth. Surprised by her move, Clay reached for her elbows to push her away. "What are you doing?"

With a coy smile, Arianna said, "I've been wanting to kiss you. I don't see anything wrong with that. Do you? I've always been attracted to big, rugged men like you. John's not rugged. He's handsome all right but not rugged. You know what I mean?"

Clay said firmly, "Why are you doing this?"

"Why? Because I'm not seeing John anymore." She paused to let her words sink in. "It was fun while it lasted. But now, without him…"

"Without him *what*?"

"Well, with Hayden being Hayden and, of course, me being me…"

"Spell it out. What do you want?"

"I thought you and I—"

"You're out of your mind. I'll remind you that you're married, and, as tempting as you are, I don't have affairs with married women. Not to mention that my life span would be reduced to that of a gnat if your husband ever learned I was involved with you."

Arianna threw her head back and laughed out loud. "I'm *tempting*, huh? That's a start." She did not relent, "You know, Clay, I understand what you're saying, but if John and I were able to keep our affair quiet all this time, I'm sure you and I could do the same."

Clay realized Arianna's intentions were to seduce him to ensure he would not divulge her affair to Hayden. "Now I get why you're here. Listen to me. I told you I'm not going to tell your husband about John Grainger. There's no reason to throw yourself at me."

The doorbell rang. Clay checked the clock on the end table. *Seven o'clock.* "Must be my pizza. Now, listen. I'm going to answer the door. Please, stay here and be quiet until the delivery guy leaves."

"I'll be as quiet as a church mouse." Arianna pulled her forefinger and thumb across her mouth to show Clay she was zipping her lips.

Clay retrieved his wallet from the foyer table and opened the door.

It was Allie.

"Hi, Clay."

"You're early."

"I hope it's okay."

"Yes, of course it's okay."

"Whose BMW is in the driveway?"

"It belongs to a woman in the living room who wanted to talk to me about my hit-and-run case."

"Oh, I see. Looks like I shouldn't have come early."

"No, not at all. We're through. I've asked her to leave."

From the living room, Arianna purred, "Clay, honey, is it okay for me to come out?"

Allie was confused. "What's that all about?"

"Maryland, look, it's a long story. I interviewed this woman last week. She came over totally unannounced to tell me something else about the case."

"It looks like you've gotten to know her well. You're wearing her lipstick on half your face."

Clay instinctively used the back of his hand to rub off the lipstick.

Arianna breezed into the foyer and said, "Clay, thanks for the wine." She examined Allie from head to toe. "Oh, hello. Who are you?"

Allie shook her head and did not answer.

Arianna reached for Clay's hand and announced, "I'm sorry, but I can't stay any longer. I've really got to go." She leaned into Clay and planted a kiss on his lips. Clay jerked his head back in response.

"Clay, sweetie, don't be embarrassed." Arianna turned back to Allie. "What is your name, honey? You look awfully cute in that skirt. Where'd you get it?"

Allie winced and continued to say nothing.

Arianna did not let up. "Seriously, Clay, I am sorry, but I have *got* to go. Call me later, okay?"

Allie shot daggers at Clay. "Boy, did I have you pegged wrong." She turned on her heels and walked toward her car before Arianna could exit.

Clay gave Arianna a look of disgust then followed after Allie as another car was pulling up to Clay's house. A teenage boy got out carrying the pizza Clay had ordered.

"Maryland! Please hold up," Clay shouted after her. "Stop for a second so I can explain."

Allie snatched the pizza from the delivery guy and sailed it at Clay. "Explain this!" Pizza flew out of the box. Some splatted against Clay's chest and the rest slid on the walkway, leaving a trail of tomato, pepperoni, and hot mozzarella cheese.

"He'll pay you," Allie shouted to the pizza guy then climbed into her car.

Clay tried again. "Maryland, I can explain."

Allie threw her car into reverse and backed out of the driveway. Through the open window she yelled, "Do not call me again. Ever!"

The pizza guy stood wide-eyed. "Uh, sir?"

"What?" Clay shouted at him.

The boy extended his hand to be paid.

Arianna walked out of the house and tiptoed around the pizza. She stood next to Clay. "My, my, she's got quite a temper, hasn't she?"

"Why did you say all that? I happen to care for her."

"I saw the way you looked at me. I think we should get to know each other better."

Clay said, "Arianna, get out of here before I change my mind about telling your husband." He pulled out his phone and dialed Allie's number. She did not answer. He left a message, "Maryland, nothing happened with that woman. *Nothing.* Call me back. I can explain."

Arianna contorted her face. "Clay, I can stay a while if you want."

"All I want you to do is leave. Now!"

She shrugged. "If you insist, but remember, I don't give up easily." She got into her BMW, opened the window, and blew Clay a kiss as she drove off.

The pizza delivery boy stood with his hand still extended. He coughed, "Sir?"

CHAPTER 22

Clay called Allie again but to no avail. He decided to drive to her condo, perch on her doorstep, and insist she listen to his explanation.

Traffic was backed up on Vista Chiara. A dispatcher's voice crackled through Clay's car radio that an accident had occurred in the area. "11-83." *No other details available.* Though officially off duty, Clay was obligated to see if he could help. He turned on his flashers to bypass the traffic jam and get to the accident scene.

The first responders had not yet arrived. *It must have just happened.* As he approached the accident, he saw a Jeep Cherokee on its right side in a ditch. He immediately recognized it as Allie's. Two men were helping Allie climb out the driver's side window.

Clay parked half on, half off the road and hurried to her. "Allie! What happened? Are you hurt?"

She thanked the two Samaritans who had extracted her from her car. She ignored Clay.

"Are you okay?" Clay asked again.

She looked at him and gave a blunt, "I'm fine."

A cop arrived on the scene, recognized Clay, and gave him a perfunctory salute. It was the same cop who helped Allie when she sought refuge at the 7-Eleven a week earlier.

The cop said, "Miss Marland, I've called an ambulance. Do you want to sit in my car until it arrives?"

"No, thanks. I'm fine. And I don't need an ambulance. You can call them off. I bumped my head, but I'm okay."

"What happened?"

"Someone ran me off the road—hit me from behind and pushed me into the ditch."

"Do you know who? Can you identify the car?"

"No, it came up behind me so quickly. The next thing I knew I was in the ditch. These men helped me get out of the car." Allie thanked them again.

The cop asked the two good Samaritans, "Did either of you see what happened? Did you see the car that ran her off the road?"

The men shook their heads in unison. "No." The cop took down their names and told them they could leave.

The cop next took a statement from Allie. She did not go into detail other than to say someone hit her from behind and forced her into the ditch. "Could it have been the same vehicle that tailgated you last week?"

"I couldn't swear to that, no."

A tow truck arrived to pull Allie's car from the ditch. The entire right side of her car was pushed in and the car was not drivable. Traffic had stopped in both directions to allow the tow truck driver to maneuver his truck alongside Allie's car to pull it from the ditch.

Allie asked the driver, "Where are you taking it?"

"Stewart's Auto Repair in the northeast."

Clay asked, "Allie, can I talk to you?" He tried to gently take her by her elbow to lead her away from the people who had gathered, but she shrugged his hand off. He insisted, "Please, I want to find out what happened." They walked to his car. "Tell me."

"I swear it had to be your girlfriend. She must have followed me. I'm lucky I didn't get killed. What is she, a psycho or something?"

"She's not my girlfriend. I've been trying to explain—"

"I don't want to hear what you have to say."

"At least tell me why you think she rammed you off the road."

"It had to be her. Who else could it have been?"

"That's what I'm trying to find out. Did you actually see her?" Clay asked.

"No."

"I'm sorry this happened, but I can't imagine she would do this to you."

"Oh, yeah, like she didn't try to annoy me earlier, right?"

Clay could not imagine Arianna purposely trying to hurt Allie, but supposed it was possible. "Can you give me *any* more details about what happened?"

Allie did not look at him. "I've already told you and the officer what happened. And I told you I think it was your girlfriend."

"She was driving a BMW 550. Is that the car that hit you?"

"I told you I don't know what car hit me. Stop asking me the same questions over and over."

"Okay, I get it. You're mad because you think I'm screwing around with that woman, but I'm not."

"No, I'm mad because she almost killed me."

"Well, since you're not going to give me any more details about what happened, I might as well leave."

Allie shot back, "What do you want to know? I saw headlights coming up fast behind me. No other cars were coming, so I thought the car was going to pass me. Then, all of a sudden, it smacked me from behind and the next thing I know, I'm in the ditch."

"Any chance you caught a glimpse of the license plate?"

Allie looked at Clay and responded angrily, "No, I did not get a license plate number. Are you not listening? I told you everything happened quickly. And what's so hard to believe about your girlfriend wanting to hurt me?"

Clay was not sympathetic. "Since you never saw who hit you, you're doing nothing more than assuming it was her."

The sound of Allie's Jeep being pulled from the ditch and onto the flatbed truck put an end to their conversation. The tow truck driver secured the Jeep then signaled to Allie that he was leaving.

Clay said, "Let me give you a lift home? I want to make sure you're okay."

Allie whispered, "No, thank you. I don't want a ride from you. And, besides, do you really care?"

"Of course I do. That's why I asked. Come on, let me take you home."

"Fine. It's not like I have a lot of choices," she said, and got into Clay's car. The drive to Allie's condominium took less than ten minutes. Allie refused to look at Clay or acknowledge his attempts to explain the events of earlier that evening. "I don't want to hear another word about your girlfriend."

"One more time. She's not my girlfriend. Clay was unable to break through Allie's mindset. When he pulled into her development, he made yet another attempt to explain the situation. "Allie, I'm sorry about what happened. Please, hear me out."

"No. I said I don't want to see you again. I don't care how you try to explain it, I know what I saw."

"If you'll listen, for a second—" he said.

"I will not." She got out and slammed the car door behind her. She did not look back and hurried to her condo. Once inside, she slammed that door too.

CHAPTER 23

Sunday morning, ADA Hank Kincaid rode his bicycle on Via del Santo, a winding roadway with multiple climbs, descents, and blind turns five miles southwest of his home in Santa Fe. Beginning at dawn on most Sundays, Hank went out alone to exercise his passion for cycling. It provided Hank with quiet time and much-needed exercise to counter the stress of his prosecutor duties. An early start to his ride allowed his wife and children to sleep in. He usually cycled a two-hour route on remote, traffic-free roads and was back home in time to prepare his breakfast specialty of banana pancakes for the entire family.

The New Mexico morning was clear and brisk. The temperature hovered at an invigorating fifty degrees but promised to warm up to the mid-seventies by noon. A mile out on Via del Santo, Hank saw an SUV heading in his direction. The vehicle veered over the center line into his lane.

Hank occasionally experienced obnoxious drivers who swerved into his lane to see how close they could get to him. Not everyone liked to share the road with cyclists. Most failed to understand that the slightest tap to a bike would send a hapless rider reeling to serious injury or death.

Hank always made sure he was visible. His bike was outfitted with front and rear blinking lights and he wore colorful cycling jerseys that stood out against the backdrop of desert roads and mountains. He decided to not take any chances with the erratic driver of the SUV. *He's probably texting.* Hank rode at the farthest edge of the road to give the car a wide berth.

The driver did not correct the vehicle's path.

The memory of a recent fatal accident flashed through Hank's mind. A cycling friend was hit by a car driven by a young man who had lost control of his car when he reached down to retrieve his cell phone that had fallen off the seat.

Hank elected to not chance the same thing happening to him. He got off his bike, walked onto the dirt shoulder along the metal guardrail and waited for the car to pass. That did not deter the driver, who drove onto the sand and gravel shoulder along the guardrail, about a thousand feet ahead of where Hank was standing. A cloud of dust trailed behind. Hank thought the car was going to crash into the guardrail but it straightened out and drove parallel to the barrier. It barreled straight toward him.

He's coming right at me.

With the SUV now only one hundred yards away, Hank climbed over the guardrail onto a craggy, three-foot-wide granite ledge that overlooked a deep canyon. He tried to hoist his bike over the guardrail, but the ledge was too narrow. He left the bike on the shoulder.

Unable to gain traction because of his cleated, rigid cycling shoes, Hank slipped and fell to his knees. He grabbed the sharp outer edge of the guardrail and held on as the car continued to run along the barrier. It crashed into his bike amid a cloud of dust and a cacophonous sound of metal on metal as his titanium bike was being mangled.

The bike was pinned to the undercarriage of the car and dragged onto the road where it finally worked itself out twenty yards later, its fork and components sheared off.

The car sped off and was out of sight before Hank could clear his eyes of dust. He clambered back over the barrier, hurried to his crumpled bike, and extracted his phone from the saddlebag. The phone was crushed. Another vehicle appeared on the remote road ten minutes later. By then, the SUV was long gone.

CHAPTER 24

Police physicians hold significant power over the lives of cops who are injured or ill and unable to serve on duty. The doctors serve as general physicians as well as mental health advisors, and can restrict an officer from retuning to field work until his or her physical and cognitive abilities meet the department's standards.

Two weeks to the day after Clay was hit by the still unidentified vehicle, he was examined by the police department physician to determine his fitness for duty. The doctor checked Clay's knee and elbow abrasions, which had nearly healed. He removed the stitches from the wound on his temple and replaced the large bandage with a smaller one.

"I have to say I'm surprised to see how diligent you've been about taking care of your wounds. Good job, Clay. Keep it up."

"Yeah, thanks. I know how important it is to change my bandages to prevent infection." *No need to tell him that Allie took care of me.*

The doctor gave him the okay to return to work. "But I want you back here on Wednesday for a follow-up."

* * * * *

"Good to have you back," Ellsworth said. "Come into my office."

Ellsworth closed the door behind them. "Update me on your hit-and-run. You interviewed Mrs. Arrington before you went on leave. What did you learn?"

"She confirmed John Grainger had been at her house that Monday morning, but she was unclear about the exact time he

136

left. I vowed I would not disclose her name to anyone during my investigation."

"Was she telling the truth?"

"I'm not sure. She confirmed Grainger's alibi and forensics can't find any evidence that his car was used to hit me, I can't get past the circumstantial evidence—his vanity plate, his car having front-end damage, the fact he happened to have scrubbed his car clean the same day I was hit, and, most important, his motive. Revenge—the fact he feels Hank and I ruined his life."

There was a knock on Ellsworth's door.

"Come in."

Clay turned to see who had knocked. "Speak of the devil."

Ellsworth motioned to Hank Kincaid to enter his office. The lanky thirty-nine-year-old ADA said, "Sorry to bother you, but I need to talk to you both about the Cantillo case. It comes to trial next week." Clay had been the arresting detective. "I can come back if I've caught you at a bad time."

"No, we're almost through. Have a seat."

Hank pointed to the bandage on Clay's head. "I heard you were hurt in a hit-and-run. Are you okay?"

"Yeah, I'm good. Thanks."

Ellsworth added, "He's a lucky man. He just came back from medical leave."

"Any idea who hit you?"

"Not for sure, but I have a suspect—John Grainger from last year's high desert murder case."

"John Grainger, that pretentious SOB."

"That's the one. I caught a glimpse of the license plate on the car that hit me. Truth be told it was only a glimpse, but the plate partially matches a tag on one of Grainger's car."

"A partial match?"

"Yes, that plus the car was a light-colored SUV. Grainger has a white Range Rover."

"Clay, that's a stretch—a partial license plate number and a white SUV."

"I know it is, Hank, but I used that as the basis to get Judge Wright to sign a search warrant to check Grainger's car."

"I'm surprised Wright signed off on it. You must have caught him at a weak moment."

"It helped that he remembered Grainger from the earlier case. When I questioned Grainger at his house he ranted about how I had destroyed his life. As a matter of fact, he blamed you, too. Claims no one will hire him because we destroyed his reputation."

"*We* destroyed his reputation? You're kidding. He's lucky he's not sitting in a cell in state prison right now."

"I told him that."

Hank looked at Captain Ellsworth then turned back to Clay. He shook his head as he spoke. "What about Grainger's car?"

"Forensics found slight damage to the left front fender where it would have hit me. Unfortunately, they found no trace of blood or fiber."

Captain Ellsworth added, "Apparently, Grainger had an alibi for that morning. He was with a woman."

Clay nodded. "I talked to the alibi, and she vouched he was with her, but I'm not convinced she was telling the truth."

"You realize, of course, I wouldn't have a prayer in court of making any charges stick, with no evidence to show his car was used to hit you and the fact he has an alibi."

"Yeah, you're right."

"Are you convinced whoever hit you did it on purpose?"

Ellsworth interjected, "Clay, tell Hank what you found written on your mirror."

"When I got home from the ER, I realized someone had gotten into my house and wrote a message on the mirror in my foyer." Clay pulled out his phone, scrolled to the photo of the message, then handed the phone to Hank.

Hank looked closely at the image. "Romans 12:19. I'll be damned."

"What?"

"Look at this." Hank reached into his suit jacket pocket to retrieve a tri-folded sheet of paper that appeared to have been torn from a magazine. He unfolded the paper and placed it on Ellsworth's desk alongside Clay's phone. "Someone put this in my mailbox on Saturday."

"What is it?"

Hank said, "An article from a past issue of *People* magazine about Bono and the band U2." He pointed out letters underlined in red. "It's similar to what was on your mirror. It spells out U2-T-W-E-L-V-E-N-I-N-E-T-E-E-N." Using the tip of a closed ballpoint pen, Hank recited each underscored letter. "I googled U2-12-19 but couldn't find anything. I brought the article in with me to look into it again when I had a minute. What does it mean?"

Clay explained, "Romans 12:19 is a biblical verse. To paraphrase, it's something like 'vengeance is mine sayeth the Lord.' That's the gist of it. I interpret it to mean someone is out to take revenge on me."

"That might explain what happened to me yesterday," Hank exclaimed. "Someone tried to hit me when I was out riding." Hank described his bike ride and how he had feared for his life. "At first I thought the driver was diverted or playing games to scare me. But it was clear he was flat out trying to kill me. And in the process, the sonofabitch destroyed my bike—I mean, he mangled it."

Clay asked, "Did you happen to see the license number?"

"No. I couldn't see anything because of all the dust his car kicked up. It was all I could do to hang onto the barrier to keep from falling into the canyon. So, no, I didn't get the license or see who was driving, but the car was a white SUV. I'm sure it was a Range Rover. And it probably has damage to its undercarriage from running over my bike."

Ellsworth drummed his fingers on his desk as he thought about the connection Clay was making. "How many cases have you two worked on together?"

"Besides the Cantillo case I came in to see you about, only the one involving Grainger."

"Is it possible Cantillo wants to see you both dead?"

"Sure, it's possible," Hank affirmed, "but Cantillo's probably only going to get one to four and, with good behavior, he could be out in six months. It wouldn't make any sense that he would try to kill us for that short period of jail time."

"Then Clay might be right. Think about it. The same kind of car. Two notes making a similar reference to the Bible. Revenge as a motive. Looks to me like it's got John Grainger written all over it."

Hank nodded. "Could be."

Clay wanted the forensics lab to check the torn magazine page for fingerprints. He put on a pair of latex gloves to avoid adding his own fingerprints to the page and took the sheet from Hank. "I'll have the crime lab check it out."

Hank said, "My prints are all over it. When I first read it, I had no idea what it was, so I've handled it several times."

"Let me ask you something, Hank."

"Shoot."

"If we were to find a *People* magazine at Grainger's house, and the magazine was missing this page, wouldn't we have enough evidence to charge him with attempted murder?"

Hank answered, "On its own merit, finding the magazine would be strong enough proof to charge Grainger. And if we find his prints on this page, it would be prima facie evidence of his intent to kill. It would be a slam dunk. I don't see any reason why you couldn't get a search warrant to look for the magazine as well as examine Grainger's car for signs it's the one that destroyed my bike."

Ellsworth leaned forward with his forearms on the desk. "Wait a second. Something just hit me. The message the suspect left on the mirror at Clay's house meant he had to know you survived the attempt on your life. But, how? How did he know? Did he see you being loaded into the ambulance? If so, that would mean the suspect was at the crime scene too, maybe mingling with your neighbors to see if you survived."

"That's a good point. But Detective Robles interviewed everyone on Santa Clara and no one saw any strangers at the scene. The paramedic who treated me told me later she saw someone at the front of my house. She wasn't able to describe him, though."

"What about when you were at the hospital? Could someone have tracked you there, realized you had survived the hit, then doubled back to write the message on your mirror?"

"I can't remember anyone lurking about at the hospital, if that's what you mean."

Ellsworth said, "It might be worthwhile to question the admissions people to see if anyone inquired about you."

Hank agreed, "The captain's right. If you determine how the person knew you survived, you might be able to narrow the range of suspects."

* * * * *

Back at his desk, Clay phoned St. Vincent Regional Medical Center and spoke to the admissions person who had been on duty when he was taken to the ER. "Can you tell me if anyone called or stopped in to ask about me while I was being treated?"

The clerk checked her logbook and indicated there had been two calls. "Allie Marland—one of the EMTs who brought you in—and another call from someone who said he was a neighbor. He asked how you were doing. I told him I couldn't divulge that information and he hung up."

"Did you get his name?"

"No, he didn't identify himself."

CHAPTER 25

Clay drove back to John Grainger's house with a warrant to search for the *People* magazine. Detective Robles followed in his vehicle to assist in the search. A moment later, Carton and Cook arrived in their forensics van to examine Grainger's Range Rover.

Clay rang the doorbell.

Through the door's side window Grainger saw it was Clay. He opened the door. "What do you want now?"

"I have a search warrant."

"Screw you and your warrant." With a flip of his wrist, Grainger slammed the door shut.

Clay pounded on the door, "Open up."

"I'm through talking with you," Grainger answered through the closed door.

"I told you I have a warrant," he shouted. "Let's not go through this again. Do we have to use a battering ram?"

Grainger opened the door and stood with his arms crossed. Pointing at Carton and Cook, he said, "I see you brought your goon squad back."

"They'll be examining your Range Rover again."

"What the hell for?" Before Clay could answer, Grainger looked to Robles and asked, "Who's he?"

Robles showed his badge. "I'm Detective Tomás Robles."

Clay said, "He's here to assist me. We're searching for a magazine—a past issue of *People.*"

"What?"

"You heard me. We're searching for *People* magazine."

"Why don't you just buy a copy?"

"Very funny. I'm tired of asking you nice. Are you going to let us in?"

Grainger stood in front of his open door, but did not move aside. "First tell me what the hell is so important about that magazine?"

Clay did not answer. "You have three seconds to move your ass and let us in."

Grainger stepped aside.

Clay handed him the warrant and walked past him into the living room. A wary Robles followed. "Where's the magazine?"

"Not only do I *not* subscribe to *People*, I don't think I've ever read a single issue, other than to leaf through it in my doctor's waiting room."

"Who's your doctor?"

Grainger rolled his eyes. He was angry. "Don't tell me you're going to try to find the magazine there."

"Yep, I am—if we don't find it here."

"Well, you ain't gonna find it here."

"His name?"

"Doctor Richard Adams, on Monument Avenue."

"Where are your bedrooms?"

Grainger pointed to two closed doors at the back of the house. "Do I need my lawyer again?"

"That's your choice." Clay turned to Robles and said, "Tomás, start with the bedrooms."

As Robles walked off, Clay said, "Let me explain to you why we're looking for the magazine. You know Hank Kincaid, the assistant district attorney who was going to prosecute the sex crime charges against you?"

"It wasn't a sex crime and, yeah, what about him? He dismissed those phony charges."

"Someone sent him a threatening note that was written in code on a page ripped from a *People* magazine. We have reason to believe you're the one who sent it to him and then tried to kill him yesterday morning." Clay studied Grainger's demeanor for any hint that he might know about the note and Hank's attempted murder.

"Well it wasn't me. I was here all day Sunday. Never left the house. And before you ask, no, I don't have any witness to verify that. Why would I want to kill Kincaid?"

"Because you blamed him, too, for losing your job at the Bend. You do remember saying we ruined your life?"

"Yeah, I said that, but I sure as hell didn't try to kill either one of you!" Grainger laughed. "You think I sent a coded note to Kincaid on a page from a magazine? I think you've been watching too many spy movies. You know, you're pitiful."

Clay shot back, "Talk about pitiful. You sit on your ass all day feeling sorry for yourself. Get a job, man."

"I don't need you lecturing me on my life. You came here to search for a phantom magazine, so, go ahead, knock yourself out."

* * * * *

Carton and Cook examined the Range Rover and informed Clay they found no evidence the vehicle had been used to run over Hank Kincaid's bike. "There are no scratch marks or paint transfer on any part of the undercarriage."

Clay and Tomás continued to search the house but failed to find the magazine. Clay spoke aside to Robles, "It's not here. If Grainger's behind all this, he's either destroyed the magazine or got it from someplace else. Do me a favor."

"What's that?"

"On your way back to headquarters, stop by the doctor's office to see if it's there."

Robles said, "I'll do that, but you know the odds are slim to none I'll find it there. If Grainger sent the note to Kincaid, he could have gotten that magazine from a dozen different stores."

"I know it's a long shot, but check it out for me anyway. I'll be back in the office in an hour. There's something else I want to talk to this asshole about."

CHAPTER 26

The Indian Bend Hotel and Casino had opened twenty years earlier—the same year John Grainger and his girlfriend Hope Archer graduated from the University of Illinois. With no job prospects or set plans, the two decided they would take a breather after college and crisscross the country before settling into what they called "real life." Their ultimate destination was southern California.

They got as far as Santa Fe.

Short on money, the graduates got jobs at the newly opened casino.

"It'll only be for a few months," John had promised Hope. "We'll make a few bucks, then get back on the road." But their temporary plans became permanent, as they fell in love with Santa Fe's diverse culture and storied history. Dreams of California were soon forgotten.

By the time they turned thirty, both John and Hope had turned their temporary job status at the Bend into significant success. Grainger was smart and ambitious, and used his innate marketing savvy to climb his way up the corporate ladder to the position of operations vice president. And Hope's drive for perfection led her to a high-level administrative position responsible for a large staff of employees.

Hope and John were together nearly ten years. The handsome Grainger knew women found him attractive, and the beautiful women who worked in the casino were too much for him to resist. In the end, Hope was unable to forgive and forget his many infidelities and their relationship fell apart. Grainger still lived in the house they had bought together on East Alameda.

Clay met and dated Hope during his investigation of the Bend employee serial killings. Sadly, their relationship ended when Hope's mental illness, hidden to that point, was exposed and led to her being committed to a psychiatric hospital.

* * * * *

With the forensics team and Detective Robles gone, Clay told Grainger, "I want to talk to you privately."

"What more do you want from me? I told you I didn't try to kill you or Kincaid."

"Let's assume you're innocent."

"I am."

"Then follow my logic. The Bend murder case is the only one Hank Kincaid and I have collaborated on."

"And your point is?"

"We believe whoever is trying to kill us could be someone from the Bend—someone who harbors a grudge. Would you have any idea who it could be?"

Unwilling to pass up an opportunity for biting sarcasm, Grainger said, "Let me get this straight. First, the great Detective Clay Bryce accuses me of trying to kill him, and now he's asking for my help. Is that right? Are you kidding me?"

"No, I'm not kidding you."

"Bryce, how long have you been a cop?"

"What does that matter?"

Grainger did not wait for him to answer. "Let me guess—fifteen, twenty years, more or less? Which means you've arrested dozens of people, right?"

"What's your point?"

"With that many arrests, why wouldn't you suspect someone from one of those cases instead of concentrating on someone from the Bend?"

"You're not listening. I told you Hank Kincaid and I have worked on only the Bend case together, so we think whoever's targeting us is someone from the Bend."

"Well, I can't help you," Grainger said. "I don't have a clue who it could be."

"What about Hope Archer?"

"What about her?" He laughed and shook his head. "You think Hope is trying to kill you? For Christ's sake, she's in a psychiatric hospital! You're really obsessed with your hit-and-run, aren't you? I think you should be in that hospital too. You're losing your marbles."

Clay held his temper. "Obviously, it can't be Hope, but do you think she might have an idea who it could be? She was at the center of all the goings-on at the Bend. She must have heard plenty of gossip and rumors. Have you been to see her?"

Grainger lowered his gaze. "No, I have to admit, I haven't."

"You haven't?" Clay was surprised, given their past relationship.

"Why not?"

"I don't think she'd exactly be happy to see me. I have to confess, I think I'm the one who started her on the way to the loony bin. I brought her to Santa Fe all those years ago. We had our ups and downs to say the least. Frankly, I feel guilty about how I treated her."

For a moment, the two men shared a sympathetic bond. Clay said, "I feel guilty about what happened to her too. I've thought a thousand times about how I could have kept her from going over the deep end."

149

"Have you been to see her?"

"Yes and no."

"What is that supposed to mean?"

"I went to the hospital to see her a couple of weeks after she was admitted and then again a month later."

"So you did visit her?"

"Tried to, but both times she refused to see me. And I couldn't force her to see me. If I was on official business, yeah, she wouldn't have had a choice. But since I was there only as a friend, it was her right to refuse me."

Both men were silent for a few awkward seconds, neither looking at the other until Grainger broke the ice. "She and I had a good thing going when we first moved here after college. I really feel bad about her."

Clay was surprised to see another side of the normally pompous man. For a brief moment, he thought Grainger may actually have been a decent sort at one time. "We can beat ourselves up about what happened, but her mental illness wasn't because of you or me. A lot of people contributed to her paranoia—her mother who left her, her father who gave her up to foster care, and her foster parents who took away the one thing that gave her comfort—her precious teddy bear."

Grainger nodded as he remembered his former girlfriend. "Yeah, that damned bear was her security blanket. She told me a million times about how it was taken away from her."

Clay said, "The saddest thing about Hope was how she believed you and I and everyone else abandoned her."

Grainger looked squarely at Clay and asked, "Are you going to talk to her?"

"Yes. I have nothing to lose. Besides, I'm now going on official business. She's got to see me."

CHAPTER 27

Tomás Robles drove to the office of John Grainger's doctor and looked through the stack of magazines in the waiting room. He found the issue of *People* he wanted and leafed through it till he found the article about U2. The article was intact. Back in the squad room, he told Clay, "I found the magazine, but the page we're looking for wasn't torn off. I also learned that Grainger hadn't been to his doctor in over six months."

"Damn it. All right, thanks."

"Now what?"

"I'm going to drive to the psychiatric hospital to see Hope Archer. I want to see if she can give me the name of anyone from the Bend who could still be pissed at Kincaid and me."

* * * * *

Clay parked in the semicircular lot reserved for visitors at the front of the three-story Santa Fe psychiatric hospital for women. The fortress-like complex was located on seventy-five acres a half-hour drive southeast of Santa Fe. The hospital itself was surrounded by a twenty-foot-high fence. A security officer at the entrance checked the credentials of service vehicles and directed visitors to the facility entrance.

Patient rooms, though spartan in nature, afforded basic amenities—a stark bathroom with a small shower, a metal locker for clothes and belongings, a three-drawer bureau, and a TV mounted on the wall above the bureau. The average daily population was two hundred patients. Some of the women were heavily sedated to keep their violent tendencies at bay. Hope Archer was one of those women.

151

Clay entered the lobby carrying a plain brown shopping bag. Signage directed him to check in with a security officer who sat behind a secure window. The lobby was empty except for a heavy-set woman and her daughter. The women sat on two of the dozen straight-back chairs that lined the walls. The only sounds were those of Clay's shoes on the tile floor and the older woman's crying. The younger woman looked at Clay. He nodded at her. She held her mother's hand and was trying in vain to calm her crying.

An outline stenciled on the floor in front of the guard reception area indicated where visitors were to stand. Clay stood patiently for a few seconds, waiting for the guard to acknowledge him. In no particular hurry, the guard lifted his chin at Clay and asked through a squawky intercom, "Yes?"

Clay pressed his badge against the window. "Detective Clay Bryce of the Santa Fe Police Department. I'm here to visit a patient, Hope Archer. I called earlier to tell your security people I needed to talk with her about an attempted murder investigation I'm working on."

"Yeah, I was the one you talked to." The guard turned to his computer and accessed the hospital patient list. "I'll have her brought down to one of the meet rooms." The rooms were secure rooms used by family and friends to visit with patients. "After you go through screening, a guard will escort you to meet with her. What's in the bag?"

"A gift for Miss Archer. I told you about it when I spoke with you."

The guard nodded toward a scanning device located on the far side of the lobby. The scanner was manned by another security officer. "Yeah, okay, I remember. You'll have to run it through screening." Visitors were allowed to bring patients one gift and one snack, both of which had to be scrutinized by security and passed through the conveyer scanner.

"No problem."

"Are you packing?"

"Yes."

"You'll need to check your weapon with me." The guard pushed a button to open a secure pass-through drawer.

Clay placed his service revolver in the drawer, signed a property release, and was instructed to sit in the lobby. "Have a seat. When we bring her down, you'll be called to go through the security screening."

Clay sat diagonally across from the older woman. Tears streamed down her cheeks, some escaping her tissue, falling to her breast and dotting her dress. The daughter explained why they were there by mouthing the words "My sister's here." Clay nodded again and looked away. He did not want to get into a discussion with her. He thought about Hope instead. He had not seen her since her breakdown. He had fallen hard for her and needed time to accept the realities of her mental illness.

Two minutes later, the guard announced. "Detective Bryce, you're up." Clay went to the screening station and emptied his pockets, took off his belt and shoes, and placed the paper shopping bag onto a conveyor belt to be checked for weapons and contraband. He then stepped through the X-ray machine for his own screening. Afterward, the guard unlocked the interior door and escorted him down a long corridor to one of three meet rooms. A plain metal table with two chairs on opposite sides sat in the center of the windowless, concrete-block room.

Hope was seated in the chair with her back to the door. A stocky nurse who had escorted her to the room was standing in a corner. The nurse greeted Clay with a stern, "No physical contact."

Clay sat at the table and placed his bag on the floor at his feet. He addressed Hope gently, "Hello, Hope. I came to see how you were doing."

Hope looked into Clay's eyes with a vacant stare. She showed no sign she knew who he was.

Clay looked at the nurse then back at Hope. The nurse explained, "She's been sedated because she attacked another patient this morning. She's almost always sedated. She's aggressive and fights with other patients. Since she's been here, she's attacked nurses, patients, and a couple of doctors too." The nurse continued as though Hope was not in the room. "But don't be fooled—she knows what's going on around her. Every now and then, she's as sweet as can be, aren't you, Hope? Occasionally she's quite lucid and pleasant. But most days, if she's not sedated, she's mean as a snake and totally out of it, which is no different from most of the women here. You can't turn your back on any of them or you get punched or hit with a chair to the back of your head. We have dozens of assault incidents each year."

Clay reached across the table to hold Hope's hand, but the nurse stopped him. "Don't do that! I said no touching. Physical contact is *not* allowed."

He pulled his hand back. He wondered if Hope recognized him. Her eyes were empty, expressionless. A year earlier, Clay thought she was the prettiest woman in Santa Fe and was shocked and saddened to see how she looked now—her cheeks were sunken, her once-flowing brown hair was now mostly gray, and she wore a formless hospital-issued cotton dress. "Hope, do you remember me?"

She tilted her head at him first one way then the other.

"I'm Detective Clay Bryce. You used to call me Mr. Detective-man. Remember?"

Surprisingly, she murmured, "Hello, Mr. Detective-man."

"Hi, Hope. I'm pleased you remember me," although he thought that perhaps she had simply parroted his words.

Hope showed a tight, almost imperceptible smile.

"I brought you something," Clay said. He reached into the shopping bag he had placed under the table and brought out her teddy bear. Before he could give it to her, she screamed, "Teddy, oh, Teddy," and lunged for the stuffed animal.

The nurse stepped forward to intervene, but Clay put his hand up to stop her. He kept his eyes focused on Hope as he explained to the nurse, "It's hers. I just got it released from the police department's evidence room. She named her bear Teddy. It's a long story, isn't it, Hope?" The nurse took a step back when she was convinced Hope's actions were under control. Clay continued, "Teddy is her best friend. I'm sure she's missed him all these months." As an aside to the nurse, he added, "Maybe having her teddy bear back will calm her down."

Hope embraced her bear tightly with her right hand, her cheek against its cheek, kissing it repeatedly.

"I'm glad you're happy to have Teddy back."

Hope mumbled to the stuffed animal, "Have you come to take me home?"

"He won't be able to take you home yet, Hope. You've got to stay here a while longer, and you need to behave yourself. I'll visit again if you want me to, but, now that you have Teddy, you've got to be a good girl."

Hope nodded mechanically, again leaving Clay uncertain if she really understood his words.

She used Teddy's paw to point to Clay's head. "Hurt?"

Clay was surprised she had noticed. "It's bandaged because I had an accident a couple of weeks ago. That's another reason why I came to see you. Someone's trying to hurt me. I was wondering if you could help me find out who it might be." Clay looked for a response from Hope—a nod or assent—but got none. He continued. "You remember John Grainger, don't you?"

Hope's face was expressionless, her eyes blank.

The nurse said, "Hope, do you remember the man who was here to see you a few weeks ago? He said he was your friend. That was Mr. Grainger."

Hope shook her head slightly and uttered something beneath her breath.

Clay thought she uttered, "Not *friend*. "What did you say, Hope? I didn't hear you."

She did not respond.

Clay looked at the nurse. "Did you say Mr. Grainger—a John Grainger—had been here a few weeks ago? Are you sure?"

"Pretty sure."

"Can you tell me if other people have been in to visit her?"

"I don't remember any other visitors, but you'll have to check with the security guard at the front desk to be sure. He logs in all the visitors."

"Not friend," Hope uttered again.

Clay heard her clearly this time, "Hope, I understand why you feel he's not your friend. But I am." *Why did Grainger lie to me that he had never visited Hope?*

"Nurse, may I have a couple of minutes with her?"

The nurse looked at Hope who continued to hug her bear. "That's fine. Remember, no touching." She left the room and watched Clay and Hope through the door's security window.

"Hope, did John talk about me when he visited you?"

She looked through him and did not answer.

Clay tried again, "Did John ever say anything about me—or about Hank Kincaid from the district attorney's office?"

Hope continued to be unresponsive.

"Do you remember Mr. Kincaid?"

Nothing. Her head dropped to her chest and her eyes were closed.

"Hope, do you remember the people at the Indian Bend? I was wondering if you knew of anyone who..." She appeared to Clay to have fallen asleep. "I was hoping you could tell me..." Clay realized it was fruitless to continue. "I am so sorry for what happened to you, Hope. I wish I could turn back time. I was never going to leave you." Clay stopped. He had seen enough. He stood and nodded to the nurse that he was through.

The nurse reentered the room. She took gentle hold of Hope's elbow and guided her up from the chair.

"I'll come back when she's not so sedated."

"Yeah, well, lots of luck on that." The nurse said to Hope, "It's time to go back to your room. Detective Bryce has to leave now. Say goodbye."

"Hope, I'll be back to visit again sometime. I hope you'll agree to see me." He spoke deliberately as though to a child.

Hope showed no emotion.

Clay was saddened to his core by her condition. He had wonderful memories of their times together and wanted to remember her the way she was and what could have been—not as he saw her at this moment.

He said to the nurse, "I'm going to give her a hug goodbye."

"I'm sorry. That's not allowed."

"That's B.S." Clay disregarded the nurse's warning and embraced his former lover.

Hope lifted her head to Clay. Her eyelids fluttered as though she was trying to remember who he was.

"Goodbye, Hope."

A solitary tear rolled down her cheek. She used her teddy bear's paw to wipe it away.

* * * * *

Clay retrieved his service revolver from the lobby security guard. "Can you print me a list of everyone who's visited Hope Archer since she was admitted?"

"Yeah, give me a couple of minutes. Have a seat."

Several other visitors were now seated in the lobby. The mother and daughter were still waiting to be called through security. Clay idly thumbed his way through magazines piled on an end table. The U2 issue of *People* was at the bottom of the stack. He turned to the table of contents. The article about U2 was on pages twenty-nine and thirty. Clay turned the pages till he reached page twenty-eight. The next page was thirty-one. Pages twenty-nine and thirty were missing. He closed the magazine and flipped it to check the address label. The label had been torn off.

Clay said, "Well, I'll be a sonofabitch. Here it is. This is the magazine." He stood abruptly and returned to the security window. "I need to take this magazine with me."

The guard shrugged, "Why?"

"I need to check it for fingerprints for a case I've been working on."

"Yeah, fine. Help yourself."

"Do you know who left it here?"

"Don't know. People bring in magazines and books to read while they're in the waiting room and sometimes they leave them behind."

Clay approached the daughter of the woman who had been crying. "Excuse me, miss. By any chance, were you here when this magazine was brought in?"

The young woman was suspicious of Clay's question. She shook her head rapidly and turned away.

"I'm not accusing you of anything. I'm a detective and am asking if you saw who brought the magazine in."

The woman turned back and responded, "My mother and I got here only a little before you did. These other people just came in. I didn't see anyone bring in any magazines. It was probably here when we came in."

The lobby guard spoke through the intercom. "Detective Bryce, here you go." He placed a sheet of paper into the pass-through window. "Here's the list you wanted. Only a couple of people."

Clay studied it briefly. Three names appeared. He recognized Jason Adams as Hope's attorney. He had visited her twice shortly after she was admitted to the hospital a year earlier but had not been back since. Clay's name appeared twice a couple of weeks apart.

The third name on the list was John Grainger. He was listed as having visited Hope three weeks earlier. Clay wondered why Grainger would lie to him.

Clay asked the guard for any information he could provide about John Grainger. "Nope, he's only another name to me. Like all the others I see." Then, in obvious frustration about the tedium of his job, he added, "All day, every day."

Clay described Grainger to the guard, "He's good looking. Dark hair, about six feet tall. Walks with a swagger."

The guard asked, "Does he have a beard?"

"No, he doesn't."

"The guy I'm thinking of had a beard. Yeah, I'm sure of that. That's about all I can tell you, though. Oh. That, and he wore a New York Yankees baseball cap."

* * * * *

Grainger had told Clay he had never visited Hope, but the visitor log showed he had been there three weeks earlier. *Why the hell did he lie when I told him I was going to visit her? What an idiot. Didn't he think I'd figure out sooner or later that he'd been there?* As eager as Clay was to get the People magazine to forensics to have them check for Grainger's fingerprints, he decided to first go back to Grainger's house to confront him about his lie.

Grainger answered the door, surprised to see Clay again only hours after his previous visit. "Did you visit Hope?"

"Yes. I need to talk to you about her."

"All right. Come in." Grainger led Clay through the living room and out to the patio at the rear of his house. He pointed to a chair for Clay to sit and said, "What did you find out?"

"I found out you lied to me."

Grainger rolled his head and looked up to the sky. "Here we go again. What the hell are you talking about?"

"What did you think—that I wouldn't find out you went to see her?"

"What are you talking about? I told you before I haven't visited her. I'll say it again. I have not visited her. Period. End of story."

Clay handed the visitor log printout from the hospital to Grainger. "Then explain this."

Grainger put on his reading glasses and read the list. He was surprised to see his name there. "What the hell is this? I have *never* been there. Never!" He slapped at the list with the back of his hand. "This was not me."

Clay studied Grainger. "You're telling me you have never visited her?"

"That's correct. I haven't. Someone's using my name to get in to see her. It wasn't me."

"If you're lying—"

Grainger did not let him finish. "Why the hell would I lie to you about that? I'm telling you I have not been to see her. I don't even know where the hospital is. You want me to take a lie detector test?"

"If it wasn't you, who was it, and why would they sign in as you?"

"Damned if I know. You're the detective—you tell me."

CHAPTER 28

Clay could not understand why Grainger would lie about visiting Hope. *He knew I was going to see her. Could her visitor have been an imposter pretending to be Grainger? Why would someone go to that measure?*

Clay phoned the hospital and spoke to the head of security. "I was at the hospital earlier today to visit a patient, Hope Archer, about a case I'm investigating. Someone who visited her three weeks ago signed in under the name of John Grainger. I have reason to believe that person was an imposter. I need to review your surveillance tape from the lobby camera to see if we can determine who it was."

Security said they would confirm Clay's status with the Santa Fe PD, then stream the surveillance footage to his laptop. "Give me an hour."

Clay returned to police headquarters and went straight to the forensics lab. "Dan, I need your help."

"Sure thing, Clay. What's up?"

"Can you verify that the magazine page Hank Kincaid received matches up to the tear I found in this magazine?" Clay handed him the *People* he had picked up at the psychiatric hospital.

Carton immediately paired the page to the magazine. "It aligns precisely."

"Good. Now I need you to examine the magazine for John Grainger's prints. If his prints are on it, I can link this magazine to the Romans 12:19 message that was written on my mirror."

Back at his desk, Clay received an email from the hospital that the CCTV had been streamed to his laptop. He played the grainy video several times but could not discern if the person who signed in as Grainger was actually Grainger or someone posing as him. The person in the video was camera savvy. He purposely avoided identification by ducking his head whenever he faced the surveillance camera. He had a full beard and wore tinted glasses and a New York Yankees baseball cap pulled down to the top of the glasses. With his back to the camera, the same person was shown leafing through the stack of magazines in the waiting area. When the video ended, Clay looked at the ceiling and shook his head slowly back and forth. The footage did not provide a clear view of the man's face.

*   *   *   *   *

Clay arrived home exhausted after his first day back on duty from medical leave. He pulled off his tie and stretched out on his couch to watch a ball game on TV but fell into a deep sleep as soon as his head hit the pillow. A little before midnight, his cell phone rang, snapping him awake. The caller ID showed it was Grainger. "Yeah?"

"I wasn't sure if I should call you about this, but—"

"But what?" Clay said.

"Never mind. Forget it about it. Nothing."

Clay was irritated. "You call and wake me up in the middle of the night and then decide not to tell me why. Come on, man, what's the problem?"

"All right, I'll tell you, but don't piss me off by saying I'm imagining things."

"Yeah, okay. What is it?"

"I went to visit a friend after you left this afternoon."

"Who, Arianna?"

"Are you going to hear me out? Who I visited is not important. A half-hour ago, when I got back to the house and pulled into my garage, I saw the shed light was on. Now, that's not a big deal, right? But I hadn't been in the shed for three or four days, so there was no reason for the light to be on."

"Okay, and?"

"And this is the second time in the past couple of weeks I think someone's been here, rummaging through my stuff in the garage and who knows what else."

"Have you been burgled?"

"Nothing's missing that I can tell. But things are out of place, like someone's looking for something."

"I don't know what the hell you're getting at."

"I *knew* I shouldn't have called you. Just drop it."

Clay apologized. "Sorry, go on. What are you trying to tell me?"

"How else can I say this so you understand? Someone's been in my shed and garage."

"And you're sure you didn't simply forget to turn the light off?"

"I didn't turn the damned lights on in the first place! I know I'm OCD. I don't apologize for how I am. I can tell when the slightest thing has been changed or moved out of place. You know what I mean? My keys are always in my car. I park my cars in the same spots. I put my tools away in the exact same place. I turn the lights off *all the time*. And that includes the shed lights."

"When you went out today, did you set your security alarm?"

"Yes."

"Did the alarm go off?"

164

"No."

"Who else knows your alarm code?"

"No one."

"What about Arianna?"

"No. There's no reason for her to know it."

"As far as you can tell, no one got into the house, right? Only the shed and garage?"

"That's correct. The door from the garage into the kitchen has an alarm. Unless whoever's been here knew the security code, they wouldn't have been able to get into the house without setting off the alarm."

"But you haven't seen anything to suggest they've been inside your house. What about the landscaper? Could they have left the shed lights on?"

"No. I've told you I can't afford maids or gardeners anymore."

"All right. If you want, I'll stop by in the morning to see what you're talking about."

CHAPTER 29

John Grainger opened the front door and greeted Clay with a brusque, "It took you long enough. Thank God I wasn't hanging by my thumbs."

Clay had checked in at headquarters before making the trip to Grainger's house. He answered, "Oh, you're right. Of course. I should have been here at the crack of dawn because I have nothing else to do except be at your freakin' beck and call."

Clay's sarcasm did not faze Grainger. "Just follow me." They walked through the kitchen and out the door to the garage.

"What's been moved?" Clay asked.

"Look at this." Grainger walked past his cars to the far wall alongside the shed door. He stopped in front of his workbench. A peg board above the bench held pliers, screwdrivers, and hammers. Some were still in their original packaging. All hung facing the same direction. One screwdriver, a Phillips head, lay on the bench. "See this screwdriver? It's not where I left it. It should be hanging on the pegboard."

"Give me a break, Grainger." Clay shook his head. "You've got to be kidding me. You're saying you know if a screwdriver's been moved from the pegboard?"

"Yes, I do. I like things to be organized—everything in its place and a place for everything. Trust me, I can tell if something's been moved. I've had no reason to go to my workbench, so I *know* that screwdriver's been moved."

Clay scanned the garage. "What else?"

"A box along the wall has been tampered with."

"Show me."

Grainger pointed to a row of storage boxes along an adjacent wall. Each box had a label that listed its contents in alphabetical order. "This one here. See how the sealing tape was removed then reattached? I wouldn't have done that. I'd use a box cutter to cut the tape then apply new tape over the old."

Clay looked at him and shook his head. "How did you spot this?"

Grainger shrugged as if to say, "That's the OCD in me."

"What's in this box that someone would have taken?"

Grainger pointed to the label and said, "Nothing of value. It's mostly Christmas stuff. You want me to show you?"

"Yes. Let's check it out."

Grainger opened the box and laid the contents out on the floor. Towels, coasters, napkins, candles. "You see, just Christmas odds and ends."

"Right."

"Leave it all here. I'll put everything away later."

"Let's check the shed. Did you notice if anything was different there?"

"Everything looked the same."

Clay recalled the shed could be entered from both inside the garage and outside in the back yard. "Was the outside shed door locked when you came home last night?"

"Yes. When I went to turn off the shed light I checked if the door was locked, and it was."

Clay put on gloves to turn the doorknob and exit the shed. He walked out onto the paver path that led to the patio and the infinity pool at the back of the house. "Do you have a spare key hidden someplace to get into the house if you get locked out?"

"Yes. It's a spare to the shed, but it's hidden. It's up ahead underneath one of the pavers."

"Show me."

Grainger pointed to the paver. "Here." He lifted the paver to expose a two-inch square metal box. "Wait a second. Something's not right. It's been moved. I always put the box with the hinges toward the pool. It's in the opposite direction now." He reached down to retrieve the box from its hiding space.

"Don't touch it," Clay said. With a gloved hand, he picked up the box. "I'll have it dusted for fingerprints." He opened the box only to find it was empty. "There's no key." He looked at Grainger. "Are you sure it was in here? If it was, someone's taken it."

"I told you someone's been in my garage. That's how they've been getting in, isn't it?"

Clay pulled a plastic evidence bag from his pocket and dropped the key box in it. Grainger replaced the paver and the two men reentered the garage through the shed. Clay asked if the Range Rover and Z were parked in their normal places.

Grainger eyeballed his cars and answered without hesitation. "Yes, they're in the exact same spot they always are."

They next walked around the interior perimeter of the garage, looking for signs of intrusion. Clay asked, "Could someone be coming in through the shed when you're not here, driving your car out of the garage, and returning it before you notice it's gone?"

"I told you my cars haven't been moved. Besides, the person would have to know where I was going, how long I would be there, and when I was coming back."

"You mean someone like Arianna?"

Grainger stopped short. "God almighty, keep it down. What the hell's wrong with you?" He looked over both shoulders. "Stop bringing up her name."

Clay looked around too. "Is someone else in the house? What are you so jumpy about?"

"No, but stop saying her name. What if someone walked in on us?"

"You're kidding me. Like, who? One of your other girlfriends?"

"Drop it, okay?"

"Did you see Arianna last night?"

"No, I did not," Grainger said. "We're not involved anymore. And what difference would it make if we still were?" After a moment's hesitation, he leveled with Clay. "I was with another woman."

"Someone I know?"

"Whether you know her or not is not important. But forget about that. I've got something else to tell you. It's totally confidential."

"Okay."

"I mean, you can't tell anyone."

"I get it. What?"

"Hayden Arrington rehired me to become the operations vice president at the Bend."

Clay said, "Are you serious?"

"Yes. Simon Learner isn't hacking it, so Arrington's hiring me back to straighten things out. Things are in such bad shape, the Bend is on the verge of bankruptcy. He knows I can fix what ails the place and get gamblers to come back. When I was in charge, we were the best casino in New Mexico for a reason. I worked my ass off to make it the best. So why does he want me back?" Grainger answered his own question by reverting to his egotistical self. "Because I'm that good."

"You always said Simon was sharp—Ivy Leaguer, photographic memory, genius—all that. Why do you suppose he hasn't been successful?"

"I can't answer that. He worked for me for ten years and I thought he was qualified to take over if I ever left—not that I wanted to leave. I loved my job. It doesn't make any difference what I thought of Simon. He had a great opportunity to showcase himself, but he's blown it. Arrington infused the Bend with a huge amount of cash to shore it up, but revenues have plummeted to half what they were a year ago. The operation used to be a cash cow, but now it's an albatross. And the man does not take kindly to failure."

"So Arrington's going to hire you in spite of all the bad publicity about the serial murders at the Bend and the charge against you? Isn't that what started the problems in the first place?"

"Arrington thinks enough time has elapsed so people won't remember what happened a year ago. Attendance dropped because people thought they might end up being the next murder victim. If you hadn't dragged out the investigation, none of this would have happened. It's like now—instead of going after real criminals, you're spending all your time investigating an automobile accident."

Clay glared at Grainger. "Believe what you want."

"Well, that's a fact. It's all on you."

"So, to thank him for rehiring you, you turn around and screw his wife. You're a prince of a guy, Grainger. Salt of the earth."

"That's not true. I haven't seen Arianna once since Arrington told me he was rehiring me. I'm not sure why the hell I'm telling you all this. Remember, you can't breathe a word of this to anyone."

"Why the big secret?"

"Arrington plans to meet with the Bend's board of directors Friday morning. The directors don't know anything about my rehire. Arrington's obligated to go through them, but it's only a formality. As far as he's concerned, it's a done deal. He said the directors will probably grouse about it, but he made it clear they serve at his bidding and have no real say in the matter. You've got to give the man credit. He doesn't take shit from anyone."

"Well, congratulations. I'm happy you got your job back."

Grainger eyed Clay with skepticism. His words had come across as disingenuous. "I know you don't mean that, but I don't care."

"No, I was being sincere. But, think about it. Do you suppose Arrington found out about you and Arianna and, by hiring you back, thinks he'll be able to keep you away from her?"

"I don't think he knows about us. If he did, I probably would have been dead by now. Ever meet his Ukrainian bodyguard, Anton whatever-his-name-is?"

"No."

"Well, I have. Arrington brought him along when he came to my house. If Arrington were to ever unleash Anton on me, the man's stare alone could kill me."

"Is that right?"

"You know, Bryce, getting my job back means everything to me. It's over with Arianna. The risk of losing my job a second time is not worth it—not even for her."

How long before he breaks that vow? "Yeah, right, I believe that. So what's going to happen to Simon?"

Grainger shrugged, "Not my problem."

"Doesn't the fact that Simon is married now and has a kid cause you any pangs of guilt about him being fired and you taking his job from him?"

"I'm not sorry enough that I would turn down the job." He shrugged then repeated with a smirk, "Nope, not at all. You know why? Because I've learned over the years that, in this dog-eat-dog world, it's survival of the fittest—every man for himself. Simon had a chance to haul in a high six-figure salary, but now he'll be lucky to get a severance package. Arrington considers failure a disease and quarantines anyone who fails him. The bastard's tough, all right. Simon knew that going in."

"Have you talked to Simon over the past year?"

"No. We didn't part on the best of terms. He turned his back on me when everything came out about that underage girl. He hasn't asked for help—the arrogant sonofabitch—and I haven't volunteered any. I could have helped him. Anyway, enough about Simon. Can we get back to why I asked you here?"

Clay nodded.

"Why do you think someone got into my garage? Do you think it could have been the same person who signed in as me at the hospital?"

"Sure, it's possible," Clay said. He had a sudden thought. "Hold on." He walked behind the Range Rover and bent down to get a close look at the license plate.

Grainger followed him. "What are you looking for?"

"What if the car that hit me used your license plate—not the car, just the plate? What if the guy got your spare key, entered your garage through the shed, used the Phillips head screwdriver that was on top of the bench to remove the license plate from your Range Rover, and then put the plate on his own car? Then, after he ran me over, he returned the plate to your car using the same screwdriver."

"Why the hell would someone do all that?"

"To frame you? To have me think it was you who ran me over?"

"You finally come up with something that makes sense," Grainger said.

"I'm glad you approve."

"But, why me? Why would someone try to frame me?"

Clay looked hard at Grainger and shook his head. "Think about the husbands of the women you've slept with who would like to put your head in a vice. The only question is, which one has the balls to do it?"

CHAPTER 30

Clay called on forensics once again, this time to determine if the license plate on John Grainger's Range Rover had recently been removed and replaced. He also asked Carton and Cook to check for fingerprints on the plate, the spare key box that was uncovered from the paver walkway, the shed door knob and light switch, and the screwdriver. His final request was for them to check the garage floor. "See if you can find latent footprints that go from the shed to the workbench to the back of the Range Rover. I realize I'm throwing a lot at you, but do what you can."

"We're still checking out prints on the magazine you gave us yesterday. As you probably gathered, there are dozens of prints, but we should have all your answers by late afternoon."

* * * * *

As promised, Carton and Cook reached their conclusions and met with Clay at police headquarters to explain their findings. "First off, we checked the fingerprints on the People magazine. There were a number of prints, but none we could identify as belonging to Grainger."

"What about the license plate?"

"We determined the plate *may* have been removed recently. Under microscope, we noticed a slight amount of rust on the screws had been scraped off, probably when they were removed. And we found a microscopic amount of rust clinging to the tip of the screwdriver which matched the rust on the screws. We're checking on the speed of oxidation of the screws to determine when they might have been removed, but we won't be able to narrow the timeline down to an exact number of days."

"Any fingerprints on the plate?"

"None. Nor did we find any on the shed door, the screwdriver, or the key box. Your suspect used gloves or wiped the surfaces clean."

"Were you able to determine if there were footprints on the garage floor that did not belong to Grainger?"

"In fact, we did. We used ultraviolet lighting to check the floor for latent prints and found some. We electrostatically lifted dust from the impressions made by the shoes. There were a lot of different prints, including yours, mine, and Dick's. Some of the other prints could have been there for weeks or even months, so they don't prove a thing. But you might find one set of prints to be of interest. We determined they were from a size nine shoe that went from the shed to the workbench to the back of the Range Rover, then back to the bench and out to the shed. We asked Grainger to show us his shoe. He wears a size eleven."

"What about the type of shoe that made the prints?"

"Smooth-soled with a slight cut an inch from the front of the right shoe. Find who is wearing that shoe and you have your intruder."

CHAPTER 31

On his way home from work, Clay stopped at the grocery store to pick up a few things. He tossed a box of Cheerios and other groceries in his cart and was headed to the dairy section when his phone rang. It was Tomás Robles. Robles seldom called him. "Hey, Tomás, what's up?"

"John Grainger is dead."

"What? How?"

"I was still at HQ when the call came in. There was a fire. A cop on routine patrol spotted smoke pouring out of his house and reported it at 6:06. The fire department had the fire under control in twenty minutes. It was confined to Grainger's bedroom, but the fire crew found Grainger dead in his bed."

"In his bed? It's not seven o'clock yet."

"I'm at his house now. The fire marshal just got here. Grainger left a note. It might have been suicide."

"Suicide? That doesn't make sense." Clay was incredulous. "I saw him this morning. He was flying high as a kite. Arrington had just told him he was getting his old job back. I'll be there in fifteen minutes."

Clay abandoned his shopping cart mid-aisle and hurried out the store to his car. He raced through city traffic with his lights flashing and siren blaring. He and the medical examiner, Aaron Safford, arrived at Grainger's house at the same time. They double-parked their cars alongside the forensic van. Clay exited his car and cupped his hand above his eyes to minimize the intensity of the combined flashing lights of the firetruck, four cop cars, the fire marshal's car, and a paramedic ambulance. The scene was chaotic. Cops blocked traffic from entering East Alameda at both ends and another cop was stretching yellow police tape around the entire front of the house.

A man who stood behind the growing number of onlookers lit a cigarette, then ducked his head, turned, and casually walked away.

Clay flashed his badge at the uniformed cop at the front door and hurried inside. The dense smell of smoke took his breath away. He swallowed hard and breathed through his mouth. He could never understand how firefighters were able to withstand the intense and lingering taste of smoke. He put on gloves and walked to Grainger's bedroom where Detective Robles was talking with Dan Carton. Dick Cook was photographing the bedroom from all angles, and Joe Sweeney, the fire marshal, a veteran of thirty years with the Santa Fe Fire Department Investigative Unit was taking measurements and collecting samples of burnt fibers from where he perceived the blaze might have originated.

The bedroom ceiling, walls, and carpeting were blackened and the curtains burned, but the extent of fire damage was minimal, thanks to the fire crew's use of dry chemical extinguishers rather than water hoses.

Grainger's fully clothed body lay in his bed. His face appeared ghost-like from the residue of chemicals used to fight the fire. The ME bent over the body to begin his examination into the cause of death.

Robles said to Clay, "Let's go to Grainger's study. That's where the suicide note is."

When Clay and Robles left the bedroom they rounded the corner in the hallway and nearly collided with a paramedic. "Sorry," Clay said. In the darkened hallway he did not immediately recognize the paramedic as Allie. When he realized who it was, he called out, "Hey, Allie."

Allie glanced at Clay but continued down the hallway and entered the bedroom without acknowledging him.

Robles noticed Allie's snub but said nothing. He led Clay through the kitchen and into the study. "Here's Grainger's note. We found it on his desk."

1 Kings 16:18

"This is it? This is the suicide note?" Clay asked. "Another biblical reference? How do you figure it's a suicide note? What does it mean?"

Robles took out his phone. "It says, 'When Zimri saw that the city was taken, he went into the citadel of the king's house and burned the king's house over him with fire, and died.' I take that to mean he committed suicide."

Clay's reaction was swift. "Grainger didn't write that. I don't care what that verse implies. There's no way he committed suicide. The note is a fake."

"Why do you say that?"

"For a lot of reasons. First, Hayden Arrington rehired him to work at the Bend—back at what he called his dream job. Second, he loved this house. He was OCD—*seriously* OCD. He kept everything immaculate. All the times I've been here, I've never seen a thing out of place. He especially wouldn't set a blaze in his own bedroom. That would be too messy, go against the grain of his personality. And, knowing him like I did, I can't imagine him setting a fire that could mar his appearance. He was too much of an egoist. He would worry about how he looked—even in death. None of this makes sense. *If* he was going to kill himself, he might have taken pills—a much cleaner, neater way to die. He would never kill himself using fire—and definitely not now when he was about to have his old job back."

"So you think he was murdered?"

"Tomás, there are no two ways about it. Last night he called and told me he suspected someone had been getting into his house. I came here this morning to see what he was talking about. We found that someone had taken the spare house key he had hidden under a paver behind his house and used it to get in through the shed. The fire was probably set by the same person who took the key."

The two detectives returned to Grainger's bedroom. Robles handed the suicide note to Carton. In a low voice he said, "Dan, check this for prints. Let us know what you find."

"You got it."

Allie was in the bedroom standing next to the fire marshal. "We're heading out. Nothing more we can do here. The ME will arrange to transport the body back to the morgue."

"Okay, thanks, Allie," Sweeney replied.

Clay called after Allie as she walked out of the room, but she pretended not to hear him. He said to Robles, "Give me a minute. I've got to talk to that paramedic." He hurried after Allie and caught up as she was nearly out the front door. "Maryland."

She responded angrily, "It's Marland. It's Allie *Marland*, not *Maryland*. Get it?"

Clay looked around to make sure no one was within earshot. "Okay, fine, Ms. Allie Marland. Will you please let me explain what happened on Sunday night?"

Allie rolled her eyes. "I don't want to listen to your explanation. The truth is, you hurt me. I was way more than embarrassed by the stunt you pulled. Does dating two women at the same time make you macho? Are you so stuck on yourself?"

"That's not what I am. I would never do anything to embarrass you. I'm telling you, that woman was trying to make me look bad. And all that crap she threw out at you and me... I don't know what she was trying to prove."

Allie looked into Clay's eyes to gauge his sincerity.

Clay said, "I've got to get back in there. Can I call you tonight?"

Allie spun around and walked away without answering.

Clay shook his head in frustration at her obstinacy and returned to Grainger's bedroom. He asked the ME what he had found.

"Much too soon to know for certain," said Safford, "but I've discovered trauma—a cranial contusion—to the back of the head that may have contributed to his death. From the redness of the eyes, the burns on the corneas, and the blueish color of the skin, I'd say he died of smoke inhalation. I'll know more when I get the body back and do the autopsy. I should have results for you Thursday at the latest. As of now, I can't tell you much more."

Clay and Tomás next approached the fire marshal to find out what he had learned.

Sweeney said, "As you both know, fire crews are instructed to notify me immediately when there's a fire death. At first I thought this was an accidental death. Typically when there's a fire in a bedroom, it's a mattress fire. But that wasn't the case here. There's no sign of fire on or near the mattress. The point of origin seemed to be at the outlet underneath that window." Sweeney pointed to one of the curtained windows at the east end of the large bedroom. "I checked to see if there was an electrical circuit overload. At closer inspection, I determined the fire actually started on the floor in front of the outlet, not in or from the outlet itself. I looked for signs of a flammable liquid, like gasoline, and found nothing. I now know the cause. Let me show you."

Robles and Clay followed Sweeney to the ignition point of the fire and huddled around him as he explained his findings. Clay motioned for Carton and Cook to join them. Sweeney dropped to his haunches. "You see this?"

"Yeah. Looks like wax."

"It is. It's residue from a candle." Sweeney pointed to the center of the burn area on the carpet. "There's residue from some kind of paper on the carpet underneath where the curtain hangs down. You can still see ashes around the wax. I'd say someone propped a candle in the middle of a lot of crumpled paper. The intention was to have the candle burn down to the same level as the paper around it, at which time the burning wick would ignite the paper."

Clay added, "And that, in turn, would ignite the curtains."

"Exactly. This is a common method used by arsonists to set a fire—one which allows them to be long gone before the fire is noticed."

"What's the burn rate of a candle?"

"It's based on the diameter of the candle. Let's say, for example, if a candle is nine inches long, one inch in diameter, and tapered, it would burn down about one inch every forty-five minutes. If a similar candle was used here, it would have taken six to seven hours to reach the level of the paper around it."

Robles asked, "So, the candle could have been lit at about ten or eleven o'clock this morning?"

"Yes, if it had burned down to an ignition point. But there's a lot of wax here. My guess is the candle may have fallen over at some point—for whatever reason—and it ignited the paper earlier than the arsonist anticipated."

"Like, how much earlier?"

"I can't answer that. One thing that would help determine the ignition time is knowing the original size of the candle, and there's no way I can tell that. Again, the longer the candle stayed lit, the more time the arsonist had to get away and establish an alibi."

Clay said, "You're saying that, while all this was going on, Grainger is lying in his bed, probably not dead yet, while the arsonist-slash-killer was creating the scenario you described."

"Most likely," Sweeney said.

Robles asked Sweeney, "Is it possible to determine the type of candle? If we can figure that out, maybe we can track it to a retail shop and learn who might have purchased it."

"It was probably an ordinary candle—the kind you can buy at a lot of stores."

Clay said, "Wait a second. I think I know where it came from." He turned to Carton and Cook. "There are boxes stacked up along the wall near the workbench in the garage. Each box has a list taped to it showing what's inside. One box has Christmas stuff in it, and the list includes an exact number of candles inside. Check to see if any of the candles are missing.

Cook said, "You're kidding me."

"I'm not," Clay responded. "The guy was OCD."

Clay squatted alongside Sweeney to examine the candle residue. "Is it your opinion Grainger did not kill himself?"

"Anything's possible, but if he wanted to commit suicide by fire, why not throw gasoline around the room and light a match? That's quick and fatal." Sweeney shook his head as he spoke. "There are a hell of a lot of easier ways to kill yourself. I sure wouldn't recommend death by fire."

"You're saying suicide by fire is rare."

"Extremely rare. Self-immolation might be done by people like the monks in Tibet, but not in our country. No, Clay, my preliminary conclusion is that the fire was set by someone else—someone who needed time to get away so he could establish an alibi. A slow-burning candle is an arsonist's ideal weapon. Wax from fires set this way is not usually detectable in post-fire debris. We're fortunate in this case because our firefighters knocked the fire out quickly, which let us find the wax and determine the cause. The walls and furniture were not engulfed. If that had happened, the fire would have been more intense and the wax would have been burned off. In this case, there was a lot of smoke, but not much fire."

Clay asked, "Would you say the smoke is what killed him?"

"Probably. That is, if he wasn't dead already. But that's for the ME to determine."

"Anything else, Joe?"

"Yes, one last thing. Even if he had set the fire in a suicide attempt, he would instinctively have tried to flee."

"What do you mean?"

"His survival instincts would have kicked in, in which case, we might have seen signs of him stumbling out of bed trying to escape. In my opinion, he wouldn't still be in bed the way we found him unless he was either already dead or incapacitated in some way."

Carton and Cook returned with plastic packaging designed to hold three nine-inch tapered candles. Two candles were still in the package. "I think we have the answer about the type of candle that was used. If it's okay with you, Joe, we'll collect the wax residue from the carpet. We're all but certain it'll match these candles. We'll also try to determine how much residue went unburned, then use the burn rate to come up with a window for when the candle was lit."

Sweeney said, "Keep me informed."

The ME had Grainger's body transported to the morgue. Two hours later, after the fire scene was secured, everyone left Grainger's house–except Clay. He decided to take one more pass through the house. He started in the garage. Nothing seemed different from when he had been there that morning. He stared at the tool bench and recalled Grainger's compulsion about every tool needing to be hung or positioned a certain way. One hammer on the pegboard was hung in the opposite direction of the other tools. He removed the hammer and placed it in an evidence bag. *Forensics can check this to see if anyone else's prints are on it.*

Clay ensured that the outside shed door was locked, then left the garage and walked through the rest of the house, room by room. He flicked on the light in Grainger's bedroom and looked around. The smell of smoke was still strong. Something he had not noticed earlier caught his eye. A small, black device was attached to one end of the curtain rod above the window located the farthest from the fire incineration point. Close up, he noticed it was a tiny, motion-activated stealth camera. He could not reach the device from the floor, so he climbed onto a chair to retrieve it. He opened the camera to remove the memory card, only to discover the card was missing.

What a helluva guy. He was probably recording his sexual encounters.

Clay searched the room but did not find the memory card.

CHAPTER 32

The image of Grainger's body lingered with Allie on her drive home. She blasted the volume on the radio. Music helped her cope with the emotional toll of her job and cleared her head of the image of pain, suffering, and death.

Tonight she also thought of her encounter with Clay at John Grainger's house. Her feelings about Clay were jumbled. She had been attracted to him from the time she first treated him at the hit-and-run accident. Allie admitted to herself that Clay had awakened senses she had not felt toward any man since her divorce years earlier.

He played me for a fool. Just when I was feeling good about him. Damn him. She felt she would never be able to forgive Clay. He had been deceitful to her. *Now he's trying to tell me I didn't see what I saw.*

Allie parked her car and entered her condo. A relaxing soak in a warm bubble bath would remove the smell of smoke from her skin and hair and relieve some of the stress she carried from her job.

She poured a glass of white wine, drew the bath, and set the wine and her cell phone on the edge of the tub. She waited until the bubbles were nearly to the top of the tub before turning the water off and stepping in. She took a sip of wine then lay back and immersed herself up to her chin.

Her soothing and healing soak was interrupted by the shrill ring of her phone. She read the caller ID.

Clay.

He had asked at the fire scene if he could call her and she had not responded. Now she debated if she should answer. She let the phone ring three more times, then answered in a cold, impersonal way.

"Yes? What is it?"

"It's Clay."

"What do you want?"

"Can I come over to talk? I won't be more than five minutes."

"No. I'm taking a bath. You can talk to me on the phone."

Clay did not want to push it. "Then hear me out?" Allie said neither yeah nor nay. Clay took her silence to mean yes, and explained, "I am totally innocent." Several more seconds passed without a word from her. He thought she had hung up on him. "Are you there?"

She was still skeptical but relented. "I'm waiting."

"I was really looking forward to seeing you on Sunday, but an hour before you arrived, that woman knocked on my door."

"That woman? You mean you didn't know who she was?"

"No, I do know her. I interviewed her about my hit-and-run. I had no idea why she came to my house or even how she knew where I lived. I told her I was expecting company, but she waltzed right in and sat herself down on my couch anyway."

"Why didn't you tell her to leave?"

"I did, but it didn't matter to her. She made herself at home. She even asked for a glass of wine."

"You're kidding me."

"No, I'm not. Then, just before you came, I told her again that she had to leave. That's when she threw her arms around me and kissed me. I tried to push her away."

"I bet you did."

"I know you don't believe me, but that's exactly what happened. I asked her what the hell she was doing."

"Why was she making a play for you?"

"I can't get into too much detail, Allie, but I can tell you this. My original suspect in my hit-and-run case named her as his alibi. When I interviewed her, she confirmed that my suspect was with her and she admitted she was having an affair with him. She panicked that I was going to tell her husband, so she came to my house to throw herself at me, hoping I'd take her bait to have sex with her. In her distorted mind, having sex with me was going to be her safety net."

"I don't get it."

"Think about it. If I were to disclose to her husband that she was having an affair, she would threaten to tell my boss that she and I had a sexual relationship. That would be the end of my career."

"I saw her. She was beautiful. You're telling me you didn't reciprocate? You didn't kiss her back? I find that hard to believe."

"I'm telling you, I did not."

Allie struggled to accept Clay's story. "Go on. What happened then?"

"When you rang the doorbell, I thought it was the pizza guy and I'd still have time to get rid of her before you showed up. After that, well, you know what happened. She came into the foyer and tried to make it look like I was her lover."

Allie asked, "If that was her motivation, I don't understand why she acted toward me the way she did."

"I don't either. She probably wanted to make you mad or jealous. I don't know. I swear, Allie, I'm not the least bit interested in her."

"For your information, I was *not* jealous" She paused for a second, then said, "Well, okay, maybe I was a *little* jealous."

Clay hoped he had convinced her of his sincerity. "Maryland, I'd really like to pick up where we left off." Allie said nothing. "You should know I got kudos from the police doctor about how well I was taking care of my wounds. That was all thanks to you. But, I have to tell you, I'm still hurting from my accident." He was milking it now. "Do you know where I can find a good nurse?"

Allie chuckled. "Yes, I believe I do know someone who might be available."

"Will you please tell her I look forward to seeing her?"

The warm bath was stoking Allie's senses. "Okay, Mr. Silver Tongue, but listen to me. If I find out you've been lying to me, I promise you, as God is my witness, you will regret it for all eternity."

"Good Lord! I don't want to risk that. How can I prove to you that I really am a good guy?"

"Hmm. Let me think. All right, here's your test. There's an art and wine fest on the Plaza on Saturday. You can be my date. We can have lunch and check out the music and art exhibits."

Art festivals were hardly Clay's cup of tea, but he tried to sound enthusiastic. "Sounds great. I'll pick you up at noon."

"That's perfect. And, Clay, I'm glad you called."

CHAPTER 33

Police Blotter

Former Indian Bend Casino Executive Dead in Fire — Mr. John Grainger, 40, a former high-ranking executive of the Indian Bend Hotel and Casino, died Tuesday afternoon in a fire at his home on East Alameda Street in Santa Fe.

The Santa Fe Fire Department was dispatched shortly after 6 p.m. and had the fire under control in twenty minutes. Fire Marshal Joe Sweeney said the fire was confined to Mr. Grainger's bedroom, where his body was found.

Detective Clay Bryce of the Santa Fe Police Department announced the discovery of a suicide note, the details of which have not been disclosed. However, the fire marshal has determined that the circumstances surrounding the fire are suspicious, and foul play has not been ruled out. Investigations at the fire scene are ongoing. The Medical Examiner is performing an autopsy, after which more information about the cause of death is expected to be made available.

Mr. Grainger had a brief but meteoric career at the Indian Bend Casino, starting as a dealer and working his way up to Operations Vice President. He was dismissed a year ago in the aftermath of a highly publicized criminal case regarding his involvement in an improper sexual relationship with an underage female employee. Mr. Grainger was not employed at the time of his death and leaves behind no family.

*   *   *   *   *

By Thursday, the ME had completed the autopsy on John Grainger. Safford concluded Grainger's skull had been fractured. Blood and hair traces that matched Grainger's were found on the hammer Clay had removed from the pegboard above Grainger's workbench, which led the ME to conclude that the hammer was likely the weapon used to fracture Grainger's skull.

Clay asked the ME, "Was Grainger already dead when the fire was started?"

Safford responded, "No. The cause of death was smoke inhalation. He wasn't dead, but neither was he capable of fleeing the fire due to the blow to his head."

Clay surmised that the assailant had unlocked the shed door using the spare key taken from underneath the paver, then entered the garage, where Grainger probably discovered him. The assailant used the hammer to subdue Grainger, then carried him into the bedroom. The killer typed the fake suicide note on Grainger's computer and left the message on the desk for the police to find. Afterward, he set the fire using the candle he had found in the garage.

*   *   *   *   *

Forensics reported they found only Grainger's fingerprints on the suicide note. However, Carton observed, "The prints appear to have been physically forced onto the paper after Grainger had been incapacitated. Let me show you."

Carton placed a sheet of paper on Clay's desk and said, "Now, pick up the paper and hand it to me." Clay did as instructed. "See how you picked it up? Your thumb print was on the top right of the page, and your forefinger and middle finger were on the back. That's not how Grainger's prints showed. They were laid on the page as though he was being fingerprinted. I don't think Grainger typed that note. Someone forced his hand on the paper, inserted it into the printer, then typed the note and left it on his desk. In our opinion, the suicide note was bogus."

* * * * *

Clay met with Captain Ellsworth to discuss Grainger's murder. "One thing is clear," Clay said. "The biblical verse on the alleged suicide note links Grainger's murder to the assaults on both Hank and me. If we find whoever killed Grainger, we've got the guy who tried to kill us."

"What about those verses? Do you have a profile on the kind of person who would leave them as a signature?"

"Yes. I spoke to the FBI in Quantico. From their intel and, contrary to what we might think, the profile fits someone who is *not* especially religious. The guy is simply using the Bible to link all his actions. He could be using the internet to find verses that explain what he's doing and why. In other words he's no zealot."

* * * * *

Clay had two prime suspects—Hayden Arrington and Arianna Arrington. If Hayden had learned about his wife's affair, he had motive to murder Grainger. Arianna, too, had motive. If Grainger were dead she would not have to worry about him disclosing their affair. The challenge was to determine why either of them would assault both Clay and Hank. Although it was clear the crimes were linked, there did not seem to be a related motive.

* * * * *

Clay dialed the Arrington's home phone number to arrange an interview with Hayden. Arianna answered. "Why, Clay, how good to hear from you. Did you change your mind about us?"

"I need to talk to your husband about John Grainger. I assume from your comment that he's not there."

"Why do you want to talk to him? You promised me you wouldn't. I thought we had an agreement."

"Don't worry. I'm not going to say anything about your affair. Where is your husband now?"

"Hayden flew to Germany on Tuesday morning. He's returning tonight for a board meeting tomorrow morning at the Bend."

"Then I'll talk to you instead. Stay put. I'll be there in fifteen minutes."

Arianna purred, "Ooh, yes, I can't wait to see you again."

Clay hung up.

* * * * *

Clay pulled up to the driveway intercom at the Arrington mansion. "Clay Bryce to see Mrs. Arrington."

"Si, señor," Imelda answered. The gate opened.

He proceeded up the long drive to the house. Arianna stood at the front door to greet him. She was dressed in tight white jeans and high heels. Her hair was pulled back in a long ponytail. She looked gorgeous. With a quick check to make sure Imelda was not within earshot, she said, "Follow me so we can talk in private. Imelda doesn't speak English very well but she understands everything." Arianna led Clay through the house and out onto the sprawling flagstone patio. She closed the patio door behind them and sat facing the house to keep tabs on Imelda's whereabouts. "I have to say, I'm very happy to see you again, Detective Bryce." She moistened her lips and tilted her head coquettishly. "Frankly, I didn't expect to see you again so soon, but I'm open to anything you might suggest." She winked.

Clay jutted his jaw at her. "I'm here to ask you about John Grainger, not for any other reason, got it?"

"Oh, you party pooper."

"I need to get something off my chest first. I know what your intention was when you came to my house. You came close to screwing up a relationship with a woman who means a lot to me. You need to stop this charade. My home and personal life are off limits to you. Do you understand?"

Arianna puckered her lips and said, "Oh, Clay, do you know how much that hurts my feelings?"

Clay said sarcastically, "Yeah, I'm sure."

"What do you want to know about John?"

"When did you last see him?"

She hesitated before answering. "What's today? Thursday, right? Let me think. A couple of weeks ago. That's when I told him we couldn't see each other anymore."

Arianna did not show much emotion causing Clay to wonder if she even knew her lover was dead. "You are aware John is dead, aren't you?"

"Oh, yes. What a tragedy, don't you think?" she answered in a matter-of-fact tone.

"How did you hear about it?"

"I first saw it on TV that he had died on Tuesday. Then I read about it in yesterday's paper that he had committed suicide."

"You don't seem upset."

"Oh, I am. Can't you tell? It's just that I'm good at controlling how I feel—good or bad. I hope he didn't commit suicide because I broke things off."

"John did not commit suicide. We know now he was murdered."

"Oh, no! Who would have done such a thing?" She blinked and used a cloth napkin from the patio table to dab at her eyes, which Clay noticed were not moist at all. "Are you sure he was killed?"

"Yes, I'm sure."

"How awful. How truly, truly awful. Poor John. He was so excited about going back to the Bend."

"How did you know about that? Did you have anything to do with your husband rehiring John?"

"Yes, and no. Hayden did mention that he planned to rehire him."

"What did you say when he told you?"

"Nothing. I thought it was strange that he told me, because he never discusses business matters with me."

"Do you think he was trying to find out how you felt about John?"

"I thought that, but I didn't respond. I just nodded and said, 'that's nice.'"

"Mrs. Arrington—"

"Arianna, remember?"

"Fine. Arianna. If John was not home when you wanted to see him, were you able to let yourself into his house?"

"I don't know what you mean. He was always there waiting for me."

"I'm asking if you know the code for his home alarm system."

"I have no clue."

"Well, he must've told you where he kept the spare key to his house, right?"

"He never told me that. Why are you asking me all these questions?"

"I can't explain it at this time."

"I still can't believe he was murdered." She continued to dab the napkin at invisible tears.

"Unfortunately, he was. Did he ever mention anyone who might have wanted to harm him?"

"No, but John told me he knew some people held it against him that the Bend had fallen on hard times. Maybe it was someone who works at the casino."

"Did he mention anyone in particular?"

"No."

"Is your husband aware John is dead?"

"Yes, I mentioned it to him yesterday when he called."

"What did he say?"

"Well, I didn't know at the time that John had been murdered. I told Hayden he had committed suicide."

"What did he say?"

"Hayden cursed John out and called him 'a weak, sorry excuse for a man,' quote, unquote. Then he said he'd have to go to Plan B as far as the Bend was concerned."

"Plan B? Did he tell you what that was?"

"No, and I didn't ask."

"What about Hayden? He certainly had motive to kill John if he knew about your affair."

"That's crazy. Hayden just hired him back. Why would he turn around and kill him?"

"I'll ask you one more time. Is there any way he might have learned about your affair?"

"No. Absolutely not."

"How can you be so sure?"

"I just am. John and I were always so careful. There's no way Hayden could have known about—" She stopped herself when she finally realized what Clay had been alluding to. "You're not accusing Hayden of murdering John, are you? Hayden would never do such a thing. If he found out about us—which he didn't—but if he did, he wouldn't, I mean..." Arianna stumbled over her words as she tried to explain her feelings.

"I get your point. What about you?"

"What about me?"

"You had motive to murder John."

"What are you saying?"

"Did you kill him? The way I see it, with John dead, you no longer have to worry about him disclosing your affair."

Arianna paused. "Don't be ridiculous. I mean, *you* know about John and me, right?"

"Yes. What's your point?"

"Well, using your logic, I should want to kill you too."

"That's twisted logic. I'll keep that in mind and never turn my back to you." He stood to leave.

Arianna said, "You have to leave? You just got here."

He nodded. "Yep."

"Well, I for one, am tickled to see you again." She stood and extended her hand.

Clay hesitated. He did not want a repeat of Sunday's incident when she ended up in his arms.

"I'm not going to bite you, Clay. You can shake my hand."

Clay felt his cheeks burn but did not extend his hand to her.

"I noticed you have huge hands, Detective. John's were smaller."

Clay shrugged.

She said, "You know what they say about huge hands."

Clay played along. He winked and teased her, in turn. "Yep, I know, but you'll never find out from me."

"Oh, yes, I will. It's just a matter of time. Tell your girlfriend she's in for a fight. I'm not going to give up on you."

Arianna walked Clay back through the house and out the front door. She stood on the outside landing and watched him get into his car. As he started to drive off, she gestured for him to stop.

He lowered his window. "Yeah, what?"

She stood with her ankles crossed in a model's pose. "I want you to know you can call me anytime." She held her smile as he put his window back up and drove off.

CHAPTER 34

Police Blotter

Former Indian Bend Casino Executive Murdered – Santa Fe Captain of Detectives, Matthew Ellsworth, provided an update to an earlier announcement that Mr. John Grainger, 40, the former executive of the Indian Bend Hotel and Casino who died in a fire at his home on Tuesday, had committed suicide. Grainger's death has now been ruled a homicide. Initial evidence pointed to a suicide, but an autopsy and other evidence found at the scene prove that Grainger had been murdered.

If anyone witnessed any individual or unusual activity in the vicinity of 14289 East Alameda Street between the hours of 10 a.m. and 6 p.m. on Tuesday, please notify the police. The Santa Fe Crime Commission is offering a $10,000 reward for information leading to the arrest and conviction of John Grainger's killer. They ask to be contacted at 505-222-9999 if anyone can offer any information.

* * * * *

Friday morning, Clay drove to the Indian Bend Casino to question Hayden Arrington. He pulled under the porte cochere and parked along the curb at the main entrance. He flashed his badge at the valet and said, "Official business." Inside, the grand lobby was virtually empty. Clay approached a uniformed security guard who was posted beside the executive elevator. "I'm here to talk with Mr. Arrington."

"I'm sorry, Detective, I've been told to inform anyone who asks for him that he is not available. He's in a board meeting. The board will be breaking for lunch at noon so you might want to wait for him."

Clay looked at his watch. "It's eleven thirty. I'll wait. Do me a favor. Call Simon Learner. Tell him I want to talk to him in the meantime."

"Will do." The guard called Simon Learner's office from a house phone on the wall behind him. He turned back to Clay and said, "Mr. Learner will see you. His secretary will be down shortly to escort you up."

Clay looked around the lobby and noted its tired look—everything needed cleaning and sprucing up. The grouting of the Mexican tile flooring needed a steam-cleaning, the windows were streaked, and the once-impressive life-size bronze statue of an Indian Brave astride a rearing mustang—the centerpiece of the lobby—was discolored from dust and cigarette smoke. He looked inside the casino and was amazed at how few people there were. During the casino's halcyon days, most slot machines and table games were occupied by mid-morning and hotel guests stood in line three and four deep to check in for the night. Not today. Only two people were checking in—a woman dressed in a lime-green polyester pants suit and her husband, who was wearing white sneakers, a flowered shirt, and a floppy hat.

Clay turned when he heard the chime of the executive elevator arrive at ground level. Simon's narrow-eyed spinster secretary, Anne Garrison, signaled with a bend of her forefinger for Clay to enter the elevator.

"Hello, Anne."

"It's Ms. Garrison to you."

Clay was surprised at Anne's attitude. She had always been pleasant to him when he visited John Grainger in the past. He tried again, "How long has it been? More than a year, I guess. How are you?"

She looked straight ahead at the mirrored elevator door and did not answer. Clay noted the sour expression on her deeply wrinkled face. "Are you mad at me, *Ms. Garrison*?"

She turned her eyes toward him and spoke in a strident tone of voice, "Detective Bryce, yes, I am angry at you. *Many* of us are angry at you. Thanks to you, the Bend's present financial condition is tenuous. We're lucky we're still in business."

Clay was surprised at her accusation. "And why, exactly, am I to blame?"

Anne spoke as if she were a mother scolding her child. "You were totally unfair to Mr. Grainger. You caused havoc here. People have lost their jobs. Those of us who remain are concerned the Bend won't survive—all because of the negative publicity you caused. You single-handedly changed the tenor of the Bend. It was once a wonderful, vibrant company, and now the atmosphere is gloomy and depressing. So, yes, I am angry at you." Before Clay could respond, she added, "And that doesn't begin to speak to what happened to Mr. Grainger."

"I'm sorry you feel that way," Clay said. "But I have no intention of apologizing for doing my job."

"I only hope you can solve Mr. Grainger's murder faster than it took you to solve the murders at the Bend."

They exited the elevator at the third-floor executive level and walked in silence the rest of the way to Simon Learner's office, the same office John Grainger had once occupied. Anne rapped on Simon's door and waited for him to respond.

"Come."

She opened the door and announced, "Detective Bryce is here to see you. As you know, sir, he is not on your appointment list."

"Yes, Anne. It's okay."

She glared daggers at Clay as she closed the door behind her. Simon got up from the oversized leather office chair behind an equally oversized mahogany desk and greeted Clay with a weak handshake. He was a thin man of medium height with delicate features. His jet-black hair showed more gray than Clay remembered from a year earlier. He was impeccably dressed in a custom-made dark blue pinstripe suit, reminiscent of how Grainger had always dressed.

"Hello, Simon."

"Detective Bryce."

"Your secretary is not happy to see me. Stupid me. I thought she missed me and would shower me with kisses."

Simon smiled and shook his head. "Anne? Hardly. She's hard as nails. The only person she misses is John Grainger. What did she say?"

"She's still mad I filed charges against him."

"Anne's very loyal and efficient and, yes, she did not take John's firing well. No doubt she came across a bit irascible. I apologize if she offended you."

"No problem. I have thick skin."

With a cheerless, almost grim expression, Simon said, "Have a seat, Detective. What can I do for you?" He nodded to Clay to sit in one of the two armchairs opposite his desk.

"How have you been, Simon?"

"Okay. Things could be better here, but I can only do what I can do."

Clay remembered that Simon had a peculiar trait of rarely looking directly at a person with whom he was talking. His eyes focused, instead, on the space above the person's shoulder.

"I'm here to talk to Hayden Arrington, but I understand he's in a director's meeting. I'll wait till the meeting adjourns and talk with him then. In the meantime, it gives me the chance to ask you a few things."

"The board should be breaking by noon, so it won't be long. I gather you want to ask me about John."

"That's correct."

"Ask away. But, we've got to make it quick." Simon examined his watch. "I don't have much time."

"I'll do my best to get out of your hair quickly."

"What can I do for you?"

"Are you aware of the details surrounding John Grainger's death?"

"Yes. I first read about John committing suicide in Wednesday's paper. I was sad to think how low his life had gotten." Simon shook his head. "What a horrible way to kill yourself—not that killing yourself is good under any circumstances. Then yesterday I read the update in the Police Blotter that he had not committed suicide after all, but had been murdered."

Clay responded, "It's true. The killer tried to make his death look like a suicide, but we learned, in fact, that it was murder."

"That's awful. Do you have any suspects?"

"Not yet. What about you? Do you have any thoughts on who might have had it out for your former boss?"

Simon answered without hesitation, "You know as well as I what he was like with women. He couldn't help himself. Maybe he was killed by one of the husbands of the wives he slept with over the years."

Clay leaned forward. "Can you think of anyone in particular?"

"I wouldn't have any idea."

"Well, give that some thought. Let me know if any names come to mind."

"Detective, you should know that John Grainger and I had been estranged."

Clay was aware, based on conversation with Grainger, that the relationship between the two casino hot shots had soured, but he let Simon continue. "Why was that?"

"He thought I should have turned this job down when it was first offered to me a year ago, said I threw him under the bus."

"Did you?"

"No. I did what any other person in my shoes would have done. He was fired. I was here and the job was offered to me, so I accepted. What was I supposed to do, turn it down? It wasn't going to change the fact that he had been fired."

"I understand."

"Actually, the timing of John's death is ironic."

"Why do you say that?"

"I shouldn't be telling you this but, what the heck, it doesn't make any difference now. Mr. Arrington had put me on a three-month warning. He told me if the Bend's bottom line did not improve significantly by the end of the three months, he was going to relieve me of my position. Confidentially, you should know that today is my last day here."

Clay did not let on that Grainger had told him about Simon's firing. "What are you saying?"

"He fired me. He planned to replace me by rehiring John. That's what's so ironic, now that John's dead."

Clay feigned surprise. "Why did he fire you?"

"The casino fell on hard times because of all the negative publicity from last year and Mr. Arrington feels I should have been able to reverse the trend by now. He and the board hired me as John's replacement. They gave me the directive to stem the tide of the significant drop in gaming revenue. I, personally, think we've turned the corner, but Mr. Arrington doesn't agree. His plan was to fire me and rehire John. As far as I know, he never shared that plan with the directors. The only people who knew about it were John and me.

"What is Mr. Arrington going to do now that Grainger is dead?"

"We met this morning before his board meeting. He told me he reversed his decision to fire me and wanted me to stay on."

"He did?"

"Well, it was more like *ordered* me to stay on. He said that, under the circumstances, he had no choice but to retain me."

"I'm a little confused. You said today was your last day because you were fired. Are you telling me now that Arrington's changed his mind?"

"Today *would* have been my last day. And, yes, Mr. Arrington changed his mind."

Clay wondered if Simon, too, had motive to murder Grainger. With Grainger out of the picture, Simon might have been able to retain his job. "You've got to be happy about the turn of events."

"No. I'm really not. He didn't exactly give me a ringing endorsement. I said to myself, screw him, he can go suck an egg. I flat out turned him down."

"You did?" As quickly as Clay thought Simon had motive to kill Grainger, he dismissed him as a suspect.

"Yes." Simon showed a smug grin. "So, you see, Detective, I may be in the driver's seat, but not in the way you suppose."

"Do you know what Arrington's going to do? Who's going to run the Bend?"

"I have no clue. It's a tough job. Not too many people can handle it."

"How did he react to you turning him down?"

"Not well. He called me an ingrate and berated me for the longest time. I mean, he *raged* at me. I just sat there and took it. But, you know what? That's exactly the reason I turned him down. I don't want to put up with his violent temper and embarrassing public derisions of my abilities. He's gone so far as to demean me in front of my wife at social events. But to quiet him this morning when he was screaming at me, I told him I would think about it over the weekend, talk to my wife, and give him my decision on Monday. Between you and me—" Simon did not finish. He shook his head and grinned to show his satisfaction at taking on his powerful boss.

Clay asked, "What will you do now?"

"I don't know yet. My focus at present is to clean things up so I can leave with a clear conscience. Frankly, I don't get why John wanted to come back and work for such a man. John and I spoke a few days ago. Today was supposed to be our transition day."

Clay was sympathetic. "Rejecting Arrington's offer to stay on had to be a tough decision."

"Not really." Simon swiveled his chair. He looked out the picture window at the desert landscape and Sangre de Cristo Mountains. "At the sake of waxing poetic, I will miss the job and this gorgeous view that comes along with it. I'll do what I have to. It's not the end of the world." Simon turned back to face Clay. "Believe it or not, I'm okay the way circumstances are playing out."

"You sound as though you're relieved to have been fired. Are you?"

"The truth is, yes. I've been under a lot of stress and I now feel a huge weight has been lifted. I'm pleased Mr. Arrington offered me a second chance. And I really am sorry that John died—was murdered or, whatever—but the stress I've been living under has not been fair to my wife or our little girl. You might remember Liza. You met her when you were dining with Hope Archer and I was with Liza at the same restaurant. Well, she's my wife now, and we have a baby girl."

"I do remember her. Congratulations."

"Thank you."

"You've got a lot of guts, Simon, going toe-to-toe with Hayden Arrington. Aren't you concerned he'll blackball you from any future opportunity, like working at one of his many other companies?"

"No. Me working at another of Hayden's companies is not going to happen. He once referred to me as a virus. I remember him saying during a group meeting with some of my employees, 'Failure is a virus. It's virulent. If we don't correct the problem at the Bend, it can spread to my other companies. Either correct what's wrong with the Bend, or I will know you are my virus and you will never set foot in any of my companies or any other company in all of New Mexico.'"

"Heavy threat he threw at you, and in front of other employees too. Nice guy, huh?"

"What's he going to do that he hasn't already done to my psyche? In my opinion, this is all a blessing in disguise. As stressful as it's been, I've enjoyed the challenge of running the Bend. This was my dream job. That's why I didn't mind working for John as long as I did. Oh, sure, there are a lot more prestigious places to work, but I got my feet wet here and was able to use my MBA right out of school. I've enjoyed the experience and made a lot of money. Who knows? I may come back some day and buy this place from Mr. Arrington." Simon snickered.

"Good for you. Don't let this knock you down."

"Trust me, I won't. But, speaking of knocking you down, I read that someone tried to kill you a few weeks ago."

"Yeah, in a hit-and-run."

"How bad were you hurt?"

"A few bumps and bruises, but nothing life-threatening."

"You were lucky, weren't you?"

"I guess I was. Let me ask you a question. Can you think of anyone at the Bend who might hold a grudge against me—a grudge so strong they'd want to kill me?"

"No, I've never heard anything like that from anyone here."

"When I rode up in the elevator with Anne, she said she was angry with me because of the way I supposedly mistreated John. I'd like to ask her who else here feels the same way she does. We think his murder might be tied to the attempt on my life."

"Really? How so?"

"Sorry, I can't go into details. However, I'm hoping Anne might be able to shed some light on both cases. I'd like to speak with her before I speak with Mr. Arrington. I know you're busy, but I want you to sit in while I talk with her."

"It's quarter to twelve. Mr. Arrington wants to meet with me when the board adjourns for lunch. I'm not sure I'll have time."

"It won't take long."

Simon said, "Fine. I'll bring her in."

CHAPTER 35

Simon buzzed his secretary and asked her to come into his office. "Have a seat, Anne. Detective Bryce wants to talk to us about Mr. Grainger's murder."

Anne gave a quick and unpleasant look at Clay then returned her gaze to Simon.

Clay explained, "Ms. Garrison, there was an attempt on my life three weeks ago. I was intentionally struck by a vehicle early morning when I was jogging near my home. In addition to that assault, a threat was made against Hank Kincaid. He was the Assistant District Attorney who prosecuted your former boss. I don't need to explain the circumstances of the assaults other than to say I've concluded that the culprit is someone associated with the Bend. More importantly, we believe there's a relationship between the assaults and Mr. Grainger's murder."

Anne was ruffled at Clay's conclusion. "What does that have to do with me?"

"Nothing directly—except, when we were in the elevator, you said you were angry at me."

Anne responded, "I said that because you're the one who's made Mr. Learner's job so difficult. The ignominy of the Bend's sinking fortunes is entirely on your shoulders." She scowled at Clay, then looked at Simon to seek reassurance that she was not talking out of line.

Simon said, "Go ahead, continue. Tell the detective what you think."

Anne continued. "The negative publicity created by your police investigation of the serial murders virtually guaranteed the Bend was going to suffer attendance issues. People were not going to come here to gamble if they feared for their lives. And you exacerbated the situation by your accusations against poor Mr. Grainger." She made the sign of the cross and intoned, "God rest his soul."

Clay saw her eyes moisten. He was stunned at the extent of her anger toward him, but addressed her in a calm manner. "I'm sorry about Mr. Grainger's death and I'm sorry you feel such anger toward me. But, no, Ms. Garrison, I did not cause his death. In fact, I'm looking for insights into what happened to him. I was hoping you could shed some light on his murder."

Anne glared at Clay and said, "I can't."

Simon interjected, "Anne, in Detective Bryce's defense, I know firsthand that he worked diligently to solve the serial murders. Let's consider the here and now. Please. All he wants to know is if you're aware of any employees who've ranted against him or indicated they wanted to harm him or Mr. Grainger."

She thought for a second and shook her head. "No, I can't think of anyone who has manifested that kind of hatred toward either one. Many are unhappy, especially with the detective, but none has threatened to harm them, that I'm aware of."

Clay said, "Okay, Ms. Garrison, that's all. If you would, please let me know if you hear of anyone making threatening remarks."

She asked Simon, "May I leave now, sir?"

"Yes, thank you."

Anne gave Clay another sour look as she left the office.

Clay said, "You know, Simon, besides jealous husbands who might have a reason to kill John, a list of suspects should probably be expanded to include women. John could just as likely have been killed by a vindictive and spiteful woman he discarded in favor of someone else."

Simon nodded in agreement. "That's true."

"Do you know any of the married women John Grainger slept with?"

"No. As much as I recognized his sexually addictive personality, I didn't know who his women-friends were. He kept that to himself. There may have been dozens, but not anyone I know."

"What about Mr. Arrington's wife?"

Simon was uncomfortable by the question. He shuffled in his chair. "Oh, no, I can't imagine he would have attempted an affair with Mrs. Arrington."

"Why not?"

Simon shrugged. "No reason. I guess anything was possible with him, but I wouldn't know one way or the other. I'm just stunned you asked." He checked his watch. "Mr. Arrington should be winding up his morning session in a few minutes. As I mentioned, I'm extremely busy here trying to get everything done. You're welcome to wait for Mr. Arrington in the sitting area."

Clay sensed Simon's discomfort at the question about Arianna and wondered about Simon's own wife. He asked point blank, "Simon, did John Grainger ever hit on your wife?"

Simon inhaled deeply before giving what Clay considered a vague response. "Not that I know of. At least she never told me he did."

CHAPTER 36

Clay left Simon's office and sat in the executive waiting area for only a short while before the five directors filed out for lunch. Their grim looks told of a testy three-hour meeting. Clay recognized Hayden Arrington as the last to exit. He stood to intercept him. "Excuse me, Mr. Arrington?"

Hayden looked quizzically at Clay. "Yes?"

"I'm Detective Clay Bryce from the Santa Fe Police Department." Clay handed him his card.

Arrington glanced at it then thrust the card in his pocket. "What do you want?"

"I need a minute of your time."

"About what?"

Clay said, "I'd rather we speak in private, if you don't mind, sir."

"I'm busy. Call my secretary for an appointment."

Clay did not back down. "It's your call, Mr. Arrington. What I want to talk to you about is private. If you don't mind others hearing what I have to ask you, I'll be happy to interview you here. If you'd rather meet with me downtown, I'm okay with that too."

Arrington operated under strict compliance to schedules and did not tolerate interruptions by anyone. Seated at her desk in front of Simon's office, Anne Garrison observed the exchange and braced for the Bend owner's angry response—typical of any challenge to his schedule or authority. She heaved a sigh of relief when she heard him acquiesce.

"I can give you two minutes. Follow me." Hayden made a sharp about-face and headed back into the conference room. He slammed the door behind Clay. The two stood facing each other. "Okay, Detective Rice, what do you want to talk to me about? Make it brief."

"It's Bryce."

"What?"

"My name is Bryce, not Rice."

"Yeah, fine. Go ahead. I've got people waiting for me."

"What do you know about John Grainger's death?"

"I know he died. That's it."

"I'm aware the Bend is not doing well. I'm also aware you planned to rehire Grainger to try to turn things around."

Arrington glared at Clay and asked, "Who the hell told you that?"

Clay was not intimidated by the mogul's short temper. His response was matter of fact. "Grainger himself. It's true, is it not?"

"It figures he'd say something about it. I expressly told him not to divulge his rehiring to anyone until I was able to relay my plans to my directors. You want to know what I know about his death." Without any show of compassion about Grainger's death, he said, "Nothing. All I know is that, initially, he was supposed to have committed suicide but now you've determined he was murdered."

"That's correct. He was murdered and his death was staged to appear as a suicide."

"Frankly, it would not have surprised me to know he had committed suicide. He was an emotionally weak man—weaker than I thought. Who killed him?"

"We don't know yet. We were hoping you might be able to help us figure that out."

"How in hell can I help you? I hardly knew the man."

"Can you think of anyone who might have had reason to kill him?"

Without hesitation, Arrington responded, "No." He then tilted his head and squinted his eyes as a thought came to him. "Tell me, Detective, why were you talking with him anyway?"

"I was questioning him about a hit-and-run. Circumstantial evidence pointed to him as a suspect. We believed he held a grudge against the victim and that revenge was his motive."

"You're kidding. You mean that milquetoast of a man tried to kill someone?"

"Allegedly, yes."

"Who?"

Clay pointed a finger to his own chest. "Me."

Arrington showed neither shock nor surprise by Clay's comment, nor did he inquire into the circumstances. "Was he guilty?"

"Probably not."

"What did he tell you about returning to the Bend?"

"That you had rehired him to replace Simon Learner."

"That's a fact. When Grainger was fired last year, we hired Learner to replace him. But he hasn't worked out. It now appears we may retain him until we can come up with someone else. He and I will be discussing his position as soon as you are through interrogating me."

"I'm certain you're aware of Grainger's reputation regarding women—oftentimes going to bed with married women."

"I am."

"Do you think his murder had anything to do with his affairs with any of those women?"

"How am I supposed to know that?"

"Frankly, knowing Grainger's issues with women at the Bend, I'm surprised you wanted to hire him back."

Arrington's breathing got deeper. "Why, you impudent fool. Being a cop, you obviously don't know much about running a business." He was agitated and advanced toward Clay until they stood less than two feet apart. The tycoon's acid breath drove Clay to tilt his head back.

Arrington overwhelmed most others with his insults and aggressiveness, but Clay was unimpressed. "You're right. My expertise is not in the realm of business. It's in solving crimes—like murder. So, let's get back to my question. Why did you want to rehire the man whose sexual predilections had caused the Bend so much negative publicity?"

Arrington did not answer. His intimidating glare never wavered.

Clay would not be bullied. "I'll wait for you to think it through. I'm not in any hurry."

Arrington exhaled hard. "I'll explain it to you in the simplest way possible so even *you* can understand."

"Go right ahead."

"If I could control John's addictive sexual behavior and have him concentrate on the business at hand, he easily was the best choice to lead the Bend. He was a brilliant marketer who led us to our earlier success. Simply stated, I believe he was the most qualified person to turn things around."

Clay said, "Now that wasn't hard, was it, Mr. Arrington."

"Don't patronize me. Are we through?"

"Almost. A few more questions, then I'll let you go. John Grainger died Tuesday afternoon. Where were you on Tuesday?"

215

Arrington's anger was immediate. His voice rose sharply and spittle flew from his mouth, landing on the lapel of Clay's jacket. "I'm not going to answer that. What the hell kind of sense does that make? You're implying I had motive to murder the man I had just rehired to run my casino."

"I'm not implying anything. I asked you a simple question. Where were you?"

Arrington exhaled sharply and said, "I was over the Atlantic on my way to Frankfurt, Germany."

"You can verify that, right?" Hayden did not acknowledge Clay's question. "Yes? No?" Arrington continued to glare at Clay. "You know what, sir? I'm still uncertain why you rehired John."

"I know the man had addictive problems and was unable to pass up any woman who shook her ass at him. That was his reputation. You want to know who the murderer could be? Look for the husband of one of the women Grainger bedded. That was his reputation." Hayden looked away from Clay when he made his next statement. "Apparently, the man had no compunction against defiling another man's wife."

Defile another man's wife. Yes, John Grainger was good at that. Do you know that your own wife was defiled? "Defile," Clay said. "That's a good, strong word." He continued to push the envelope to see how the mogul would react. "Mr. Arrington, weren't you concerned that he might have attempted—to use your word—to *defile* your own wife?"

Arrington's chest rose and fell rapidly and his face turned nearly crimson. "You piss-head! How dare you ask me such an offensive question! My wife would never be swayed by a common whoremonger like Grainger. I *will* be filing a complaint with your chief of police about your impertinent and stupid line of questioning."

Clay stood his ground. "No offense intended. My question still stands. Has your wife ever indicated that John Grainger made advances toward her?"

Arrington refused to answer. "That's it, Detective Rice. We're through. I've got business to attend to."

Clay corrected him once more. "My name is *Bryce*— Detective Clay *B–R–Y–C–E*. And, of course I understand how busy you must be. I really appreciate that you've explained to this dumb cop the ways of business and all. So let me get to the point. You thought you could control Grainger's behavior. That's what you said, right?" Arrington did not react. Clay continued, "You know, I understand all that and I understand what you're saying about his reputation with women, mostly married women, right. That's the reason for my question regarding Mrs. Arrington. Could she—?"

"Detective *Bryce*, I will not answer any more questions about me or my wife. You're trying to intimidate the wrong man." Hayden opened the conference room door. "Now, leave before I have you cited for trespassing. I will not answer any more of your questions without my lawyer present. I have my rights."

He's overreacting to my question about Arianna. I think he knows about her affair with Grainger. "Ah, yes. Your rights. And I, too, have rights. For example, I could announce right here and now that you're a person of interest in the murder of John Grainger, then cuff you and drag you downtown till you answer all my questions. But, nice guy that I am, I won't do that. However, I expect to see you at police headquarters—with or without your lawyer—on Monday morning. Eleven o'clock.

That should give you plenty of time to rearrange your business schedule."

"You will pay for this," Arrington stammered.

"Show or don't show. It's your choice. But, remember, if you fail to be there, I will have a warrant issued for your arrest. Your choice, *sir.*"

Clay exited the conference room. He heard Arrington shout to Simon's secretary, "Garrison, tell Learner I want to see him—now! And get my lawyer on the phone." He slammed the door shut behind Clay.

CHAPTER 37

The unknowns surrounding the John Grainger impersonator who visited Hope at the psychiatric hospital gnawed at Clay. Someone had masqueraded as Grainger, but who, and why? The man who appeared on the security video footage remained unidentified. Clay was convinced Hope knew who it was. He decided to visit her again to find out what she knew.

* * * * *

Hope was seated in the meet room with her back to the door, clutching her teddy bear tight to her chest. The same burly nurse as before assumed her position in the corner to stand watch.

Clay entered the room and immediately recognized that, although Hope's hair was still ragged and her clothing loose on her lithe body, she was not as sedated as she had been on his first visit. "Hi, Hope. I'm happy to see you again. How is Teddy today?"

Hope put the bear's mouth to her ear. She smiled. "He says he's well, thank you." Each word was uttered in a staccato monotone.

"Are you well too?"

"Yes. I'm ready to go home now. Are you going to take me home?"

"Not today, but hopefully soon."

"John promised he was going to take me home, but he hasn't."

"You mean John Grainger? He was here to see you recently, wasn't he? What did he tell you?"

"He said he was going to take me home."

Clay looked at the nurse. "Can I have two minutes alone with her?"

The nurse nodded. "I'll be right outside."

He waited for the nurse to exit the room before continuing. "Hope, I'm here to talk to you about John." Hope tilted her head to listen. "He won't be coming back."

Hope scrunched her brow.

"Something's happened to him. There was a terrible fire at his house and he died."

She thrust out her jaw and raised her voice. "No! He did not die."

"I'm sorry to tell you, but he did die. I thought you should know."

"I said no!" Hope's voice got even louder as tears rolled down her cheeks. Clay let her vent. "He was not supposed to die," she sobbed. "He promised to take me home He said he was going to take me home. He lied to me. I'm glad he died. I'm glad."

"Hope—"

"I knew he was going to die, I knew it. Didn't I tell you, Teddy? *Every*one always dies and leaves me. Everyone! Except for you, Teddy. Don't ever leave me." She kissed Teddy's cheek. "John promised to come back and take me home. He wasn't supposed to die."

The nurse heard Hope's raised voice and opened the door to check on her and Clay. "Everything okay in here?

Clay waved the nurse off. "Yeah, we're good." He turned back to Hope after she calmed a bit. "John promised to come back for you? When was he going to do that?"

"He said he couldn't get into our house, but as soon as he was able to, he was going to come get me."

"What did he mean by that? Why couldn't John get into the house?"

"He didn't remember where the key was."

"The key? What key?"

"I told you—the key to our house. He needed the key to get into our house."

"Did you tell him where it was?"

"Yes."

"Where was it?"

"Underneath the backyard sidewalk where we always keep it."

"I bet he forgot the security code too, didn't he?"

Hope tilted her head and looked at Clay. "Yes, he did."

"You used to live with John, didn't you?"

She used the bear's paw to wipe the tears from her eyes. "Yes."

"He changed a lot since you lived with him, didn't he? He grew a beard. Did you recognize him?"

"No, I didn't."

"What did you say to him?"

"I said, 'You are not John,' and he said he was. He said he grew a beard to see if I liked it."

"And did you like it?"

"No. I could not tell he was John."

CHAPTER 38

Clay returned to headquarters as Captain Ellsworth was preparing to leave for the weekend. "Captain, I need to talk to you."

"I'm heading out. Walk with me to my car."

The two men exited the building to the parking lot. Clay briefed his boss on his latest visit to the hospital to see Hope Archer. He also described his interview with Arianna Arrington. "Arianna seemed genuinely surprised—and upset—when I told her John Grainger had been murdered. Either she's one hell of an actress or she shed real tears."

Ellsworth set his briefcase in the back seat of his car. "Clay, I wouldn't trust her more than I could throw her. She's probably an expert at shedding tears to get her way."

"Have you ever met her?"

"Yes. Once. At a benefit," he responded, and added, "She's a knockout, isn't she?"

"Yes, sir, she is. I think she may have had motive to silence Grainger. With him out of the picture, the odds of Hayden Arrington finding out about her affair drops significantly. If she couldn't trust Grainger to keep quiet, why not kill him to silence him?"

"Certainly possible, although I still find it hard to believe she was willing to risk losing everything by having an affair with Grainger in the first place."

"It doesn't make sense to me either."

"What about Arrington? Have you talked to him?"

"Yes, and it didn't go well. I questioned him about Grainger. I asked him why he wanted to rehire him after all the negative publicity he had caused the Bend. Arrington said because he was the only one who could turn the business around. I walked away believing he knows about his wife's affair. I can't nail down why, but I think he does."

Ellsworth asked, "In Arrington's defense, why would he rehire Grainger if he knew he was sleeping with his wife, then turn around and kill him? Why go through that charade?"

"To develop an alibi. And then punctuate that alibi by hopping on a plane out of the country. He's no dummy. I'm betting he knows about them."

"How did you leave it?"

"I asked him if Grainger had ever hit on Arianna."

"What did he say?"

"He flipped out on me. Overreacted. He could have simply said no, but instead, he cursed me out. Mind you, Captain, I didn't say I knew Arianna was having an affair. It was a simple question in the context of Grainger's reputation with women. He went crazy and wouldn't answer any more questions after that. He said he was going to file a complaint against me with the chief because of my *impertinence,* as he called it. And then he booted me out of his office."

"He called you impertinent? You?" Ellsworth laughed.

"Yeah, hard to believe, isn't it?" Clay chuckled. "I told him since he wouldn't answer any more questions I wanted him here Monday morning at eleven, with or without his lawyer, and if he didn't show up I'd issue an arrest warrant."

Ellsworth rolled his eyes. "You didn't really threaten him, did you?"

"I did."

"Oh, brother. He's a friend of the chief's. He'll unleash a firestorm."

"Maybe so, but the way I look at it, I'll place him under oath to find out what he knows about his wife and Grainger."

"But he has an alibi for the time Grainger was killed."

"He does. But I think it's got a hole in it."

"Where's the hole?"

Clay explained, "The candle that ignited the fire that killed Grainger was slow to burn. The killer had plenty of time to light the candle, then get away to develop an alibi. Hayden could have set the fire that killed Grainger and still had time to get to his plane and be long gone off to Germany."

Ellsworth nodded slowly and took in Clay's theory. "I guess we'll know Monday what he's going to do. If he files a complaint against you, word will get to me lightning fast. I'll have to calm everyone down. I hope he'll just show up with his lawyer to answer a few more questions and be on his way. At any rate, there's nothing we can do about it now. Let's go home. See you Monday."

CHAPTER 39

Allie was pleased Clay had agreed to go with her to the Art and Wine Festival at the Plaza, and looked forward to spending the afternoon with him. She primped far longer than she normally would and, after a half-dozen wardrobe changes, settled on a white skirt and sleeveless blue blouse tied high on her slender waist. Her outfit exposed her athletically toned midriff. Deep red lipstick added to her sensual look.

As naturally pretty and intelligent as Allie was, she lacked confidence and self-esteem. Her failed marriage weighed heavily on her psyche. She had not been able to develop a warm and caring relationship with any man since her divorce.

Until Clay.

She had developed strong feelings for him, and thought the big, tough, yet gentle, man might be the one she could settle down with. Then again, maybe not. She was uncertain. Time would tell. Yes, she was attracted to him, but unsure what he wanted from her. Was it sex or a serious relationship? He did not push her to go to bed with him, but that's clearly what he wanted. And while she had not let her guard down, something about Clay was different. He made her want to reveal more of herself than she had with any of the handful of other men she had dated.

Clay rang the doorbell to Allie's condo at noon exactly. When Allie opened the door, Clay's jaw dropped. He stood and gawked at the sexy woman who greeted him.

"Well? Do you want to come in or are you just going to stand there?" She knew she looked good and was happy to see Clay react the way he did.

"I do want to come in," he stammered. "Damn, you look hot."

"Thanks. I wanted you to know that that woman who threw herself at you doesn't have a monopoly on sexy."

"You win hands down." Clay stepped into the condo and enveloped Allie in his arms. "It is so good to see you again."

Allie looked up into his eyes. "I've missed you too."

They kissed.

Clay slid his hands down low on her back tantalizingly close to her butt. He wanted to carry her into the bedroom and make love to her. Right there, right then. Allie still was not ready. She pushed away from him and shook her head. "Oh, my God, you're doing it to me again. I can hardly breathe. We'd better get going."

Clay let out a long but silent exhale.

Allie bit her lip softly. "You're mad at me, aren't you?"

"No, I'm not mad. Really, I'm not. You're right. We have to leave, or else—"

"Or else what?" She knew what he meant.

"Or else, nothing," he insisted.

"Maybe later, okay?"

Clay was unsure what *maybe later* meant, but he was optimistic.

She giggled, "Look what I've done to you. You look silly. You've got lipstick all over your face." She pulled a tissue from a box of Kleenex on the counter and gently wiped off the lipstick.

"How about I keep it on all afternoon to show everyone that the prettiest girl in Santa Fe gave me a lipstick tattoo?"

* * * * *

Allie had made reservations for lunch at The Compound Restaurant on Canyon Road, away from the bustling art show in the Plaza.

During lunch, Clay sensed something was bothering her. Their conversation was hollow and stiff. "Are you still mad at me?"

"No."

"Are you sure?"

Allie answered, "It's not you. It's… it's the woman who was at your house. I don't want to have doubts about our relationship, but, who is she anyway? She looked familiar. Are you telling me the truth?"

"The absolute truth."

"That's what I don't understand. Why did she do what she did? What was she trying to prove?"

"All I can tell you, and I probably shouldn't, but—"

"But what?"

"Remember I told you she was an alibi for a suspect in my hit-and-run investigation?"

"Yes."

He lowered his voice. "John Grainger was that suspect."

"The man who died in the fire on Tuesday?"

"That's correct."

"Did she have anything to do with his murder?"

"I really can't go into any more details."

Allie leaned closer to Clay. "Wait a second. It just hit me where I've seen her before."

"Where?"

"In the society pages of the Times Journal. She and her husband are always in the papers for some charity or another. She's Hayden Arrington's wife. Am I right?"

Clay looked around to see if any nearby diners had heard Allie. "Shh. Please keep your voice down. Let's not talk about her anymore."

Allie was more certain than ever. She lowered her voice. "I'm right, aren't I?"

"Yes, but please forget about her," Clay said. "All I can tell you is this. If I had a choice between spending this day with you or with her, I'd pick you eleven times out of ten."

She smiled and reached for his hand. "Thank you. You just got a huge gold star for that."

"Does this mean we're officially made up?"

"Almost."

"Almost?" Clay frowned. "What more do I have to do to be totally forgiven?"

"You'll see."

Clay and Allie left the restaurant and walked hand in hand down Canyon Road to the Plaza. There was a huge selection of Native American-made jewelry displayed on colorful blankets on the sidewalk outside the historic adobe structured Palace of the Governors. Visitors browsed through tented kiosks that displayed crafts and paintings by local artists, beer from southwest microbreweries, and wines from west coast wineries. Allie and Clay strolled through a number of kiosks and sampled wines and ales. Afterward, they sat and listened to country music artists perform in the gazebo at the center of the plaza.

After a half hour, Allie looked at Clay and asked, "You're ready to leave, aren't you?"

"Whenever you are."

"You've been a very good boy." She suggested, "Let's go back to my house. I have steaks in the fridge that we can throw on the grill."

"Sounds great, but I have one more thing to do before we go."

"What's that?"

Clay led her into a Washington State wine kiosk and bought a bottle of cabernet. "This will make up for that bottle we never had with our Chinese dinner all those weeks ago."

Allie nodded. "It seems more like *months* ago."

"I've been hoping to make it up to you." From the moment he first set eyes on her, through the ensuing weeks of police investigation and her unbearable anger toward him, Clay never wavered in his feelings toward Allie. He had fallen hard. He lifted her hand to his lips and kissed it sweetly.

Allie was smitten by the gesture.

On the ride back, each wondered what the other was thinking. Moments away from her condo, Allie reached for Clay's hand and rested their interlocked fingers on his thigh. Their eyes met momentarily.

Allie looked out the side window and smiled.

Inside the condo, Clay set the wine on the kitchen table and turned to face Allie. They stood looking at each other and said nothing until he reached to embrace her. "I really had a nice time."

"Me too."

Clay held Allie close, her body folded against his until she pulled away. She whispered, "We'd better eat."

"Do we have to?"

"Yes, silly boy."

Clay uncorked the wine he had bought and poured two glasses.

"Nice," she said after a sip. "Good choice." Clay stepped out to the patio to light the grill while Allie set the table. She had flowers as the centerpiece and lit candles for an added romantic atmosphere.

Allie said to Clay through the patio screen door, "Sampling all that wine today at the fair has gotten to me."

"Good," Clay laughed. "Does that mean I can take advantage of you?" He stepped inside and once again took Allie in his arms.

She felt his arousal. He decided now was the time and slowly reached behind her to unhook her bra. She reached for his hands and pulled them away. "I can't, Clay. I can't. I'm sorry. Not now."

Clay did not understand her reluctance.

"We will—sometime. I promise. Please don't be mad."

"What's wrong, Maryland?"

She shook her head. Her eyes brimmed with tears. "It's just that... it's been so long, and..." She was unable to finish.

"What, Allie? Talk to me."

"Oh, Clay, I told you I was immature and stupid to have gotten married so young. Jordan really swept me off my feet. He was good looking and popular, the big man on campus. All the girls wanted to be with him. Unfortunately, I ended up with him. I really had no idea who he was or what he was like."

"What *was* he like?"

"I found out quickly he was cruel and hurtful, and..."

Clay waited for Allie to continue. He gave her time to compose herself. "He hurt you, didn't he?"

"Yes." Allie started to weep. "He enjoyed hurting me."

"How do you mean? Physically?"

"Yes—physically, verbally, emotionally, and every way! Oh, what a mistake I made. Sex was torture. I mean *torture*. He wanted to do all kinds of S and M stuff, and I didn't. When I refused, he punched my arms, slapped me in the face, and knocked me around. I mean, he *hurt* me. I was terrified to be alone with him. Finally, I just left him one night and took a bus back home. My parents were wonderful. They helped me get an annulment and supported me every step of the way."

"Allie, I'm so sorry. I would never treat you like that."

"I thought I was so much in love. I wasn't. I was only in love with the idea of being in love. Does that make sense? I wish I could let myself go with you, but I can't—not right now. I really like you. I mean, really, Clay. Please understand." She looked into Clay's eyes and said, "I will in time. I promise. I don't want to lose you." She cried harder.

"It's okay. Don't cry. It's okay. I'm sorry for what you went through. We'll just take our time." Clay kissed a tear from Allie's cheek and said, "When the time is right, we'll both know. We won't have any regrets. I promise."

CHAPTER 40

To avoid the attention of reporters who often hung around police headquarters looking to get the next day's headline, Hayden Arrington, accompanied by his long-time lawyer and friend, Wallace Sanderson, entered through the back entrance of the police headquarters building.

They were led to one of three interview rooms and sat facing the one-way mirror without speaking. Hayden was dressed as always in a tailored suit, a starched white shirt with monogrammed cufflinks, and a purple tie. He sat with his hands clenched on the table, staring at the mirror—his eyes frozen in a defiant look at whomever he thought might be viewing the interview from the observation room.

Hayden's anger was palpable. He could barely contain his rage. Sanderson heard Hayden's breathing become more rapid as the moments ticked away. "He's treating me like a common criminal," Hayden howled to his lawyer.

Sanderson leaned toward his client and cautioned him. "Hayden, you flying off the handle will not help the situation. Let me manage this."

Hayden glared at Sanderson but nodded that he would comply. Sanderson was the only person Hayden allowed to talk to him in a scolding manner.

Because of Hayden's stature in Santa Fe, Clay and Captain Ellsworth thought it wise to have Hank Kincaid witness the interview from the observation room. They briefed the ADA on the status of the investigation into Grainger's murder.

Ellsworth said, "We consider Arrington a suspect. If he knew Grainger was having an affair with Arianna, we believe he had motive to murder him."

Clay gave Ellsworth and Kincaid the thumbs up sign before he entered the interview room. He nodded to Sanderson, who nodded in return. Hayden looked at Clay then turned his stare back to the mirror.

"Good morning, gentlemen. Thank you for coming in to talk with me."

Sanderson said, "Make this quick, Detective. My client is a very busy man."

"I'm aware how busy he is. In fact, on Friday, he gave me a tutorial on how the world of business conducts its work. I was very appreciative." Clay's sarcasm was not lost on either Sanderson or Arrington. "Before we start, I'm going to read Mr. Arrington his Miranda rights, and I'm informing you and your client that this interview is being video recorded."

Hayden snapped. "Why the hell do I need to hear the Miranda warning?"

"Sir, we read Miranda when preparing to question anyone about a case. I'm sure Mr. Sanderson understands it's police department protocol."

Sanderson responded, "I fully understand the use of Miranda, however, we also have a right to know why you've asked my client here."

"You know full well, Counselor, that I'm under no legal obligation to inform Mr. Arrington why I asked to interview him. In due time, I'll explain. This shouldn't take long—if he cooperates."

Clay read Hayden his rights, after which he addressed Sanderson. "This past Friday, I talked with Mr. Arrington at the Indian Bend, hoping he could identify someone who would have motive to murder John Grainger. He eventually refused to answer my questions. As you are no doubt aware, Mr. Grainger was a former employee of Mr. Arrington's and had recently been rehired to lift the Bend out of potential bankruptcy."

Sanderson interrupted, "Why were you questioning him without me being present?"

"I questioned Mr. Arrington up to the point he expressed his right to have his attorney present. That's why we're all here now."

Arrington glared at Clay.

Clay said, "Mr. Arrington, jump in anytime if you think I'm misrepresenting our meeting."

Hayden did not respond.

"Do you deem my client a suspect?"

"No. Not at this point. But, back to Friday's conversation, I asked Mr. Arrington why he was going to rehire Mr. Grainger— the man who brought shame to his company, was an inveterate sex addict, and was apt to fall into the same pattern of misbehavior. Mr. Arrington said it was none of my concern who he hired to manage his business. I must say, he spoke eloquently about what's required to run a business. Isn't that so, Mr. Arrington?"

Again, Hayden said nothing.

Clay continued, "Apparently, your client took my line of questioning as an indication that I considered him a suspect. However, I did not, in any way, state or imply that to be the case. Isn't that a fact, Mr. Arrington?"

Sanderson asked, "Are you asking my client a question or are you reciting the conversation you had with him?"

"I'm bringing you up to speed. That's all."

"What do you want from him now?"

"I previously asked him if he had any idea who might have had motive to kill Mr. Grainger, with his womanizing reputation. Mr. Arrington suggested I need go no further than to interview the husbands—and I'll quote him directly—whose wives Grainger had *defiled*. I'm sure that was the word he used. Defiled. He made a very good point. Could John Grainger's murderer be a scorned husband?"

Sanderson said, "If you agree it was a good point, why aren't you out looking for the so-called scorned husband instead of wasting my client's time?"

Clay narrowed his gaze at the attorney. "I can now say to you, as Mr. Arrington said to me, that I don't need your advice on how I should pursue my investigation. The fact is, in spite of Mr. Grainger's reputation, no one I've interviewed can give me the name of a single married woman Grainger had an affair with. I'm at a proverbial dead end."

Sanderson was impatient at the pace of the interview. He held up a hand to Clay and asked, "What do you want to ask of my client?"

"Does he know if John Grainger ever attempted to quote, unquote, defile his own wife, Arianna Arrington?"

Sanderson was not pleased with Clay's line of questioning. "What are you saying?"

"Since *he* used the word *defile* and *he* suggested the murderer might be a scorned husband, logically I asked if John Grainger had ever made advances toward Mrs. Arrington. There is no gentle way to ask the question, but it demands a response. So, did he know if Mr. Grainger was having, or attempted to have, an affair with his wife, as his reputation suggests he had with so many other married women?"

Hayden slapped the table hard. "Why, you..."

Sanderson flinched at the explosion of sound. He reached over and grabbed Hayden's forearm. "Hayden, calm down."

Then, turning to Clay, he voiced his objection. "You are out of line asking such a question, to doubt the integrity and fidelity of a man's wife—"

Clay interrupted. "I may be impertinent in your client's eyes, but you know as well as I that when a crime is committed, you sometimes have to ask difficult and uncompromising questions."

"Earlier, you said you did not consider Mr. Arrington a suspect. It seems to me you are now insinuating he's responsible for, or complicit in, John Grainger's death."

"No, I'm not." Clay eyed Hayden but directed his words toward Sanderson. "Frankly, what I don't understand is why your client is making such an issue of my question about his wife. When I spoke with him on Friday, I expected cooperation on his part. Instead, he took offense at my questions and refused to answer. So, here we are, wasting each other's time when all I want to know is if Grainger ever hit on his wife."

Arrington resigned himself to the fact that this meeting with Clay would not end until or unless he answered the question. He leaned in and whispered to his lawyer.

Sanderson nodded to his client. "Mr. Arrington said Grainger never made any advances toward his wife. And if he had, she certainly would have rebuffed him."

"Did Mrs. Arrington know John Grainger?"

"No."

Clay was surprised at Hayden's answer. "No? I've been led to believe that your wife accompanied you to the Bend from time to time to attend charitable events. Wasn't it likely that you would have introduced her to Grainger during one such event?"

Arrington hesitated before answering. "It's possible."

"Since then, have you ever talked to Mrs. Arrington about him?"

"No."

"I'm sure you know how, uh, *persuasive* Grainger was. After all, how could he have garnered such success at the Bend without top-notch skills of persuasion? Skills I'm sure he employed in his personal life too."

Arrington flared again. His eyes bulged, his face reddened, and he curled his fingers into a fist. "What are you trying to imply? I told you she didn't know the man."

"Well, sir, maybe you'll see my problem. I'm asking myself how you know if Grainger never made advances toward your wife if, as you said, you've never talked with her about him."

"I know my wife. She would have said something to me if he had. She would not have an affair with anyone, much less with a common sexual pervert. I trust her implicitly."

"This isn't about trust. All I'm asking is how can you possibly know what Grainger may or may not have done, or attempted to do, with your wife if you've never had a conversation with her about him?"

Sanderson raised his voice, "My client said he has not talked to his wife about Mr. Grainger. Period!"

"There's no reason to be upset, Counselor." Clay thought it was time to reduce the tension in the room. He leaned back in his chair and said with a grin, "I know I'm not the easiest person to deal with. Ask my ex-wife." Neither Hayden nor Sanderson found humor in Clay's comment. Clay continued. "My question regarding Mrs. Arrington should not be construed as unreasonable, don't you agree, Counselor?"

Sanderson disregarded Clay's question and instead asked, "What else do you need to know?"

Clay again directed his attention to Hayden. "Mr. Arrington, you told me you were in Germany the day Grainger died."

"I said I was en route to Germany."

"Where was your bodyguard when Grainger was killed?"

"Anton? He was onboard the plane with me."

"That was convenient." He said under his breath, then asked, "Does Anton normally travel with you?"

"Sometimes he does, and sometimes the host company I'm meeting with will arrange security for me."

Sanderson said, "What does his bodyguard have to do with this? By asking questions about Anton, you are again implying that my client was complicit in Mr. Grainger's death."

"Assume all you want. All I'm doing is asking simple, straightforward questions. Again, had he answered these questions on Friday, we could have avoided this proceeding altogether."

Arrington defended his actions of three days earlier. "If you recall, on Friday I said I was not going to answer any more questions without my lawyer being present. I did not say I was not going to answer your questions."

"Sounded like a refusal to me when you said it."

Sanderson said, "Detective Bryce—"

Clay cut the attorney short to avoid another rebuke. "Let's talk about the Bend. What are you going to do now that Grainger is dead and you've fired Simon Learner? Who will run the business now?"

Sanderson asked, "Why is that germane to your investigation?"

Hayden said, "That's okay, Wallace. I can answer that. I decided it was best to keep Learner on as head of operations rather than leave the Bend rudderless. After you left on Friday,

I spoke with Learner and made him a generous offer to remain with the Bend. And he agreed to stay on."

Clay was surprised at the news. Simon had told him was he was not going to accept Arrington's offer to stay on. *I need to discuss Simon's about-face with him.*

Sanderson shook his head. "That's enough, Detective. You're heading nowhere with this line of questioning. Are we through?"

Clay looked back and forth at the two men seated opposite him. "Yes, we're through. Thank you for coming in." He stood and extended his hand to Arrington across the interview table.

Hayden looked at Clay's hand but did not offer his own in return. "Detective Rice, I'll remember what you've put me through. And I promise, you will pay for your impudence."

Clay smiled. "I'm sorry you feel that way. Just doing my job."

* * * * *

Clay watched Hayden Arrington and Wallace Sanderson walk down the corridor toward the parking lot exit. Captain Ellsworth and Hank Kincaid stepped out of the observation room as Arrington and Sanderson exited the building.

Clay asked, "What do you think?"

Hank said, "I think Arrington might have known his wife and Grainger were having an affair, but he has a bona fide alibi that places him and his bodyguard out of the country at the time Grainger was killed. We have nothing to show he was involved in Grainger's murder?"

"I have a theory, though, and it really sticks in my craw."

"Which is?" Hank asked.

"Picture this. Arrington and his bodyguard light the candle, board the plane, and they're in the clear because they're on their way to Germany when the fire finally ignites hours later. That makes for a perfect alibi, doesn't it?"

Ellsworth responded, "Yes, it does. They could have set the fire. But we don't know when the candle was lit. The arsonist could have been anyone. Nothing we have points explicitly to Arrington or his bodyguard."

Clay agreed. "You're right. Forensics tried to analyze the candle wax residue to determine when it was lit, but they couldn't narrow it down to a specific time."

Hank said, "Arrington may have known about his wife's affair but, I agree with the captain–there's no way to prove he murdered Grainger with what you have now. Arrington certainly overreacted to your questions. In his defense, however, if he knew about his wife's affair with Grainger, that doesn't mean he's the killer. Marital infidelities occur every minute of every day, but that doesn't mean the spurned spouses are going to kill the adulterers."

Clay nodded. "Yeah, I know you're both right. On another note, I was surprised to hear Simon Learner agreed to stay on at the Bend. He told me he had rejected Arrington's offer. I'm going to talk to him again. Arrington must have made him one hell of an offer."

CHAPTER 41

Clay returned to the Bend to question Simon. Contrary to his grim bearing of three days earlier, Simon exuded self-confidence when he spoke—a far cry from his behavior on Clay's first visit. He had a smile on his face, his shoulders were erect, his gaze direct and unwavering, and his handshake firm. "I know why you're back," he said to Clay.

"You do, huh?"

"Yes. You found out I was staying on and now you want to know what made me change my mind, right?"

"Right," Clay said. "I spoke with your boss this morning and learned you accepted his offer after all. I was surprised. On Friday, you were so certain of your decision to reject it."

"All true. And now you're probably wondering if I had ulterior motives."

"Did you?"

"No, I did not. But maybe Mr. Arrington did."

"What do you mean?"

"I don't know. Probably just my imagination, but he didn't appear to be unhappy about John dying. I mean, he concocted this grand scheme to bring him back, but it doesn't appear that he was distraught about keeping me on."

"I thought you said he was spitting mad at you for turning him down."

"Well, he seemed mad. In retrospect, I think he was faking, just showing me he's the boss. It's really strange how I went from being out of a job to being offered the moon and the stars. I truly had no idea I'd be staying on."

"What did he say to you after I left?"

"He made me a very generous offer and was as nice as could be.

"What was the offer?"

"He would double my salary and provide me with whatever resources I need to turn things around. He gave me a second chance, another opportunity to succeed. How could I turn down that offer? He reminded me to keep his earlier decision to rehire John between the two of us. He couldn't have been more pleasant or courteous. It was one heck of a turnaround. Admittedly, I derived more than a little pleasure seeing him squirm in his own juices. Ha!" Simon let out a shrill laugh.

"You told me you were going to consult with your wife first and then decide what to do. What did she advise?"

"I didn't need to ask her opinion. I decided Friday after you left to accept Mr. Arrington's offer."

"You must have told Liza what transpired. What did she say?"

"She was surprised at first but she understood when I told her the money was too good to pass up. She was supportive, as usual."

"Well, good for both of you."

"Thank you."

"Seems to me your career has taken you from the frying pan to the fire, first working for John and then with Mr. Arrington. Both difficult men."

"Yes, that's true."

"But, contrary to your relationship with Arrington, you and John seemed to have gotten along."

"As much as one could co-exist with him. He was full of himself, as you know."

"Didn't that bother you to work for a man like that?"

"Yes. In fact, I was sometimes embarrassed to be seen with him. He had a huge ego and thought he was God's gift to women. I always wondered what the employees here thought of me because I spent so much time with him."

"Did you worry about that?"

"I didn't want people to think I was like him. Everyone knew what he was like. In some ways, he was like Mr. Arrington. He'd lash out at me in front of people if things weren't operating smoothly. And, yes, there were times I wanted to smack him in the face and walk out of here."

"Why didn't you?"

"I can't answer that definitively. Lots of reasons. Maybe because I really liked my job. And maybe because I was making a nice salary, and maybe it was because I was learning how to manage the complexities of the casino business. John was a good teacher. People used to say he was a marketing genius. Well, he was. So, to answer your question, why did I stay on? I don't know. Pick any one or all of the above reasons."

Clay remembered what Grainger had said about Simon's wife—that he was surprised Liza had married Simon. That she was smokin' hot and Simon was not man enough to be married to her. "On Friday I asked if you were ever concerned about John hitting on your wife. You didn't answer the question. You did, however, offer the suggestion that a vengeful husband could have been responsible for Grainger's murder. Are you one of those vengeful husbands?"

"Nice try, Detective." Simon smirked and shook his head. "No, I'm not vengeful in the least. It's not in my character. Did John try to sleep with Liza? Yes. But that was before I married her. I can't control what happened in the past."

Clay said nothing but waited to see what more Simon would reveal.

"I really don't want to answer any more questions regarding my wife. I told you all I know."

"You mean all you want me to know."

"Whatever." Simon lost his smile and his face contorted in irritation at Clay's line of questions.

"Simon, you seem angry all of a sudden. Are you?"

"I'm not angry, but I don't like what you're asking about my wife. Reverse our roles. Wouldn't you be mad at this line of questioning?"

"No. I would simply speak the truth. That's all I'm asking of you." Clay turned silent, electing to have Simon face another pregnant pause.

Simon looked away, then returned his gaze to Clay and said, "With all due respect, I'm not going to answer any more questions about Liza."

"Then you won't mind if I talk to her directly."

"Oh, for Christ's sake, yes. *Yes*, they had an affair. Are you satisfied now that you got that out of me?"

"When was their affair?"

"Two years ago. Before Liza and I started dating. She had just been hired to work here and was young and gullible. He swept her off her feet. It didn't last long and she regrets it to this day."

"Did he ever try to have sex with her after you two were married?"

"No. I'm certain of that. If he had, I would have used a baseball bat against him."

"In other words, you might have killed him?"

"Threaten, yes. Kill, no."

CHAPTER 42

The following morning, Clay was in the squad room at police headquarters when he received a call from Arianna. "Yes? What is it?" He had lost all patience with her.

Arianna's voice was high pitched and urgent. "I need to see you."

"What now?" Clay responded.

"I have something to show you."

"What?"

"I can't tell you. I need to show you," Arianna said. "Can I please meet you at your house? It's important."

"No, I'm busy. If you want to see me, come to police headquarters." He was not about to be drawn into another meeting with her at his house.

"Let me meet you at your house. Please, I'm begging you. I need to talk to you in private."

"Listen, Arianna, I don't know what you're up to but you're starting to wear on me."

"I'm not up to anything. You've got to believe me."

She sounded sincere—and in a near state of panic. "Damn it. Okay. You're pushing your luck with me. I'll meet you there in half an hour. But do not play games with me."

"I won't. I promise."

* * * * *

Arianna pulled into Clay's driveway and waited for him to arrive. A few minutes later, Clay pulled up to the curb and got out of his car. He observed that she was not wearing makeup and was dressed in simple blue jeans and a gray t-shirt, a far cry from her normally sexy attire.

"Can we talk inside?" she asked.

Clay looked at her suspiciously. "No, we're good right here."

Arianna was insistent. "Oh, my God, I'm not going to do anything."

Clay sighed heavily and led her into his house. He kept the front door open and said, "Go ahead, talk. What's so important?"

"Anton picked up the normal bundle of mail and this envelope was in it," she said, and handed it to Clay. "Thank God he didn't see it."

The envelope was addressed to *H. Arrington* with block letters cut from a newspaper. There was no return address.

"It's addressed to your husband."

"It is. But don't you find it odd that someone would address an envelope this way? I had a feeling it was about me, so I opened it."

Clay looked at the envelope again, then back to Arianna. "Why would you think that?"

"I don't know how I knew, but I did. And I was right. Look."

"There's nothing in it."

"There was." She held up a tiny computer memory card for Clay to see. "I played it on my laptop. It's a video showing John and me having sex at his house."

Clay recalled finding the tiny camera mounted on the wall in Grainger's bedroom. "That explains what happened to the memory card," he said.

"What do you mean?"

"The day John was murdered, I discovered a camera hidden in his bedroom, but the memory card was missing. This is probably that missing card. At first I thought it was your boyfriend recording your sexual escapades, but now it's obvious someone else set up the camera." He checked the postmark. "The envelope is postmarked the day after his murder."

Clay reached for the card, but Arianna withdrew her hand. She shook her head and said, "You can't have it. I don't want you to watch it. You'll have to trust me about what's on it."

Clay nodded, "Okay, fine, I'll trust you. Tell me, has anyone tried to extort money from you?"

"What do you mean, like blackmail? No. No one."

"Does anyone have a bone to pick with you?"

"I'm sure some people do."

"Like who?"

"Hayden's son, Hunter, and his bitch of a daughter-in-law, Harmony, for starters."

"Tell me about them."

"They were against our marriage from the beginning—especially Harmony. Her name is laughable. She's the absolute opposite of what her name implies. She's capable of doing something like this to get Hayden to divorce me."

"Why do you say that?"

"She's mean-spirited. She hired me as a nanny to her kids but made life miserable for me right from the beginning. I think it was because she was jealous of how I look compared to her. She's a frump. Hayden would pay a lot of attention to me when he came over to the house."

"What about her husband?"

"Hunter? He cows to Harmony, because he doesn't want to cause a stink, and boy can she cause a stink. I don't understand why he puts up with all her crap. She was always nagging him and telling him how dumb he was and that he didn't have the guts to stick up for himself with his father."

"If Harmony disliked you so much why did she hire you in the first place?"

"Probably because Hayden convinced her to. Honestly, she was awful to me—and everyone else—even her kids."

"Why did you stay on as nanny if she treated you that badly?"

Arianna looked at Clay as though he were joking. "Why do you think? Hayden was at the end of the rainbow."

"Your pot of gold."

"Yes," she answered without hesitation. "I knew Hayden lusted over me and I said to myself, why the hell not? So I seduced him. And then he asked me to marry him."

"And Hunter and Harmony did not approve."

"Oh, Lord, no. When Hayden announced our plans to them, Harmony went bat-shit."

"How so?"

"I remember we were sitting in their living room and Harmony argued right to our faces that our age difference was too great and that we had nothing in common. She said, 'What will people say? The newspapers will feast on this story.' That kind of thing. When Hayden didn't buy any of that, Harmony freaked out. She called Hayden an old fool and me a slut and a gold digger and then she stomped out of the room like a spoiled brat. But she didn't fool me one little bit. It was so obvious why she was mad."

"Why?"

"She didn't care a whit about her father-in-law. That bitch was afraid Hayden was going to leave everything to me when he died."

"Is he?"

Arianna looked away from Clay. After a few seconds, she turned back to him and said, "Yes, he wants me to inherit everything. I can tell you this much. I've worked *very* hard to keep Hayden happy. So why not? Why can't I have what he wants to give me? It's not like I was lucky and hit the lottery or anything. I've earned it. I do things to keep him happy."

"What's your relationship with Hunter and Harmony now?"

"They hate me. They claim I betrayed their trust as a nanny—well, Harmony does."

"You don't think you did?"

"No. The fact is, I was a really good nanny. I never neglected their children and they loved me."

"What about Hayden? Are Hunter and Harmony on speaking terms with him now?"

"No. They haven't spoken to either one of us since Hayden divorced Hunter's mother. They won't even let Hayden see his grandkids! He adores those children. What snake would do that to grandparents?"

Clay said, "Which takes us back to the video of you and John. You agree your husband would divorce you if he viewed it, right?"

"Yes. Hayden would divorce me and Hunter would he back in the will and inherit everything. That's why this envelope had to come from them."

"How would they have known John Grainger?"

"They probably knew him from the Bend. They attended events there. They must have somehow found out we were having an affair. You'll have to ask them how they found out. Probably spying on me. Who knows? For your information, I think *they*'re the ones who killed John."

"Why do you say that? They had no reason to kill him."

249

"Well, then, what about them trying to kill me? They could be planning to kill me too."

"They don't have to go to that extreme. They only have to do what you're alleging they did—send proof to your husband that you were having an affair. There's no reason for them to commit murder to get what they want."

Arianna was not convinced. "I disagree. You've got to arrest them for killing John"

"On what basis?"

She was angry. Her voice got louder as she spelled out her logic. "On the basis that maybe they did kill John. I mean, you *must* suspect they murdered him, don't you?"

"No. I don't have any evidence of a motive that justifies arresting them. Now, if you're convinced they're the ones who sent the disk, maybe you want to file criminal charges against them for invasion of privacy."

"I can't do that. Hayden would know about my affair with John."

"That's very true. The best I can do, then, is bring Harmony and Hunter in for questioning to find out if they sent the envelope and, if they did, advise them to cease and desist. I will not pursue your idea that they killed John because there is absolutely no basis to think they did."

"Fine."

"Let me have the disk."

"No! Absolutely not," Arianna said. "You're not getting it." She put the memory card in her pocket. "You can have the envelope and check for Hunter's and Harmony's fingerprints all you want but you're not getting the memory card."

"That's ridiculous. Why not? Do you think I'm going to show it to your husband?"

"I don't know what you would do with it, but I'm through taking chances. I don't trust anybody to have it—not even you. I will destroy it. No one will ever see what's on it."

That afternoon, under pretense that Hunter and Harmony might offer some clues about a crime he was investigating, Clay asked them to meet with him at police headquarters. "I can't go into it over the phone but I'll explain when you get here."

CHAPTER 43

When Harmony and Hunter Arrington arrived at police headquarters, Clay had Harmony sit in one interview room and Hunter in another. Clay explained the reason why witnesses had to be separated. "We do that so one person does not prejudice the other witness's recollection of events."

Both Harmony and Hunter bought the explanation.

Clay elected to speak with Harmony first.

"Thank you for coming in, Mrs. Arrington. May I call you Harmony?"

"No. It's Mrs. Arrington."

"Fair enough. Mrs. Arrington it is."

"Are there people behind the mirror watching this?"

"No."

"Then why have you asked to interview my husband and me? Why didn't you come to our house to talk to us?"

"Protocol, Mrs. Arrington."

"I'm not sure I believe you. What do you want to ask?"

"We've been investigating a crime that took place last week and have been hitting a brick wall. No evidence, no witnesses, no nothing. We thought perhaps you could help us out."

Harmony shook her head. "How could I possibly help? Do you think I was witness to the crime?"

"That's the reason I asked you to meet with me. We understand a vehicle such as yours was seen in the vicinity of the crime."

"Which? We own three."

Clay had researched the make, model, and color of Hunter and Harmony's cars to support the reasoning for interviewing them. "Your metallic blue Jaguar. Now, mind you, we're not saying you were driving the vehicle in question at the time of the crime but, as I said, a blue Jaguar was seen in the neighborhood. We're interviewing everyone who drives such a car."

"Where was it supposedly seen?"

"On Upper Canyon Road. By any chance, were you in that vicinity last Tuesday in the late afternoon?"

"I don't know. I've got to think about where I was that day."

"Were you with your husband?"

Harmony tapped her fingers nervously on the table. "I don't know. I can't remember."

"Well, let's forget about last Tuesday for the moment. Do you know where Upper Canyon Road is?"

"Of course."

"Good. That means you can tell me if you've been there, say, in the past couple of weeks."

"Probably. I sometimes meet my girlfriends for lunch in that area."

Clay nodded. "That makes sense. There's a lot of good restaurants there. Do you have a favorite?"

She looked at Clay quizzically. "They're all good. I don't have a favorite."

"I used to have lunch at the Compound with a friend of mine, John Grainger. Did you know him by any chance?"

Harmony swallowed hard to drum up saliva. "John Grainger? No. Can't say I do."

"Are you sure?"

"As sure as I can be."

Perspiration developed on Harmony's forehead. Clay had her worried and decided to drop the hammer with a harsher line of questioning. "John Grainger was the former vice president of the Indian Bend Hotel and Casino. He was fired a year ago after his arrest for a felonious sexual liaison with an underage girl."

"Oh, now I remember. He got off scot-free, didn't he?"

"So you know him?"

"No. I only remember reading about him. I don't know him."

"Unfortunately, someone killed him in his home on East Alameda last Tuesday. That's the crime we're investigating."

"And you think I had something to do with his murder?"

Clay did not answer her. "You know Arianna Arrington, do you not?"

Harmony squirmed in her chair, her eyes flitting about. "Why are you asking me all these inane questions? Of course I know her. She's my father-in-law's wife. I shouldn't say *wife.* She's more like his teenybopper bride."

"Ouch. I gather you're not fond of her."

"She's a slut and a whore and a gold digger. And she had the nerve to apply for a job as my children's nanny so she could seduce my father-in-law. Our lives have been turned upside down because of her."

"Turned upside down? How so?"

"Hayden's mad at us because we told him it was a bad idea for him to marry her. You know what he did because we disagreed with his decision to marry her?"

"No, what?'

She spit out the words. "He changed his will to leave everything to her when he dies. She's going to inherit everything he owns—his money, his businesses, his properties—all of which rightfully belongs to my husband and me."

"Do you know if John Grainger knew Arianna?"

"Everyone knows about her, if you know what I mean."

Clay cocked his head. "I don't know what you mean. Tell me."

"I think she's had a lot of affairs."

"A lot of affairs?"

"Yes, before and after she married Hayden. John Grainger was probably another conquest for her."

"Why would you say that? You said you didn't know Mr. Grainger."

Harmony hesitated and looked away. "I didn't. People have told me things. I've filled in the blanks." With a shrug she added, "I don't know for sure. It's only a guess."

"A guess? That's not fair to Arianna, is it?"

"Trust me. She's the type who would sleep around."

"If you suspected she had relationships with other men, why didn't you tell your father-in-law?"

Harmony stared at Clay. "He wouldn't believe us. He slobbers over her like he's a sixteen-year-old kid."

"If your Hayden wouldn't listen to you, I'm sure you could find other ways to let him know what his wife was up to."

"What do you mean? Like what?"

"Like use hidden cameras to record her affairs."

Harmony's eyes widened and she shook her head vehemently. "I wouldn't do that."

"Actually, Mrs. Arrington, I know the truth. Please don't lie to me. Let's try this again. You've used hidden cameras to spy on Arianna, isn't that true?"

Harmony refused to budge an inch. "Why would I do such a thing?"

"Here's what I know. You and your husband sent a disk to Hayden Arrington showing Arianna having sex with John Grainger. Why would you do that?"

Clay waited for Harmony to answer but she said nothing. After a few seconds he continued. "Here's my theory, if Hayden views the recording, you expect he'll divorce Arianna. Then you and Hunter are back in his will. What we're talking about here is gross invasion of privacy with intent to do significant harm to someone's reputation. That's a felony in the State of New Mexico."

Harmony abruptly stood, smoothed her skirt, and looked down her nose at Clay. She said, "I don't want to answer any more of your questions. I want to go home. Where's my husband?"

"He's fine. I'll be talking to him shortly."

"I'm leaving now."

"No, Mrs. Arrington, you're not. Sit back down. I'm going to talk with Hunter. I'll have other questions for you later. There's a guard posted outside this room and he will see to it that you do not leave. When I return, if you wish to have counsel, we'll ensure you have the opportunity to call your lawyer."

Harmony sat down and glared at Clay as he exited the room.

CHAPTER 44

Hunter Arrington sat in the interview room waiting impatiently for Clay to arrive. After ten minutes, his anxiety got the best of him. He walked to the one-way mirror, cupped his hands to the glass, and tried to peer through to see who might be watching.

Clay entered and found Hunter with his face up against the mirror. "Hello, Hunter. There's no one there. Have a seat, please."

"Why am I here?"

Clay recalled that Arianna described Hunter as weak. Intimidation tactics would likely serve Clay well in getting to the truth. "I'm going to read you your Miranda rights before I ask you any questions."

Hunter looked back and forth between Clay and the mirror as Clay read the warning. "Are you telling me the truth that there's no one behind the mirror?"

"I am. No one's there."

"Then why did you read me my rights?"

"It's protocol."

"You *do* know I'm Hayden Arrington's son, don't you?"

Clay glared at Hunter. "I'm sure you don't care who *my* father is and, frankly, sir, I don't care who *your* father is. Do you understand your Miranda rights?"

Hunter was taken aback by Clay's blunt response. He answered with a meek, "Yes."

Clay continued, "You should know that your wife has made it clear what you and she have done and why you did it. In a way, I can't blame you."

Hunter shook his head, dumbfounded by Clay's comment. "I don't know what you're talking about. What did she tell you?"

"Well, to start, she claims it was your idea from the beginning." Clay lied and pointed the finger of blame to Hunter.

Hunter slapped the table. "Damn her! It was not my idea. She came up with the plan, and I went along with her."

"I'm pleased you're giving me the straight scoop. It'll make it easier for both you and Harmony. Well, I shouldn't say *Harmony*. She insisted I call her *Mrs. Arrington*."

Hunter mumbled, "That figures. She probably prefers I call her that too."

"I gather she's not easy to live with."

"Amen to that."

Clay leaned forward in his chair. "I bet you know the saying, in marriage you can be right or you can be happy. In my case, I thought I was more right than my wife, so my wife is now my ex-wife." He laughed. "But, getting back to you and your wife. You're saying it wasn't your idea?"

"It was not."

"Actually, Hunter, I'm really less concerned about whose idea it was and more about how you managed to do it." Clay leafed through his notepad which was filled with pages of notes from previous cases. He wanted Hunter to think the notes were quotes from his interview with Harmony.

Hunter pointed to the notepad. "What's in there? What did Harmony tell you?"

Clay said, "I would rather you tell me your recollection. For example, how were you able to get into John Grainger's house and set up the stealth camera? Did you use a spare key to get in? Did you know the passcode to bypass his security system? Let's go back to the beginning."

"We didn't have his key and we didn't know his passcode. I knew John from his time at the Bend, but I hadn't seen him in over a year. We visited him a couple of weeks ago under the pretense that we were in the area and wanted to see how he was doing. While Harmony diverted his attention out on the patio, I asked to use the bathroom. That's when I snuck into his bedroom and installed the camera. I had to stand on a chair to do it, but it took less than a minute."

"Your wife said she didn't know John. That's a lie." Clay looked Hunter directly in the eyes. "It is, isn't it?"

"Yes."

Hunter's about ready to spill his guts.

"How and when did you retrieve the camera disk from his bedroom?"

"The day before John was killed, we went to his house again, and this time we brought sandwiches and chips and snacks to share with him. We all ate on the patio alongside the swimming pool and, when I had a chance, I snuck in and got the disk."

"Why didn't you take the camera too?"

"Harmony told me to leave it in case I hadn't aimed it right, that maybe we'd have to do it again."

"That was a brilliant plan. How did you know they were having an affair? Or was it Harmony who found out?"

"Harmony was obsessed with finding dirt on Arianna. She followed her day after day and eventually found out Arianna was meeting with John, sometimes at her house, sometimes at John's."

Clay did not believe Hunter had anything to do with Grainger's death, but decided to see how he would respond to the accusation. "So you retrieved the disk before you killed John."

Hunter's breathing became hard and fast. Clay thought he was going to hyperventilate. "No! No! No!" he said. "Whoa, I didn't say that. We didn't kill him. No way. No. We read he had been killed, but we didn't do it. Harmony said we should video Arianna and John having sex and send the disk to my father, and that's all we did. Believe me, we did not kill John. Why would we? It wouldn't have served any purpose."

Clay extracted what he was after—an admission of guilt regarding the sex recording. He decided to wrap up his investigation by interviewing Harmony and Hunter together. He had no reason to believe they were responsible for Grainger's death.

* * * * *

A guard escorted Harmony into Hunter's interview room. Hunter looked away from his wife when she entered. Harmony squinted at him. She knew immediately he had confessed to the taping.

"Mrs. Arrington, Hunter has told me you set up the camera so you could catch Arianna and John Grainger having sex. And that it was your intention to send the video recording to Hunter's father. For your information, the tape never got to Mr. Arrington. The envelope you sent was intercepted by Arianna, and she made me aware of it."

Harmony looked at Hunter in disbelief and shouted, "Why in the world did you tell him we did that, you jerk?"

Hunter continued to look away.

"Mrs. Arrington, Arianna understands you did this to make your father-in-law aware of her infidelity. Was that the sole purpose?"

Harmony did not answer.

"Lucky for you, Mr. Arrington did not see it."

"I wouldn't call that lucky," she said.

"Yes, you were lucky. You see, what you did was a crime. If the disk had gotten through to Mr. Arrington, Arianna could have filed civil and criminal charges against you for invasion of privacy."

Hunter asked, "Are you saying we can't be arrested because my father never saw the recording?"

"That's correct, unless Arianna files suit against you. But she won't. She is between a rock and a hard place. She knows you know about her affair, but she can't do anything about it. If she files suit against you, her affair will become public knowledge."

Hunter looked at Harmony and exhaled a sigh of relief.

Harmony said, "We want to leave."

"Let me tell you this. I understand you disapprove of Arianna marrying Hunter's father, but here's what I suggest you do. Get over it. Leave her alone. You can't control what she is or what she does. Your only hope is to reconcile with Mr. Arrington and maybe, in time, he'll recognize Arianna for what she really is. Get it? For right now, call yourselves lucky."

"Let's get out of here, Hunter."

"One last question before you leave," Clay said. "How many copies of the video did you make?"

Hunter opened his mouth to speak, but Harmony cut him short. "We didn't make any copies."

CHAPTER 45

Clay and Allie planned to have a light dinner at Allie's condo when her shift ended on the mid-day of her new daytime work cycle. Allie phoned Clay early afternoon. "The body shop called. They've finally finished repairing my car. I need to pick it up and turn in my rental. I'll be no later than eight."

"See you then."

* * * * *

A little before eight, Allie pulled into her condominium complex and used her remote control to open the garage door. Before getting out of the car, she was startled by the shrill ring of her phone. "Clay, you scared me."

"What do you mean I scared you? What's the matter?"

"Oh, nothing. The phone startled me. I... I'm fine. I just pulled into the garage."

"You sound jumpy."

"I'm still spooked from the tailgating incident of a couple of weeks ago."

"You were followed again?"

"I thought I was. On my drive home, a car behind me made every turn I did."

"Did he follow you into your complex?"

"No. He drove past the entrance. And, actually, when they drove by, I saw a man and a woman in the car." Allie gave a nervous laugh in an attempt to hide her concern. "Everything is fine. My imagination got the best of me. As I said, I'm still a little spooked—but I'm fine."

"I'll be there in less than ten minutes. If it would make you feel better, stay on the phone with me until you get inside."

"Okay, I will." Allie closed the garage door and waited until it thumped shut. She looked in every direction to see if anyone was lurking. When she saw no one, she walked to her condo.

Clay heard beeps as Allie entered her unit and punched in the passcode to disarm the security system. "Everything okay?"

"Yes, I'm good. I'm going to hang up. I'll see you in a bit."

Clay arrived and backed his car into a visitor's parking space so the front of his car faced Allie's condo. He exited his car, walked to Allie's unit, and knocked on the front door. "Maryland, it's me." He looked out at the parking area to see if anything aroused his suspicions. Nothing did. He waited for Allie to come to the door. Half a minute elapsed.

He knocked again.

No answer.

Clay leaned toward the door to listen for noise from inside and heard nothing. He rang the doorbell. "Allie, open up. It's me."

Still no response.

He tried to peer in the window of Allie's spare bedroom at the end of the landing, but the blinds were drawn. He rang the doorbell again. *What is she doing in there?* "It's me, Clay. Open up. You okay in there?" He hated waiting for anything and was getting irritated. *She's probably changing out of her uniform and can't hear me.*

Clay pulled out his cell phone and dialed her number. He heard it ring from somewhere near the front door. The call went to voicemail. "Maryland, open up. It's Clay." He spoke louder and put his ear against the door to listen. He heard what sounded like a chair fall to the floor, then the sound of scuffling followed by a muffled shout.

"Help!"

A door slammed shut.

Clay tried unsuccessfully to break down the metal door by ramming his shoulder against it. He then tried to kick the door open. It did not budge. A middle-aged man stepped out of the condo next to Allie's. "What's going on out here?" he shouted. "I'm calling the police."

"I *am* the police! Call 911. Fast! Tell them Detective Bryce needs backup. Detective Bryce. Quick!"

The neighbor hurried back inside.

The sound of a gunshot rang out from Allie's condo.

"Allie!" He leaped off the landing and started to circle around the outside of the building to enter Allie's condo from the rear. He stopped in his tracks when he heard the front door open and Allie utter, "Clay! Help!"

Clay raced back up the steps, stood at the side of the doorway, and peeked into the unit. He saw Allie a few feet from the door, leaning against the foyer wall. She held a silver-plated pistol in one hand and massaged her throat with the other. "Allie! Are you okay? It's me. I'm coming in. Don't shoot! What happened?"

Allie was trembling and pointed to the patio door. The sliding door was open. Clay flicked on the outside light, drew his service revolver, and guardedly walked from the patio down to the cart path. When he saw no one, he returned to the condo, holstered his revolver, and took Allie's pistol from her. He led her to the sofa in the living room. "I didn't see anyone outside," he said. "Are you okay?"

She continued to massage her throat and whispered, "Yes, I'm okay."

Clay asked, "Did you fire that shot?"

Allie nodded and raised her forefinger to signal Clay she needed a minute to clear her throat.

"Do you need to go to the hospital?"

"No."

Clay went to the kitchen to get Allie a glass of water. "Here. Drink some water. When you're able to talk, tell me what happened."

She took a sip and spoke slowly, deliberately, clearing her throat every few words. "I got in... turned off the security system... Before I could turn the lights on... someone came through the patio door and dragged me into the bedroom."

She took another sip.

"What happened then?"

"He had his arm around my throat... choking me... I couldn't breathe."

Clay stroked her arm. "You're safe now. I'm here with you. He can't hurt you anymore. Did you recognize him?"

Allie continued to massage her throat. "No. He was wearing a ski mask."

Clay looked around the living room. "Your security system was on. How did he get in?"

"I don't know."

"Was the patio door locked?"

"I thought it was."

"Allie, didn't I tell—" Clay caught himself. Now was not the time to lecture her. He checked the patio door for signs of forced entry but saw no indication it had been jimmied. "I'll leave it to forensics to determine if the door's been tampered with." He sat next to Allie and urged her to continue. "The intruder was choking you. What happened then?"

"I couldn't do anything. I tried to flip him but I couldn't get any leverage. Then I heard you trying to bust the front door open and he heard you too."

"What did he do then?"

"He relaxed his hold for just a second, and I was able to twist away from him. He shoved me to the floor and ran out of the bedroom. That's when I got my gun from the bedside table. I thought he was still in the condo, so I snuck out of the bedroom. But when I saw the patio door open, I realized he had run out. I went outside and heard a golf cart head down the cart path. That's when I fired my gun."

"Did you see the cart?"

"No. It was too dark and the bushes were in the way. I fired in the direction where I thought the cart was heading."

"Do you think you hit him?"

"No, I don't think so. Well… maybe. I don't know. I don't know. I was shaking so much."

"Which way did the golf cart go?"

She shrugged and shook her head.

"Think hard, Allie." He knew the longer it took to determine the facts of the assault, the less likely he would be able to pursue and apprehend the culprit. "Did he go up the cart path to the next hole or did he go in the opposite direction?"

"I think he drove toward the next hole."

"You think? You don't know?"

"Clay, you're acting like you're mad at me. Please don't be. I'm trying my best to remember everything that happened."

"I'm not mad at you. I just want to get the sonofabitch." Clay kissed Allie on the forehead. "Thankfully, you're okay."

"The fact is, if you hadn't been here—" Allie did not finish. She looked at Clay and was close to crying. "Why me?"

"We're going to find out. I promise."

CHAPTER 46

In response to the neighbor's 911 call, two cop cars arrived at the condo with sirens wailing. The neighbor opened his door and pointed to Allie's condo. "I'm the one who called. The guy who said he's a detective is in there. Someone fired a gun a few minutes ago."

"Sir, go back inside and close your door."

Other residents stepped onto their landings or peered out their windows as the police cars flashed their presence. The cops waved everyone back into their units. They drew their revolvers and stood on either side of Allie's open door. "Police! Come out with your hands up! Now!"

Clay took out his badge to identify himself and left Allie's pistol on the kitchen table. "We're coming out. I'm Detective Bryce of the SFPD. My weapon is holstered." Clay and Allie walked out of the condo with hands raised above their heads and Clay displaying his badge in the palm of his hand.

One cop recognized Clay. He asked, "What's going on here, Detective Bryce?"

"Someone assaulted my friend in her condo."

The other cop noticed Allie was still in her paramedic uniform. He said, "You look familiar."

"My name is Allie Marland. You look familiar too. We've been at accident scenes together."

The cop said, "You're right. I'm Officer Woodruff and this is Officer Rendon. What's going on here? I understand someone fired a gun. Are you okay?"

Allie nodded and said, "It was me. I fired at the man who assaulted me."

Clay added, "The perp is gone. She scared him off."

The cops needed to confirm what had happened. "We're going to check the condo. Wait out here, please."

"It's clear, Officer," Clay said.

The cop eyed Clay. He had to take all possibilities into account, including the possibility that the incident had been a domestic dispute between Clay and Allie. "Just playing it safe, Detective."

The cops entered the condo and performed a search. A minute later, Officer Woodruff said, "It's okay. You can come in."

Allie held Clay's arm for support as they moved back inside.

"Tell me what happened," Officer Rendon said.

Allie retold her story. "I turned off my security system and, before I could turn on the lights, he barreled in from the patio and put a chokehold on me. He dragged me into the bedroom."

"Did you get a look at him?"

"No. He was wearing a ski mask and gloves... and dark clothes. That's all I can tell you. I don't know if he was white, black, or gray. The lights were off and he came at me from behind, so I wasn't able to see his face."

Clay added, "The intruder had her in a chokehold."

"Yes, and if it weren't for Clay—Detective Bryce—I'd probably be dead right now."

"How is it that you're involved, Detective?"

"Allie and I are friends. We had a dinner date. When I got here, I heard scuffling inside, Allie's cry for help, and then the gunshot. I tried to shoulder the front door open, but couldn't budge it. When she got free from the guy, she let me in."

Allie said, "The man relaxed his hold on me for a second when he heard Clay trying to break the door down. The next thing I knew, he threw me to the floor, slammed the bedroom door shut, and ran out the patio door. I got my gun and ran after him. That's when I shot at him."

"Did you hit him?"

"I don't know."

Officer Woodruff said, "Hospitals will notify us if someone comes in with a bullet wound."

The cops continued their questioning to better understand what had transpired and if this was a domestic dispute, a burglary, or a sexual assault. "Could you have known the perpetrator, maybe a boyfriend jealous of your relationship with Detective Bryce?"

Allie said, "No. I have no idea who it was."

"You said he dragged you into the bedroom. Do you think he was trying to sexually assault you?"

"I don't know. I... I guess that's possible."

"You and Detective Bryce are friends? Did you have a disagreement of some kind?"

Clay took control. He said, "I see where you're headed but, no, this is not a domestic dispute."

Allie shook her head. "We were not fighting, if that's what you're getting at."

Rendon asked, "You said your assailant left through the patio door. Can you show us the direction he took off in?"

Allie went out to the patio, followed by the two cops and Clay. She explained where she thought her attacker had gone. "This is the seventeenth hole." She pointed in the direction of the final hole on the course. "I think I heard a golf cart go toward the eighteenth hole, but I'm not totally certain that's how he got away." The shock of the attack was so overwhelming Allie was unable to recall every detail. Clay understood that can happen when someone is traumatized by an assault.

All four looked toward the eighteenth fairway. Headlights flickered some five hundred yards in the distance. "Those headlights, are they on the road leading to the clubhouse?"

Allie said, "Yes. The golfers have to go through a tunnel under the road to get to the eighteenth tee box and then on to the clubhouse."

Clay said, "It's possible the perp had a car parked somewhere nearby to use for his getaway—maybe at the clubhouse or on that road."

"We'll check it out," Woodruff said.

"If you find the cart, secure it so forensics can check it for prints and possibly blood spatter from a bullet wound."

"Right."

Clay gave Woodruff and Rendon his card. "Call me either way."

"Will do. We're going to question the neighbors to see if they saw or heard anything, then we'll see if we can locate the golf cart." The officers left to talk to the neighbor who had called 911.

Clay was concerned about Allie. "Maryland, listen. Someone who attacks a woman like you who lives alone will often return to try again. I don't think you should stay here tonight."

Allie started to object.

Clay continued, "Let me finish, please. Here's another reason for you to stay away—I want to secure your condo to preserve whatever evidence our crime scene guys can uncover. Is there someone else you can stay with tonight?"

Allie thought for a moment. "I'd rather not put anyone else in harm's way."

Clay hesitated for a moment before saying, "Allie, take this at face value, please. You're welcome to stay at my house. No ulterior motive on my part."

"If you're okay with it, then I will. I'll stay with you."

"Good. Go ahead and pack a few things."

Allie threw some clothes and toiletries into an overnight bag. "I'm ready. If you don't mind, I'll drive myself to your house. I'll need to get to work tomorrow and don't want to trouble you to chauffeur me around."

"That's fine. You can park in my garage, out of sight. I don't want this guy to know you're staying with me."

"And, Clay, I'm going to bring my gun with me."

Clay laughed. "Good grief, you don't trust me, do you?"

"Of course I do," Allie said. "It's that I need to be able to protect myself until you find whoever's trying to hurt me."

"Which I'm hoping is sooner rather than later."

"I've never carried my gun before. I've always left it in my bedroom, but I'm going to have it with me from now on. My father was right. When I started living alone after my marriage ended, he insisted I learn how to use a gun so I could protect myself. I think he was thinking my ex might try to hurt me, but Jordan was totally out of my life. He joined the army and, from last I heard, he was stationed in South Korea. Until tonight, I've only fired my gun at a firing range. However, starting this minute, I'm going to make it my new best friend."

"Allie, is it possible Jordan's the person who attacked you tonight?"

"Oh, don't frighten me like that. I hope not, but, yes, I guess it's possible."

* * * * *

Clay was on guard as he escorted Allie to the garage. Suddenly, Allie latched onto his elbow and jerked him to a stop. "What's the matter?" he asked.

"The garage door is open. I closed it, Clay. I know I did. I watched it slam shut before going to my condo. I was talking to you when I closed it."

"I know you did," Clay said. "I heard it close."

"This guy can't be in the garage, can he? It's so small in there, there's no place to hide."

Clay looked around to see if Woodruff and Rendon were still in the complex, but they had left minutes earlier. Clay whispered, "I'm going to check your car. That's the only place he could be. Stand aside. When I say go, use your remote to open the Jeep's cargo door."

Allie pulled out the car keys and waited for Clay's signal. Clay drew his revolver and slowly advanced to the Jeep. Looking back to Allie, he used his fingers to count out one, two, three!"

CHAPTER 47

The cargo door popped open. Clay looked in, saw nothing, then checked under the car. "All clear." He went to the keypad at the side of the garage door. "Who else has the code to open your garage?"

"No one. I've never given it to anyone."

"Where do you keep your garage remote?"

"In my purse."

"Could you have accidentally pushed the button to open the door when you were assaulted?"

Allie considered Clay's question. "Maybe. I was holding my purse when I got into the house. It fell to the floor when he grabbed me, so maybe the remote was activated by the fall."

"I don't know if dropping the remote would open the door, but we can look into that another time. Come on. Let's head out to my place. I'll follow you. Just don't lose me at any traffic light." He walked to his car.

Allie got into her car and started the engine. She put the car in reverse and was half out of the garage when she noticed a sheet of paper on the passenger seat. She honked the horn to get Clay's attention.

He got out of his car and asked, "What's the matter?"

"Here's why the garage door was open." She handed Clay the paper. "Someone left this on the passenger seat. It wasn't here when I pulled into the garage."

Acts 22:15.

Clay said, "Look it up on your cell to see what it says."

"'For you will be a witness for him to everyone of what you have seen and heard,'" Allie said. "What does that mean? A witness? To what?"

"Let's think this through. Whoever left this note thinks you were a witness to something he did."

"Like what?"

"He might be the same person you saw standing at the front door of my house the morning of my hit-and–run. Maybe he thinks you can identify him."

"Clay, I told you, I have no idea who that was. I can't identify him."

"I know that and you know that, but he doesn't," Clay said. "This is the fourth biblical verse left at a crime scene. There's no question they were all left by the same person. We can say for sure that the guy who attacked you tonight is the same person who tried to kill me and the same one who killed John Grainger."

"That's all very scary."

"Come on. Let's head to my house."

Before getting back in his car, Clay looked around for direct visual access to the garage door keypad. He pointed to several parking spots about fifty yards away. They were lined up diagonally from Allie's keypad.

Allie wondered what Clay was doing. "What are you looking at?"

"It's possible someone saw you enter your access code if they watched from that angle—maybe with a pair of binoculars. What's your code?"

"One, two, three, four."

Clay shook his head. "Really? Are you kidding me? That's one of the most common passcodes people use. Half the world probably uses that code. Tell me that's not also the code for your house alarm?"

Allie's sheepish look answered Clay's question.

"We need to change both codes. This guy knows where you live and he's figured out your security codes. You'll be fine at my house tonight but, beginning tomorrow, I think you need to go to a safe house—somewhere you can stay until we nab him."

Allie got her back up. "No! Absolutely not. I'm not going to stay in a safe house. I agreed to spend tonight at your house, but I won't be confined in a safe house. I might as well be in prison."

"Don't look at it that way. It's for your own safety. The guy is bent on killing you. You've got to be smart. We'll arrest him sooner or later, but if you're out in the open, he'll try to get you again."

"Remember, I'm going to be carrying my gun from now on."

"Trust me when I say I'm not thrilled with that."

"Clay, truth be told, that gun is going to help me be safe. I can't expect you to be around every time that crazy SOB comes after me."

CHAPTER 48

Clay set Allie up in his spare bedroom. He checked all the doors and windows, pulled all the shades down, and reassured her. "You're safe here. For double measure lock your door."

"If I'm safe here, why do I have to lock my door?"

"Allie, good grief. Would you just do it? Please? And get some sleep. You've had a tough night. I'm just down the hall."

Allie had changed into silk pajamas and was standing next to the bed. "Thanks for looking out for me, Clay. I'm going to be fine. I promise you I can take care of myself. Just you wait and see." She gave Clay a peck on the lips then closed and locked her door. Exhausted from her ordeal, she found sleep quickly.

Satisfied the house was secure, Clay turned on the TV in his bedroom and kept the volume barely audible so it would not disturb Allie. He placed his service revolver on the night stand. Still in street clothes, Clay propped himself up on his pillows and flipped channels for the next half hour, going from sporting event to sporting event. Sleep was not going to come easy. He could not get Allie off his mind. Her stubborn trait worried him. *Even after being attacked by someone who's hell bent on eliminating her as a witness, she doesn't seem to understand the danger she's in. The guy is relentless. If I can't get her to agree to go to a safe house, I've got to get her to stay here.*

Clay's thoughts turned to how sexually attractive he found her. He was frustrated by her reluctance to be intimate but he vowed to be patient and understanding. *She's not ready. I need to calm down. She'll let me know when she's ready.*

Click.

The sound of a latch opening caught Clay's attention. He turned off the TV, reached for his revolver, and inched to the door, listening for sounds. He opened the door a crack. The display from a digital clock in the living room cast a faint light. Clay waited for his eyes to acclimate to the darkness then stepped out of the bedroom and edged a few steps toward the foyer. He heard a shuffling sound behind him. He spun around, dropped to one knee, and aimed his revolver in the direction of the sound. The light from the clock reflected off something shiny, metallic.

A drawn pistol.

"Drop it," Clay shouted.

"It's me."

"Jesus, Mary, and Joseph! What are you doing up?"

"Oh, Clay, you scared the heck out of me."

He turned on a lamp. "I could have shot you."

"I thought I heard someone outside my window and I was coming to wake you."

"What did you hear?"

"I don't know. It was... I don't know... a noise. I can't describe it. It was like rustling outside."

"Could it have been the wind, or maybe you were dreaming?"

"I don't think I was dreaming. But, I... I guess that's what it could have been. Just a dream." Allie shook her head. "I'm a mess, aren't I? I'm so sorry to wake you."

"It's okay. I wasn't asleep anyway. I'll check outside. You stay right here. Keep your gun handy. I'll give you fair warning when I come back in."

Clay turned on the outside floods and circled the house with his gun drawn. He saw no one or anything suspicious and went back inside. "It's me, Maryland. We're okay. No one's about."

278

"Thank you for checking."

"Now, come on. Let's get you back to bed." Clay put his arm around her waist to walk her back to her bedroom and said, "I'm going to sleep out here on the couch tonight, just to play it safe."

"But—"

"No buts. Go back to bed. Lock the door behind you. But, let me hold onto your pistol. I'll give it back to you in the morning."

Allie handed her gun to Clay for safekeeping.

Clay set both his revolver and Allie's pistol on the coffee table, and lay down on the couch. With his senses heightened by the encounter with Allie and the image of her in her pajamas, he was unable to sleep. Thirty minutes later, he heard the door to her bedroom open again. Light from the lamp on her nightstand filtered into the living room, enough for Clay to see Allie walk slowly toward him. He feigned sleep to see what she was up to.

She stood over Clay and touched his sleeve. "Clay, are you awake?"

"Yes. What's the matter? Are you still scared?"

"I want to ask if you'll stay with me tonight."

"Of course. I'm not going to leave."

"I don't mean that."

"What do you mean?"

"I mean, will you... will you...?" She could not ask what she had been practicing to say for so long. "I know what I want to tell you when we're apart, but then I don't have the courage to say it when we're together."

"Try."

"Maybe I'll just show you instead." She sat alongside Clay on the couch and gave him a long, open-mouthed kiss, then reached for his hand and moved it to her breast.

Clay could not believe what was happening. He had hoped they would become intimate, but was surprised it was happening now, out of the clear blue—without warning or expectation. How far was she was going to go?

The answer was clear. In the dim light, Allie stood up and slowly removed her pajama top and dropped it to the floor with a shy smile. She wiggled her bottoms to the floor then kicked them away. Clay sat up, gaping at this beautiful woman standing naked in front of him stunned at what was happening. Allie held his hand and coaxed him off the couch. When he stood, she purred in delight as he smothered her lips, cheeks, and neck with kisses.

Allie pulled away just enough to unbuckle Clay's belt and help him remove his trousers. She reached down to his arousal. "Oh, my God," she said.

Clay picked her up, cradled her in his powerful arms, and took her into the bedroom. He set her down gently on the bed and stood over her, kissing her breasts, and every sensuous part of her body. He lay down alongside her and watched her as she stroked and kissed him in turn.

When they were at the height of their desire, Allie rolled on top of Clay and let him penetrate her. They moved in unison and climaxed together in bursts of intense ecstasy. It had been a long time for both of them.

* * * * *

Clay woke early the next morning. The smile Allie wore as she slept made him smile too. Dressed in nothing but his boxers, he went to the kitchen, made a pot of coffee, poured a cup for Allie, and went back to the bedroom. He stirred her gently to awaken her. "Hey, pretty girl, time to wake up."

Allie was still smiling when she opened her eyes and saw Clay standing over her, She sat up, unashamedly naked, and happily accepted his early morning offering. "Good morning. How sweet of you," she said.

She set her cup down, wrapped her hands around the back of Clay's neck, and pulled him onto the bed. "This is my thank you." They kissed and fondled each other until their passion exploded again.

Afterwards, they lay in bed, looking at the ceiling, breathing hard. "Whoa," Clay said. "And to think I was unsure if we were ever going to have sex."

Allie said. "One thing for sure, you've opened up the floodgates for me."

"That's good news. Happy to be of help," Clay said with a broad grin. "Now, I hate to say this, especially with your floodgates open, but we need to talk. Reality is around the corner for both of us."

Allie groaned at the thought.

"You know, I'm really sorry you've been dragged into this mess because of me."

"It's not your fault, Clay. I look at the positive side. Last night would never have happened if you hadn't suffered a hit-and-run." She stroked his chest.

"Will you do me a favor, Allie?"

"Yes, of course. Anything."

"Stay here another night? It will give me a chance to talk to Captain Ellsworth to come up with a plan to protect you. You'll be safe here."

"Is that the only reason you want me to stay?"

"No! I can think of at least one, no, make it three more reasons."

"Three? Then the answer is yes."

* * * * *

Allie called her manager and explained she needed the day off for personal reasons.

On his way out the door, Clay reminded her, "Please, don't leave the house. And don't answer the door or tell anyone you're here."

"I won't. I promise." She kissed him goodbye and, before closing the door behind him, asked, "Since I'm housebound today, why don't you come back for lunch? I have a delicious dessert in mind."

"I'll try, but in case I can't, keep that dessert on hold for tonight."

CHAPTER 49

At police headquarters Clay asked Captain Ellsworth for five minutes of his time.

Ellsworth pointed with his pen to a chair for Clay to sit. "What's up?"

"Do you remember me telling you about the paramedic who treated me after the hit-and-run? Allie Marland."

"Yes. What about her?"

"We've been dating."

"Well, good for you, but you don't have to go into your dating life with me. It's none of my business what you do outside of work."

"I know that. I never thought I needed to tell you, except I think the person who killed John Grainger and who tried to kill both Hank and me is now after her, too."

"Go on." Ellsworth twirled his forefinger in a circle, a sign to Clay to get to the point.

"Allie was assaulted last night in her condo."

"By who?"

"I don't know. However, I do believe the person who attacked her might think she can identify him as the person who tried to run me over. Remember, she saw someone outside my house the morning I got hit."

"You told me she couldn't identify him."

"She says she can't."

"Tell me about the assault. What, exactly, happened?"

"She and I had plans for dinner at her house—a condo north of the city. It's on a golf course, on the ground floor, easy to break into. And that's exactly what happened. When I got there, she didn't answer my knock. A few seconds later I heard a struggle and then a gunshot. By the time she opened the door to let me in, the perp was gone. He escaped when he heard me trying to break down the door, so I never saw him."

"Who fired the gun?"

"Allie. She shot at him when he was fleeing in a golf cart he had parked outside her condo."

"Did she hit him?"

Clay shook his head. "She doesn't know. I've checked with every hospital and none of them treated anyone with a gunshot wound last evening."

"Can she identify the perp?"

"No. He was wearing a ski mask."

"Were you able to locate the golf cart he used to get away?"

"I asked two uniforms to look for it, but they didn't find it. It probably got garaged with the other carts at the clubhouse."

"Could the attack have been a sexual assault?"

"It wasn't. I'm sure of that."

Captain Ellsworth raised an eyebrow. "How can you be so sure?"

"Afterward, she found a biblical message in her car similar to the others we've found."

"Another? What did this one say?"

"Here." Clay held up an evidence bag that held the note. "I have to get it to Dan to check for prints."

Ellsworth read the note. "Acts 22:15. What does that mean?"

Clay pulled out his cellphone and read. "For you will be a witness for him to everyone of what you have seen and heard."

Ellsworth said, "Sounds as though the intent is to make it clear he believes your girlfriend witnessed your hit-and-run."

"I agree," said Clay.

"She obviously needs protection. Where is she now?"

"At my house. She stayed last night and has agreed to stay again tonight. I'm okay with that but I'd really like to see her in a safe house under twenty-four-seven protection until we solve this."

"Well, go ahead and arrange it."

"She won't go to one."

Ellsworth leaned forward in his chair. "Why not?"

"She said she might as well be in prison if she has to be confined to a safe house. She wants to get on with her life. She's right, in a way. We're not close to solving these crimes. I can't know how long she would have to be holed up."

Ellsworth grew suspicious. "Clay, your girlfriend is in jeopardy, pursued by someone who wants to kill her, yet she doesn't want to take the simplest precaution of staying someplace where she can be protected. Don't you find that strange?"

"I agree. She's headstrong, to say the least."

Ellsworth fidgeted with his pen, clicking and unclicking it. "Let me get this straight. She said she was attacked by someone last night, but she can't tell you anything about her attacker. She somehow got free, got her gun, and then shot at him as he escaped in a golf cart, but she's not sure if she hit him. The getaway cart is nowhere to be found. And, to top things off, you never saw this phantom assailant either." Ellsworth leaned back in his chair. "Do you see where I'm heading with this?"

"Yes, sir. You think Allie is fabricating the attack."

"The thought hasn't occurred to you? And what about the note referencing Scripture? Might she have written the note herself to get you off track?"

Clay shook his head. "No, I believe her," he said. "I can't answer what happened to the cart or how the perp got away, but I don't doubt her story. Not one bit. Other things have happened to her which probably involved the same man who attacked her last night. There's no reason why she'd lie."

"What else has happened?"

"Someone ran her off the road while she was driving. That was the worst incident. She was lucky to survive that crash."

Ellsworth asked, "I assume she was unable to identify the driver who ran her off the road."

"She was not."

"You see? It's the same pattern. I'm not accusing her. I'm simply asking if it's possible she's making all this up. She's never able to identify her assailant and there's never a witness to back up her story."

Clay turned defensive. He did not like that Ellsworth was accusing Allie of a sham assault. "Captain, she's not making this up. There's no question the assailant believes she can identify him. Unfortunately for her, she's now linked to me."

"Let's say you're right. How do we divert his attention away from her? We can't have a uniform follow her around twenty-four seven. And, unless she agrees to it, we can't insist she remain at your house or go to a safe house."

"I've been thinking about this," said Clay. "What if you contact the *Times Journal* reporter who writes the Police Blotter and ask him to write a follow-up about the hit-and-run, that we're at a dead end in our investigation and we have no witness or credible evidence to charge anyone?"

"What then?"

"Maybe Allie's stalker reads the column, realizes she's not a threat, and stops pursuing her."

"How will you know if he reads the column?"

"Time will tell."

"You know, Clay, retirement is fast closing in on me. I have less than a year to go. After all my years in this business, I'm sad to say I've become suspicious about everything and everyone. I've learned to distrust the obvious, your girlfriend included. Hell, if my mother were alive, I probably wouldn't trust her. Here's my word of advice to you. If your Miss Marland is going to stay at your house, I suggest you sleep with one eye open."

CHAPTER 50

Clay returned home late that afternoon and was greeted by the aroma of sautéed garlic and herbs wafting throughout the house.

"What smells so good?"

"We're having pasta. I made spaghetti sauce with the cans of diced tomatoes and herbs I found in your pantry."

"Can't wait. My mouth is watering."

"Before we eat, I need to tell you what I've decided to do. I thought about it all day. Come with me." Allie took Clay's hand and walked him into the kitchen. The table was set and a bottle of red wine was uncorked. She filled two glasses and handed one to Clay, then cleared her throat. "Don't be mad at me, but I've decided to leave tomorrow morning. You must know how much I love being with you. Last night was wonderful. But I need to get back to my job and my home. I can't stay hidden here forever. We both have to get on with our lives."

"I understand how you feel about wanting to get back to a normal life, and I agree. But I have a plan too."

"I know what you're going to say."

"Well, please listen anyway. My captain has arranged to have the *Times Journal* run a blurb in the Police Blotter column saying that the investigation into my hit-and-run is at a standstill. It'll say we have no witnesses and the case has turned cold. We're hoping that whoever has been assaulting you will read the column and believe he is in the clear."

"Are you thinking that, if he reads the column and believes the investigation has stopped, he'll stop attacking me?"

"Yes."

Allie did not respond immediately. She took a sip of wine and shook her head. "That is such a longshot."

"I know it is. But it's worth a try. It just means you spend one more night here with me. Is that so bad?"

She smiled. "You are such a smooth talker." She paused for a few seconds. "Okay, I'll do it. I'll stay another night and go back to work the day after tomorrow."

* * * * *

The following morning, Clay retrieved the *Times Journal* from his driveway.

Police Blotter

Police at Dead End – Captain Matthew Ellsworth of the Santa Fe Criminal Investigations Division gave the Police Blotter an update on the June 28 hit-and-run attack on Detective Clay Bryce. Ellsworth reported that the vehicle used in the assault against Detective Bryce has not been identified nor has any evidence been uncovered that could lead police to the culprit. The captain of detectives went on to say, "Frankly, we are at a dead end. We have no witnesses or any indication why the assault occurred. As a result, we have put the investigation on hold. Fortunately, Detective Bryce is fully recovered from his injuries and back on active duty."

* * * * *

Allie read the article and wasn't convinced. "I don't understand how we'll know if this works."

"I knew you'd be skeptical. Frankly, you're right. We won't know if it works until we arrest the guy who's been assaulting you."

"What other options do I have?"

"How about this? Go back to work starting tomorrow. At the end of your shift, you come back here to spend nights until we find your assailant."

Allie nodded, then smiled. "Spend nights here? I like it. I like that plan. I'll do it, but on one condition."

"What?"

"I'll do it if you agree not to worry about me."

"Of course, I'm going to worry about you."

"Clay, I'll be careful—extra careful. And I'll keep my gun handy at all times. Take me out to the range to see for yourself that I can handle it."

Clay shook his head at Allie's boldness. "I'm keeping my fingers crossed you won't need to fire your gun for any reason."

Before leaving for work the next morning, Clay advised Allie, "Please, play it safe again today. I'll be home as soon as I can tonight."

CHAPTER 51

Clay phoned Allie at seven that evening. "I'm running late. I'll be there in ten minutes. Anything I can pick up on my way? Take-out for dinner?"

"No, I'm cooking for us tonight. Since you were delayed, I went to the grocery store to pick up some groceries. I'm heading home now."

"What? You went to the grocery store? I asked you to stay in the house until I got home."

"I know, but I was going to make us dinner and there's nothing in your house."

Clay fumed. "Dammit, Allie."

"Don't worry. I'm almost back home. I'm being careful."

"You know you're going to drive me crazy? Are your car doors locked? Can you tell if anyone's following you?"

Allie checked the rearview mirror. "I don't see anyone. Don't worry. Nothing's going to happen. I should never have told you I went out. Besides, my gun's right next to me." She patted her purse.

"When you get to the house, pull your car into the garage, then lock yourself inside until I get there."

"Okay, don't worry. I'm fine. See you in a few," she said.

Clay turned on his flashers and raced the rest of the way home, mumbling to himself, "I don't know what I'm going to do with her."

Allie ignored Clay's order to park in the garage and instead parked in the driveway. Unable to take all the grocery bags into the house in one trip, she left the remaining bags in the Jeep with the cargo door open. A minute later, Clay arrived and pulled in behind Allie's car. *I told her to pull into the garage.* He glanced at the house and noticed the front door was wide open. He immediately thought the worst and darted into the house. "Hey, Maryland, for crying out loud, you left your car in the driveway and the front door is wide open. I don't think you're taking this serious—"

A bearded man wearing jeans and a New York Yankees baseball cap slammed the door shut behind Clay. Allie came out of the kitchen. "What was that?"

The man waved his pistol at her. "Nice to see you again, Ms. Marland."

Clay reached for his holstered service revolver.

"The man fired his pistol over Clay's head. I wouldn't if I were you, Detective. Take your hand away from your gun. Leave it holstered." His disguised voice sounded like Marlon Brando's in *The Godfather.*

"Now, remove your revolver from your holster. Use your thumb and forefinger. Two fingers only, please. If you use any other finger to extract the revolver I'll have to shoot your girlfriend."

Clay removed his revolver.

The man said, "Now, put the gun on the floor and slide it over to me with your foot."

Clay slid the revolver toward the man.

"Now, Detective Bryce, remove your cell phone from your pocket and slide it to me."

Clay complied.

"Good. Now Miss Marland where is your phone?"

"In the kitchen. In my purse."

"If you're lying, I promise you it will be the last time you ever lie to me. I don't like liars."

Allie snapped back, "I told you it's in the kitchen. Do you want me to get it?"

"Don't be a wiseass. No, I don't want you to get it. Stay there and be quiet."

The man kicked Clay's phone and revolver to the wall then waved his pistol. "Both of you, in the living room. Now!"

CHAPTER 52

"I'm so sorry, Clay. You were right. He must have found out I was here and followed me from the grocery store."

"Shut up."

Allie asked, "Are you the one who attacked me in my condo? And forced me off the road while I was driving? I have the right to know."

"The right to know? That's funny. Yes, that was me."

Allie shook her head, "Why have you been trying to hurt me?"

"It's simple. You saw me when I exited Detective Bryce's house the morning of his accident. I've been concerned you would run into me one day and identify me to the police."

"Where in the world would I run into you?"

"At the pool, golf course, community center. Who knows! You and I might meet again and I don't want you to suddenly realize I was the person you saw that morning. You might recognize the way I walked, or my build, or something."

"What are you talking about?"

"I live in the same development as you—on Camino de Brisa."

"You have got to be kidding me."

"I'm not. That golf cart I was in when you shot at me the other night?"

"What about it?"

"It's mine. I own it. Ha!"

Clay recognized the high-pitched laugh that burst from deep in the man's throat.

"The cart's in my garage, not at the clubhouse, where I'm sure the police looked for it. Oh, and for your information, when you shot at me, I think you may have killed a coyote. Ha!" He laughed his irritating laugh again.

Allie said, "I would never have been able to identify you. It was too dark that morning. You were only a silhouette."

The man raised his gun and aimed it at Allie's chest. "Remember what I said about lying. Are you telling me the truth?"

"I swear on a stack of Bibles."

Clay interceded. "If she could identify you, don't you think we would have arrested you by now?"

"Well, if she's telling the truth, that's too bad. Then all of this will have been to no avail. It doesn't make any difference now. I can't take any chances."

"She told you she's telling the truth. Let her go."

The man's laugh told Clay he had no intention of letting Allie go.

"I read an update about the hit-and-run in this morning's paper. It said you didn't have a witness."

"That update was written specifically for you to read."

The man stood nodding his head. "It gave me pause, I have to admit. But I couldn't take the chance that the article was only a ploy to get me to stop pursuing Miss Marland."

"Who are you, anyway?" Allie asked.

"Detective Bryce knows who I am, don't you, Detective? I can tell by how you're studying me."

CHAPTER 53

Allie turned to Clay and asked, "Who is he?"

"Simon Learner."

Simon dropped his disguised voice. "How did you know?"

"Your laugh. You laughed like that when you told me how you hoodwinked Hayden Arrington at the Bend."

Allie was confused. "What does he have to do with the Bend?"

"Simon works there. He used to work for John Grainger, the man he killed in that fire. Right, Simon? You killed John Grainger?"

Simon hesitated. He raised his eyes to the ceiling as though in thought. "Do I tell the truth about John? Let me think. Yes or no? Dead men can't serve as witnesses, right? So, the answer is, yes, I killed him."

"Why? Because he was going to take your job away from you?"

"Heck, no."

"Then, why?"

"Because he was the lowest creature in the food chain—a pompous, lying, cheating, lowlife."

"That he was. But that doesn't explain why you killed him."

Simon looked away and grimaced. Clay thought he was trying to keep from crying. "You want to know why?"

"I do."

"Because he was having an affair with my wife."

"You told me that happened before you and Liza got married."

"I didn't tell you everything. No, the sonofabitch was sleeping with Liza even afterward."

"I'm sorry."

"It's worse than that."

"How so?"

"It took me a while, but I finally realized our daughter wasn't mine. You know, I always thought she resembled John."

"Are you saying John's the father of your daughter?"

"That's right. He got Liza pregnant, not me."

"How did you find out about them?"

"I followed her one day after we were married and she went straight to his house. Not only that day, but two and three times a week, for weeks on end. I was devastated. I wanted to kill him. And her, too. How could she have an affair with that snake? I didn't know what to do about it. And then she told me she was pregnant and when the baby was born I pretended to be happy. But I knew, I just knew the baby was John's."

"Why did you try to kill me—and Hank Kincaid? What did we have to do with John getting Liza pregnant?"

"As much as I wanted to kill John, I couldn't drum up the nerve to actually go through with it. I knew he held a grudge against you and the ADA, so I came up with a plan to make it look like John tried to kill both of you."

Clay asked, "What was your plan?"

"I have a white Range Rover identical to John's. I realized all I needed to do was put John's license plate on my car and I'd go out and make it look like I was trying to run you both over. You'd think it was John behind the wheel and place the blame on him. He'd be arrested for attempted murder, and bang, he'd end up in prison."

Clay said, "Let me guess how everything went down. You needed access to John's garage to get his license plate. To do that, you impersonated John at the psychiatric hospital and got

Hope Archer to tell you where the spare key was to get into John's house. How am I doing so far?"

"Very good. That's why you're the detective. And poor Hope. She was so sedated I could've gone in wearing a top hat and told her I was Abraham Lincoln and she would have believed me. Ha!"

"That doesn't explain why you wanted to kill me," Clay said.

"Like I said, my plan was to only bump you, hurt you a little."

"You put on a good act, because your *bump* damn near killed me."

"Yeah, my fault. When I got close, you crossed over then jumped right in front of me. I actually hesitated after I hit you. I know this sounds strange, but for a second I thought about stopping to help you."

Clay was incredulous. "So, instead, you left me on the street to die?"

"Oh, don't get melodramatic. You survived, didn't you? All I wanted was for you to read the license plate, identify John's car as the one that hit you, and arrest John for attempted murder. But, no. Obviously neither you nor Mr. Kincaid were smart enough to read the plate number."

"It *was* a little hard to read the license when you hit me so hard I went flying through the air."

"It was your fault, not mine. You ran right in front of me."

"What about the biblical verse on my mirror?"

"Yes. It was obvious later that you survived, but I had to be sure you read the license plate number. If you didn't, then the whole thing would have been simply a hit-and-run, nothing more, nothing less. To have you think it was John who ran you over, I left that biblical about revenge on your mirror."

Clay said, "It was a good plan but it didn't work."

"I've got to tell you, I was terribly disappointed that, between you and Mr. Kincaid, you couldn't come up with the evidence needed to charge John with attempted murder. I couldn't have made it any easier."

"So you went to plan B. You killed John."

Simon waved his pistol in the air. "Yes. All I could think about morning, noon, and night was getting even with that bastard. I was obsessed. It was driving me crazy. I wanted to extract revenge."

"You do realize revenge is not justice."

"But revenge is what I wanted."

"Tell me about the fire that killed John."

"I researched the internet and learned that using a candle to start a fire is a brilliant way to commit arson. It gave me plenty of time to establish my alibi. I first got into John's garage, then sneaked into the kitchen. When he walked in, I hit him across the back of his head with a hammer. I carried him to his bedroom, set up the candle that would eventually start the fire, and returned to the Bend to establish my alibi. Voila. That was it."

"You know what I don't get, Simon?"

"No. What?"

"Leaving biblical verses behind after every crime. Logic would dictate that the person who left those messages was religious. Obviously, religion has nothing to do with any of it."

"You're right. I'm not at all religious. You'd be amazed the stuff you can find on the internet. Pretty cool, heh? An eye for an eye—that kind of thing."

"Eye for an eye? I assume you've heard of the commandment that says thou shalt not kill?" Clay said.

"Of course. However, that commandment is superseded by the one that says thou shalt not covet thy neighbor's wife. As I've said, I didn't want to kill him. I didn't want to kill anyone. He forced me to do it all."

"And now you're bent on murdering Allie and me?"

"Yep. Sometimes you do what you have to do."

"You're big on revenge, aren't you?"

Simon sat on a nearby chair and rested his pistol on his knee. He kept his gun aimed at Clay. A wide smile indicated he was pleased about something.

"What are you smirking about?"

"Smirking? Is that what I'm doing? Yeah, I guess I am. I'm thinking how I manipulated the great Hayden Arrington so I could retain my job at the Bend."

"You manipulated him. How?"

"He isn't as great a negotiator as he thinks he is. I plotted that whole charade about turning down his offer to stay on at the Bend. I knew he had no choice after John was killed. He had to keep me on. It would've taken him forever to find someone else to run the place. I also figured he was going to sweeten the pot to get me to stay. I told him my wife and I were going to talk about it and I'd tell him afterward if I would accept his offer. Of course, I wasn't going to talk to Liza about anything. That was just a bluff. Pretty smart, huh?"

"Yeah, it was. You put one over on him. Speaking of Liza, what are you going to do about her?" Clay wanted to keep him talking.

"I don't know. I want to forgive her, but I can't get past the fact that our daughter is John's daughter, not mine. I do love Liza, you know. I just don't know what to do. What do you think I should do?"

"If you kill her, you'll become an immediate suspect. Either forgive her or get a divorce."

"Yeah, maybe I'll divorce her."

Clay nodded toward Allie. "Simon, why not let Allie go? If you let her go, I'll help you navigate through all this. I've been divorced. I could advise you."

Simon said, "Ha! As tempting as that is, you must know I can't do that. Besides, your Miss Marland is the one who caused me all this angst in the first place. Nope. Can't do it." He stood and aimed his pistol at Clay. "I'm sorry. I really am. However, thanks. I feel so much better talking it out to you."

"If that's true, why kill us? You could probably beat the rap for killing John. A jury would be sympathetic. If not, the most I see you serving is three to five years."

"Ha!"

CHAPTER 54

Clay recognized it was now or never to attack Simon. Even if he was not able to overwhelm him quickly, Allie might have an opportunity to escape. It was time to risk it. He needed only the slightest diversion. As Clay was about to strike there was a loud knock on the front door. "Detective Bryce, are you in there?"

Simon jumped out of his chair. "Who's that?"

"Probably my neighbor. He's always asking to borrow a tool or something."

Simon waved his pistol at Clay and Allie to move to the middle of the living room where he could keep an eye on them as he peeked out the front window. Two uniformed cops stood at the door talking to each other. Simon saw one cop motion for the other to go to the back of the house.

Simon murmured, "Sonofabitch. It's not your neighbor. It's a couple of cops. I should kill you right now."

"What are you talking about?"

"The flashers on your car are still on."

Clay's neighbor, Alan Strickland, noticed the flashers had been on for a while and got concerned something was wrong. He called 911. The two cops who stood outside had been dispatched to the house.

"I must have forgotten to turn them off when I pulled in. I rushed into the house thinking something had happened to Allie. Someone must've reported it to the police."

"You did that on purpose, didn't you?"

"No, it was unintentional. How would I have known you'd be holding us hostage?"

The cop who had circled around back pounded on the kitchen door. "Detective Bryce! It's the police!"

Simon motioned to Allie. "Come here. Quick!" Allie strode cautiously to Simon. "I said *quick.*" Simon grabbed her left elbow and bent it behind her in a hammerlock.

"You're hurting me," Allie said.

"Not as much as you're going to hurt if you don't listen to me. Understand?"

"Yes."

Clay saw Simon's agitation grow to near panic, his eyes flitting to the front and back doors and his voice trembling. "Simon what are you going to do with her? Why not give it up? The cops aren't going to go away."

"Keep quiet. If they come in here, you're both dead. And she goes first."

"Let me answer the door and tell them I'm okay. I'll tell them I left the flashers on by accident."

Simon shouted, "Shut up! Stay where you are."

The cop in the back was now looking in a side window and saw Simon with his gun aimed at Clay and Allie. He ran low to the ground around to the front and told his partner what was happening inside the house. They called for backup.

Clay said, "You can't get away, Simon. Let her go. They'll have a swat team here in minutes."

"I said shut up!"

Allie caught Clay's eyes and looked down at her right shoulder. Clay understood her intentions immediately and nodded once.

Allie yelled, "Now!" She bent forward, letting her left arm go straight, then twisted her left shoulder to the right in one swift karate move. It freed her arm from Simon's hold. She elbowed him high on his cheekbone then dropped to the floor. Simon's hand flew to his face. "Why, you bitch..." He reached down and tried to pull her back but Allie knocked his hand away. She crawled and rolled away.

Clay barreled into Simon and grabbed his wrist to divert his aim, but Simon was surprisingly strong and held onto his pistol. The two men struggled for control of the pistol, bouncing into furniture across the room. Finally, Clay lifted him up and slammed him to the living room floor. But Simon continued holding the pistol, his finger still on the trigger. Clay slammed Simon's wrist against the floor trying to force him to release his hold, but the gun went off, the bullet nearly striking Allie.

Allie crawled to the coffee table and grabbed her gun. She stood over the two men and aimed it at Simon, but could not get a clear shot. "I'm going to shoot," she shouted. "I'm going to shoot."

Simon continued to struggle but his grip on his pistol eased with Allie's threat.

Clay yanked the pistol away, flipped Simon onto his stomach and, jammed his knee into the middle of his back.

Allie shouted, "Should I shoot him?"

"Yes! Shoot me. Please. I have nothing to live for." Simon sobbed.

"Shoot me, please." He begged.

Clay looked up at Allie. Her face was contorted in anger at this man who had caused her so much anguish. Clay shook his head. "Allie, no. Put the gun down. It's all over."

* * * * *

A week after Simon's arrest, Clay was back working his usual caseload and Allie was back home, well settled into her new work schedule.

CHAPTER 55

The doorbell at the Arrington mansion sounded. Two seconds later it sounded again. Then again.

11 p.m.

Arianna was still awake. *Who the hell could that be this late at night? Probably Hayden back from Phoenix. I didn't expect him back until tomorrow. Anton must have dropped him off. I'm surprised he didn't call me. Oh, God, I hope he's not expecting to have sex tonight.*

She took her time getting to the front door. The doorbell sounded a fourth time. "Hold your horses, Hayden." She knew she would have to put on a show of affection for him, but she would not go overboard. She opened the door. It was not Hayden. She quickly tried to slam the door shut. Too late. Her visitor shoved her aside, brandishing a pistol.

"What do you want?" she said.

"Well, hello to you too."

"Hayden's upstairs. He's coming right down with his gun."

"I don't think so."

"What do you want?"

The visitor grinned, "I came to ask for a loan. Lord knows you don't have to worry about money, so I came to ask you to share some of your wealth."

"Are you serious? You're here for a loan?"

"Duh, no."

"Then what do you want?"

"I'm not sure yet. What about that engagement ring you're wearing? Give it to me."

"No."

"Pretty please. Do it or I'll shoot it off."

"No. I'm not taking it off."

"You know, you're a pain in the ass. Don't give me a reason to shoot you. Now give me your ring, bitch."

Arianna realized she had no choice. She squeezed the ring off and handed it over.

"Nice. It almost blinds me looking at it. How many carats? Like a hundred, I bet. I remember reading in the newspaper when you got married that the engagement ring was one of the biggest diamonds ever. You won't miss it, will you? Your husband will just get you another one, I'm sure."

"You're right. He will. You can have it."

"Thanks for your generosity."

"You got what you wanted, so why don't you leave?"

"Nope, not quite yet. Take me to your safe."

"What safe?"

"Your house safe."

"We don't have one."

"I know you do. All rich people have a safe in their house. That's where they keep all their jewels and loose change. So don't tell me you don't have a safe."

"You're right. There is a safe, but I don't know the combination."

"That's B.S." The intruder fired a shot over Arianna's head. She instinctively ducked. "If I aim lower will you remember it?"

Arianna did not answer.

"I thought so. Your silence speaks volumes. Start walking."

Arianna led her visitor up the staircase to the master bedroom.

"Get a move on. I don't want to be here all night."

Arianna removed a Salvador Dalí painting from the wall above a chaise lounge to expose a wall safe."

"Open it."

She did.

The intruder tossed a black plastic bag at Arianna. "Now, empty everything into the bag."

Arianna complied and handed over the bag.

"Let's go back downstairs," the visitor said, then followed Arianna into the living room.

"Tell me something. Truly, honestly, don't lie to me. What do you see in your husband? He isn't a looker, that's for sure. So what is it? His wealth, right? Power? What else could it be? It's certainly not his personality. Has it been worth it? Sleeping with him can't be fun. Are you happy giving up your body to satisfy his lust?"

"Yes, he's given me everything I've ever wanted. I love him."

"Yeah, you love him all right."

"Why don't you take what I've given you and leave? Hayden will be back from his business trip soon."

"I'll leave in just a moment. First, I'm going to do what I came here to do. The clock is ticking."

"What else do you have to do?"

"Tell you goodbye, whore."

The visitor fired one solitary shot into the center of Arianna's chest.

CHAPTER 56

Clay was in his car when a police dispatch report came across his radio. "Code 246, gunshot victim, 2019 Coyote Ridge. Any unit in five or less."

Clay said out loud, "That's the Arrington's address." He radioed the dispatcher, "I'm five minutes."

Captain Ellsworth called seconds after Clay heard the dispatch. "Arianna Arrington has been murdered. She was shot to death in her house."

"Holy mother of God. You can't be serious. I got the 246. I'm heading there now. What happened? What can you tell me?"

"I don't know much, Clay. She was found this morning by her maid. Robles is out there now. I'm going to assign him the case."

"No, Captain. Let me have it. Her murder has got to be related to John Grainger's."

Ellsworth thought for a moment. "Okay, have Tomás assist. I'll get forensics and the ME out there on the double. Keep me informed."

In spite of Clay's contempt for Arianna, he was saddened by her death. *What a beautiful, yet wretched, woman. She had everything, but everything wasn't enough.* As Clay raced through Santa Fe to the Arrington home, he conjectured what may have led to her murder. Was it her husband who found out about her affairs and killed her in a fit of passion? Was it a burglary gone bad? A sexual assault?

* * * * *

Allie was in the kitchen sipping coffee and watching the KOB 4 morning show. The meteorologist was reciting the day's forecast when a Breaking News banner scrolled across the bottom of the screen.

News anchor Lauren Ashleigh appeared on camera and interrupted the weather report. "Breaking news just in. Arianna Arrington, wife of Santa Fe billionaire entrepreneur, Hayden Arrington, has been found murdered in the Arrington's Coyote Ridge mansion. Our reporter Jim Cortez is on the scene. What can you tell us, Jim?"

The beat reporter appeared on a split screen with Ashleigh. "Lauren, shocking news this morning. Police have confirmed the death of Hayden Arrington's wife, Arianna Arrington. If the camera will zoom in behind me, you can see significant police activity with multiple official vehicles entering and exiting the long, gated driveway. We're not allowed access beyond this point. As you know, Hayden Arrington is the prominent Santa Fe entrepreneur, philanthropist, and political power broker."

Ashleigh said, "Tragic death. Fill us in on what else you've been told."

"Understandably, details of the crime are being closely guarded at this time," Cortez said. "There's not a whole lot to report. The police are not telling us much at all."

"When do you expect to learn more?"

"We've been informed there will be a news briefing this afternoon."

Ashleigh asked, "Do you know, Jim, if Mr. Arrington was present when his wife was killed?"

The reporter answered, "From what I understand, Mr. Arrington was in Phoenix last night. Upon learning of his wife's murder, he flew back immediately. In fact, our camera caught a glimpse of him in the back seat of his Rolls-Royce as he was being chauffeured up the driveway to his home."

* * * * *

Clay showed his badge to the cop on duty at the front door of the Arrington home, then walked into the living room. Detective Robles was standing over Arianna's body, which was face down on the floor in a pool of dried blood, her left arm tucked awkwardly under her body.

Clay said, "Hello, Tomás. Fill me in."

"Nothing much to go on yet. I made a quick pass through the house as soon as I got here and didn't find any sign of a break-in. However, there was a wall safe open in the master bedroom and it looked like it had been emptied."

"A burglary?"

"Could be."

"Any signs of a struggle?"

"No, nothing."

The sound of a woman crying came from another room. "Who's that?"

"The maid, Imelda Gomez. She's in the kitchen. She's the one who found Mrs. Arrington dead when she came to work this morning."

"Where's Mr. Arrington?"

"In his den. He was in Phoenix on business overnight. He flew back this morning and was picked up at the airport by his bodyguard."

"How's he doing?"

"He's not showing any emotion. He's almost catatonic. Stares straight ahead into space. I think he's in shock. Mumbles 'Shoulda been here,' over and over."

"I'll talk to him in a bit."

Carton and Cook arrived and received a similar briefing from Robles. The forensics team immediately began the arduous task of collecting evidence, dusting for fingerprints, photographing the body and every square foot of the room, and collecting evidence impressions outside the house at every window and door.

Next to arrive was ME Safford. He acknowledged Clay and Robles and put on gloves. He knelt alongside Arianna, gently grasped her shoulder, then turned her partially over.

Clay asked, "When do you think she was killed?"

"I'd say, based on rigor mortis and lividity, roughly twelve hours ago."

"That would make it about 11:30 last night. The cause?"

"Appears to be from a single shot to her chest, but I won't know for certain if that's what actually killed her until I autopsy the body."

Clay crouched near Arianna's body. He looked to Robles. "Did you notice when Aaron turned her over, she wasn't wearing any rings?"

"I did," Tomás said. "That, along with the empty bedroom safe, points to a burglary—or made to look like one."

Clay said, "Let's talk to the maid first. I've met her before. She doesn't speak much English, so you may have to interpret for me."

In the kitchen, Imelda was sitting at the table, her eyes red and swollen. When she saw the two detectives, a new tide of tears cascaded down her cheeks. Clay said, "Imelda, I'm very sorry about this. Tell me what you found when you arrived here this morning."

Imelda responded in Spanish. "I came to work at nine. I saw la Señora Arrington on the floor and the blood. There was a lot of blood. I didn't know what to do. I called Anton right away. He called the police. "

Clay signaled to Tomás that he understood what Imelda was saying. "Ask her if there was anyone in the house and if she saw any car outside."

"No," she answered.

"Was the front door open or closed?"

"Closed."

"Did you touch anything?" Clay asked.

"No. I was scared. I went outside and waited for Anton."

"What did Anton do?"

"He called Señor Arrington and, when the police came, he went to the airport to pick him up."

Clay directed Robles to gather whatever additional details he could from the maid. He patted Imelda's hand and thanked her, "Gracias, Imelda. Por favor, hable con el Detective Robles." He then told Robles he was going to talk to Arrington.

CHAPTER 57

In the den, Hayden was sitting stiffly, his hands folded on his desk, his eyes cast in a blank stare. Anton stood at the window, gazing at the desert landscape. Both men looked to Clay when he entered the den.

"I'm sorry for your loss, Mr. Arrington." Hayden still harbored a grudge against Clay and did not acknowledge his expression of sympathy.

Clay said, "I know you have issues with me, sir, but you can trust that we will find out what happened to your wife. To do that, I'll need your help."

Again, no acknowledgement from Hayden.

Clay shifted his attention to Anton. "Who is this gentleman, Mr. Arrington?"

Hayden broke his silence. "His name is Anton Yushenko. He's many things to me. My bodyguard, assistant, driver, my personal attendant and, more importantly, he's like a son to me—more so than my own son."

Anton bowed his head in acknowledgement and stepped forward to shake Clay's hand.

Clay asked Hayden, "Mr. Arrington, when did you last see or talk to your wife?"

"Yesterday morning about eight o'clock, before I flew to Phoenix for meetings. Anton drove me to the airport."

"Anton did not accompany you?"

"No."

"Did you speak with your wife last night?"

"Yes. I called her about seven o'clock."

"Did you normally call her when you were away overnight?"

"Yes, to check in and see how she was doing."

"And how was she doing last night?"

"Fine. She said she would be going to sleep early."

Clay turned to Anton, "When was the last time you saw Mrs. Arrington?"

"Yesterday afternoon about five o'clock." Anton spoke each word precisely. "Mrs. Arrington had taken the BMW to meet some friends for lunch at the country club. I saw her when she returned."

Clay eyed the big man. With no obvious sign of a break-in, Arianna may have known her killer and willingly allowed him in the house. Arianna knew Anton well and, as bodyguard and aide to her husband, he had free reign of the house.

"What did you do all day yesterday when Mr. Arrington was away and Mrs. Arrington was out?"

Anton looked at Hayden for direction.

Hayden nodded. "It's okay. Answer the detective."

"My usual. I washed and serviced the cars in the morning and after Imelda made me lunch I ran some errands for her."

"Errands, like what?"

"I picked up some things at the grocery store, went to the cleaners, that kind of thing."

"You say you washed and serviced the cars?"

"Yes, except for the BMW, which Mrs. Arrington was using."

"What time did Mrs. Arrington return?"

"About three o'clock. I stayed in and around the house until five when I left for the day. Imelda and I left together. I said goodbye to Mrs. Arrington and then..."

"Then what?"

"I went home."

"Where is home?"

"White Rock."

"Will your wife confirm that?"

"I'm not married. Why are you asking?"

"Just gathering facts."

Anton glanced at his boss.

"Tell me what transpired this morning."

"I went to the post office to get the Arringtons' mail as I normally do first thing in the morning. That's when Imelda called me. She was hysterical. She told me Mrs. Arrington was on the living room floor, covered with blood."

"Do you speak Spanish?"

"Enough to get by."

"Who called the police?"

"I called 911 as soon as I hung up with Imelda. Then I came here as fast as I could. I got here before the police arrived."

"Were you Mrs. Arrington's bodyguard also?"

Anton looked at Hayden for an instant before he answered. "Yes."

"Why weren't you in Phoenix with Mr. Arrington?"

Anton hesitated, causing Hayden to turn and look at him.

"Mr. Arrington told me he did not require me in Phoenix. He had arranged for security through his business associates there."

"And Mrs. Arrington?"

"She did not want me around. She often forbade me to follow her because she told me her friends were intimidated by my presence."

"She didn't want you around at night either?"

"Correct. She wanted to be left alone." *Because she was having her affairs.* "I was concerned about her safety but I was not able to protect her as well as Mr. Arrington would have liked. Mr. Arrington was aware of his wife's disdain for my intrusion on her space."

"That's an unfortunate circumstance, as it turns out," Clay said.

"Yes, I'm sorry to say I wasn't able to protect her when she needed it most. I'm to blame for what happened."

Hayden came to Anton's defense, "It's not your fault, Anton. I should have returned from Phoenix last night." He leaned forward and spoke directly to Clay. "My wife was headstrong about certain things and I couldn't do a thing about it. And now we know I was right to be concerned."

"Right about what?"

"I felt she was always in danger because of our affluence. I am heartbroken I was not able to convince her to have Anton protect her. I argued with her that she needed protection— round the clock."

"But Anton couldn't be here twenty-four seven, could he?"

"I'm aware of that. Our home security system should have protected her when Anton wasn't around."

"Anton, do you know if Mrs. Arrington was expecting anyone last night?"

"Not that I was aware. She said she had a long day and wanted to be left alone. She said she was going to open a bottle of wine, watch a movie, and that she didn't want me around. I tried to convince her I should stay, that I would make myself invisible, but she was adamant that she wanted me to go. There was nothing I could do to change her mind, so I left."

Hayden said, "Detective, Anton feels bad enough about Arianna's death. I don't fault him for what has happened. Now, if we can get to the crux of my wife's murder, what do you think happened?"

"One theory at this time is that her death was the result of a burglary gone bad. We noticed she wasn't wearing an engagement ring or wedding band. Those items might have been stolen. We need to know if other valuable items are missing. You'll have to tell us that. Do you keep cash here?"

"Yes, in a wall safe with some documents and jewelry."

"I understand from one of our detectives that the safe has been opened and is empty. Will you take me to it?" Clay, Arrington, and Anton left the den and went up to the master bedroom. "Don't touch the bannister—or anything else, for that matter," Clay said.

In the bedroom, Clay noticed a painting had been removed from the wall and now stood on the floor against a chaise lounge. The door to the wall safe above the chaise lounge was wide open. "Mr. Arrington, did your wife know the combination to the safe?"

"Yes.

"Can you tell what's missing?"

Hayden approached the safe.

"Sir, please, look only. Don't touch anything."

Hayden peered inside and immediately realized the contents had been removed. "*Every*thing is gone. Arianna kept most of her jewelry in here. It's all gone. Her jewels, the cash—everything. I probably had ten thousand dollars in here."

"Our crime scene investigators will comb the safe and the entire room for evidence." Clay ushered Hayden and Anton out of the room. "Please wait for me in the den. I'll be down as soon as I give instructions to the investigators."

Hayden asked, "One more thing."

"What's that?"

"When can my wife be removed? I don't want her on the floor exposed for everyone to see." His breathing was rapid and his voice tremulous. He whispered to Clay, "I was deeply in love with her. I'll miss her more than you'll ever know."

"I'm sure you will, Mr. Arrington. As soon as our medical examiner finishes his examination he'll remove her body. He'll stay in touch with you."

In a gesture that surprised Clay, Hayden extended his hand and, out of character, said, "Thank you."

"You're welcome."

"If I can help with anything."

"One thing that will be of immense help is a detailed list of what's missing."

"I'll have Anton provide you with a list of the missing jewels. Everything's scheduled under our insurance policy, Arianna's rings included."

"Good. The sooner the better. We'll use that information to check on known receivers of stolen goods and pawn shop owners who deal in stolen items."

"We can provide you with that itemization forthwith." Hayden looked at his aide and said simply, "Anton."

"Yes, sir. Right away."

"Detective Bryce, if you think it will help, I'll offer a reward of one hundred thousand dollars to anyone with information leading to the arrest and conviction of the person who did this to my sweet wife."

Sweet wife, my ass.

CHAPTER 58

Clay asked Robles, Carton, and Cook to meet with him in the bedroom. "Gentlemen, we've got to keep every detail about Mrs. Arrington's death sealed. I don't want her cause of death disclosed to anyone, especially the media. As we search the room, keep your eyes out for a video memory card about this big." He held his thumb and forefinger less than an inch apart.

Robles asked, "What's on it?"

"Arrington's son and daughter-in-law secretly recorded Arianna—Mrs. Arrington—having sex with John Grainger. They mailed the disk to Arrington, but Arianna intercepted the envelope before he saw it. I have reason to believe she hid the video card, maybe here in her bedroom."

"What were they trying to accomplish by sending the video?"

"Arianna was slated to inherit the entirety of Hayden Arrington's fortune when he dies. Hunter had been taken out of the will. Hunter and Harmony's aim was to have Mr. Arrington view the sex tape, realize Arianna was being unfaithful, and hope he would strike her from his will and reinstate Hunter."

Carton said, "Unbelievable, the lives of the rich and famous, eh?"

"Okay, let's go at it and see if we can find out who killed her and why."

The four men spread out to begin their search for evidence. Cook dusted the safe for fingerprints while Robles and Clay searched the bureau, nightstands, and clothes closet. Carton checked the bathroom. Ten minutes later, Carton shouted, "I've got something here."

Everyone moved into the expansive bathroom to hear what Carton had discovered.

"There was something written on the mirror with lipstick. Someone tried to wipe it off, but they didn't get it all. I was able to highlight the lettering using our fluorescent light."

Clay asked, "What does it say?"

"Whore."

"Whore?" Clay repeated. "That's it? Just whore?"

"That's all I could pull up."

"Let's think about that. That word is almost always used in anger. Jewels and cash are missing from the safe which suggest a robbery. However, the word *whore* presents a new motive for the murder. Now we're talking crime of passion."

"You know how some of these cases go," Robles said. "Jilted husbands and wives have been known to kill their cheating spouse. I don't want to jump to conclusions, but the odds are strong that Hayden Arrington may have killed his wife."

Clay responded, "I agree. If Arrington learned about his wife's affair, a likely scenario is that he arranged to have someone kill her. He wouldn't do it himself. He would have needed help to pull it off."

"Someone like Anton?"

"Let's play this out. Arrington finds the video in the morning and watches his wife having sex with Grainger. He rages at what he sees. He writes *whore* on the mirror and his anger overwhelms him. Arianna finds the word on her mirror, tries to wipe it clean, and begs for forgiveness. He won't have any part of it and storms out of the house. He flies to Phoenix to establish an alibi and enlists Anton to kill his wife that same night. From what I know about Anton, he would do anything for Arrington. Conceivably that would include committing murder."

Robles agreed with Clay's theory. "That makes sense. So Anton murders Arianna, takes her rings, and empties the safe to make it look like a robbery."

"And if that scenario occurred, she had to know the murderer."

"I agree. Since there was no sign of a break-in she had to know the killer. Otherwise, why would she let him in so late at night?"

Clay said, "We've got a long way to go to prove that's what happened. As of now, Arrington and Anton are our prime suspects. Tomás, find out what time Arrington left for Phoenix, the hotel he stayed in, if he stayed the entire night, and the time his flight manifest showed he returned to Santa Fe. We need corroboration of his alibi. He's our prime suspect. And talk to Anton. Does he have an alibi for last night? Find out where he was and what he did."

"Will do."

Clay said, "I'm going to talk to Hunter and Harmony Arrington."

CHAPTER 59

The front door to Harmony and Hunter Arrington's home swung open as Clay approached. Harmony stood in the doorway with Hunter behind her. "We were expecting you," she said. "We knew you were going to think we killed her. Might as well come in."

Clay's stare was intimidating. He read them the Miranda warning. "... Anything you say may be used against you..."

"We know our rights," Harmony said.

"Did you kill her?"

"Of course not," Harmony said. "We agreed with you there was no benefit to us killing her."

Hunter added, "Yeah, we've thought about it, but, no, we did not go that far. Who shot her anyway?"

Clay hesitated, then answered, "We don't know."

"Her murder's been all over the news since this morning. When we saw the news conference with your chief of police earlier this afternoon and they showed you as the lead detective we knew you'd be knocking on our door sooner or later."

"Where were you last night?"

Harmony answered, "Right here. With our kids. Actually, I wasn't feeling well. I was in bed with a cold. I slept in our spare bedroom to avoid giving Hunter and the kids my cold."

"Can anyone confirm you were both here last night?"

Hunter and Harmony looked at each other and shook their heads. "Our kids."

"What about your nanny?"

Harmony said, "Nanny? Are you kidding? After the move Arianna made on Hunter's father, there's no way I will *ever* hire another nanny. The next one could try to take *my* husband away from me."

Sheepish as usual, Hunter shrugged at Clay and said nothing.

"When I interviewed you at police headquarters you told me you didn't make copies of the memory card."

"That's correct. We did not." Harmony replied, her voice void of emotion.

"If I find out you sent a copy of the disk to your father-in-law, not only will I charge you and Hunter with felony invasion of privacy, I'll also charge you with obstruction involving capital murder."

Harmony spoke up. "You know, Detective Bryce, I'd like to extend my thanks to whoever killed that bitch."

Hunter tried to hush his wife. He turned to Clay and said, "She doesn't really mean that. No one deserves to be murdered no matter what the reason. Isn't that right, Harmony?"

Harmony answered, "Yeah, right, whatever. But now we'll get back what is rightfully yours and mine. Hopefully, you'll find out who killed her so we can thank the killer for his service."

Clay nodded. "It looks like you got what you wanted, Mrs. Arrington."

"What's that?"

"Arianna will be out of Mr. Arrington's will by default."

"All we wanted was what was rightfully ours."

"Explain to me again what, exactly, is rightfully yours?"

"The Arrington family enterprise is rightfully Hunter's. His family built the company over generations with blood, sweat, and tears. Frankly, we could give a rat's behind about Arianna.

She's gone now and out of our lives forever. And you know what? I'm happy she was killed."

"Harmony, don't say that," Hunter said.

"No. I *can* say that, because that's how I feel."

CHAPTER 60

Dan Carton called Clay.

Clay listened for a few seconds then beamed broadly. He shouted into the phone, "Dan, of course. It all ties together. How did you match it?"

Carton answered, "We got it off the car door handle. Dick followed the car to the post office this morning and lifted the prints when it was in the parking lot."

"Awesome, man. You guys are awesome."

* * * * *

Clay and Robles went to Harmony and Hunter's home accompanied by four cops in bullet-proof vests.

Hunter and Harmony looked out at the scene as they opened the front door. "What now?" Harmony asked.

Clay and Tomás barged in. Clay reached for Hunter's elbow and jerked him around. "Hunter Arrington, I'm arresting you for the murder of Arianna Arrington." Robles handcuffed him.

"What are you doing," Hunter shouted.

Harmony looked on incredulously.

"Help me," Hunter shouted to her.

Harmony screamed, "Stop hurting him. He couldn't have killed her. He was here with me and the kids when she was killed."

Clay said, "He was—before and after he shot Arianna. All while you were sleeping off your cold in the spare bedroom. Isn't that true, Hunter?"

Harmony shouted, "Hunter, you didn't, did you?"

Hunter looked at her and dropped his head to his chest.

"Oh, my God, you did. You did. What is wrong with you?"

Clay said, "Hunter, you asked me yesterday who shot Arianna. How did you know she was shot? That information was purposely sealed from the media and never made public. How would you have known she had been shot unless you were the one who shot her?"

Harmony said, "You're crazy. You're telling me you think Hunter killed her because he guessed she had been shot?"

"No. Here's how I know he killed her. The word *whore*. A word you both used on multiple occasions to describe Arianna."

"That's what she was."

"And that's the word Hunter wrote on her mirror."

"What are you talking about? What mirror?" Harmony asked.

"After Hunter killed Arianna, he went into her bathroom, found lipstick in one of the drawers, and used it to write *whore* on the mirror. He didn't realize at first that his father would be accused of killing her, but then he had second thoughts. Didn't you, Hunter? If your father was accused of murdering Arianna, there was no guarantee you'd be back in his will, so you cleaned the mirror—or tried to. The problem is, you didn't get all the lipstick off. We found traces."

"I didn't write anything on her mirror."

"Yes, you did."

"You have no proof."

"Oh, but we do."

"What?"

"Your fingerprints on the tube of lipstick."

"Oh, my God. Why, Hunter? Why?"

"Because of you."

"I didn't ask you to kill Arianna."

"You wanted me to. I knew that."

"No, we decided not to kill her. That's why we sent the tape to your father."

"I know what you really wanted, Harmony. All you could talk about was my inheritance and that you wished Arianna was dead. I had to prove to you I was a man—not a jerk and a loser. You've called me that a thousand times. I couldn't take it anymore."

"What's going to happen to me now? What am I going to do?"

"I know what you can do."

"What?"

"You can go to hell."

EPILOGUE

Simon underwent a mental health evaluation and was declared sane. He pleaded innocent to John Grainger's murder and to the attempted murders of Clay, Hank, and Allie.

Simon's lawyer used a crime-of-passion defense in seeking the murder charges be lowered to manslaughter. At trial, he argued Simon meant only to scare his victims, not harm them. The jury found Simon guilty on all charges, including voluntary manslaughter as a third-degree felony. Simon was sentenced to thirty years imprisonment.

Hunter pleaded no contest to the charge of first-degree murder of Arianna Arrington and was sentenced to life in prison.

Hayden would not reconcile with Harmony or his son. He agreed, however, to provide Harmony with a generous allowance under an arrangement in which Hayden had visitation rights with his grandchildren.

The end.

ABOUT THE AUTHOR

Tony Spallone is a retired executive who, when not traveling with his wife Patti or clocking miles on his bike, devotes his time to writing. He has a graduate degree in psychology, served as an officer in the U.S. Army, and has held various executive positions in business. His first three novels *Murder at Breeze Canyon*, *Murders in the High Desert*, and *Murders on Pigeon Mountain* have received high praise. He and Patti live in Chester Springs, Pennsylvania. You can reach Tony on his website www.tonyspallone.com.

Your review is valued.

Tony welcomes feedback via email at:
tony@tonyspallone.com

Made in United States
North Haven, CT
28 December 2022

30294837R10186